Thomas Kendall

HOW I KILLED THE UNIVERSAL MAN

Published in the United States and Canada by Whisk(e)y Tit: www.whiskeytit.com. If you wish to use or reproduce all or part of this book for any means, please let the author and publisher know. You're pretty much required to, legally.

ISBN 978-1-952600-36-4

Cover design by Shaw at Multifold mltfld.com.

HOW I KILLED THE UNIVERSAL MAN

CONTENTS

THOMAS KENDALL

THERE IS NO PLACE LIKE HOME

KEY BISCAYNE, FLORIDA.

L akerman's a visitor here, a tourist in every sense of the word. The world he's moving in is one of large air-conditioned apartments, of rooms where the horizon became something ornamental. He is not used to this. He is used to the prolonged immediacy of loss, to the sour milk and onion shit smell of bodies openly and actively uncared for, to tarpaulin beds left out in large multipurpose rooms, converted school gyms. To emergency spaces and borderlines where the symbolic made unholy pacts with the real and a cross the colour of blood could still mean salvation. The opposite of where he is now, basically, but forever connected to it like the dual faces of a coin.

Twenty-three-year-old John Lakerman, orphaned since birth and former eight-year occupant of the notorious Roscoff migrant camp, is standing at the windows of Patrick Diaz's Abuela's fourteenth floor apartment, thinking again of how the sea holds no sense of awe for him in the US of A. This part at least. It's something to do with the height of the buildings and the fact that they were apartments, that this was designed as living space. It had to be that. What could be less holy or reverent or awe-inspiring than this way of living?

He finishes his drink and steps away from the view and wanders into the apartment's heavily dated kitchen. The kitchen counter and cupboards are constructed out of a plastic it's illegal to produce now and crowded with the kind of bulky gadgets familiar from late night shopping channels. The kitchen surfaces and appliances seem a little out of focus to him, as if the image of the future the kitchen had once derived itself from had lost resolution. He looks over the retro counterware. Had that peppermint green ice cream maker referenced the ambitions of the 1950s for the Abuela? It might have done. It was entirely possible. The whole apartment was a prolapse of merchandised time, of branded objects measured out in disjointed impulse.

Lakerman opens the freezer and rakes some ice into his glass. He didn't trust the ice maker to be clean. Lakerman mixes another Negroni, finishing the ickily gummed bottle of Campari he'd found tucked away behind the washing machine's industrial sized drum. He's willing to bet he'd find another in one of the four toilets peppering the apartment.

Lakerman sits on a couch in front of the window. He puts his feet up on the coffee table. The sea, mediated as it was by the distance and his central nervous system, is a monochromatic blue. The horizon appears a little thickened, like an ageing scar. The sea wall remains partially visible despite the best efforts of engineers to erase any trace of the calamity from the more affluent residents' day-to-day perception of the world.

Lakerman is waiting for the sky to darken, for time to coincide with his desires. For night to come. He notices his feet on the coffee table are in violation of the framed cross stitch hanging on the wall to the right of him. Who cares? No one. *Bless this house.*

And that's entirely true, no one cares, the apartment is otherwise empty. Patrick's not here and his Abuela is long dead. Lakerman couldn't comment on the providence of the latter's eternal non-existence but Patrick was a total dick and his absence has been the sole blessing of their arrangement. Lakerman had messaged his old university acquaintance on a whim after finding out his assignment would take him to Miami and then, after Patrick had pretty much offered him this apartment for free, he'd ended up blowing his meagre expense allowance via a goodwill gesture he hadn't expected Patrick to accept.

Lakerman's here on assignment for *donkeyWolf*, one of the online media brands he regularly produces content for. *donkeyWolf*'s a self-consciously edgy multi-social new(s) presence with a polyamorous approach to truth and ethics and an existentially confused understanding of its purpose. The brand being owned and commissioned by the very type of corporation its better work railed against. Any meaningful stories they published, or worthy documentaries they funded and made, were forever underwritten by this essential irony. Lakerman has a whole host of arguments for why that shouldn't matter but of course it does. It's what *donkeyWolf* is in a very real way. Same as the world is. *Incorporation, it's how you know you're real.* An old joke. He'd sucked at standup.

He's in Miami to investigate a new designer drug tantalisingly described as fifty times more emotionally and philosophically poignant than DMT. That's the story's designated angle. Lakerman's thought about opening his report with a quote from Bergson outlining the literal impossibility of quantifying the qualitative but he needs to find a suitably throwaway turn of phrase so that no one has to actually confront the idea behind it. The drug was one in a recent crop of smart drugs, of chemicals laced with biotechnology. This wasn't in itself particularly interesting to him, Lakerman having partaken in the collective sense of exhaustion at the mere anticipation of the think pieces, debates, and comment sections that would emerge around this marriage of flesh and robotics. The preemptive exhaustion had resulted in a near total absence of uproar and was, Lakerman thought, a sociological phenomenon waiting to be recognised.

The simple truth of it was that everyone knew it would happen. Like the future, it didn't seem worth thinking about.

More interesting to him than the drug was the narrative behind its discovery. Developed as an antidepressant, its visionary side effects had apparently come as a total surprise to the research team involved. That struck Lakerman as something he could work with, comment wryly upon. Secondly, on discovery of the drug's actual effects one of the scientists, a Doctor Kenneth Marker, had apparently gone rogue, leaked the drug and aspects of its program to the public, and posted its chemical makeup online. All this before disappearing the moment a warrant was issued for his arrest. This disappearance alone should have been news. It was almost impossible to disappear unless you were dirt poor, Lakerman knew, so what was the evidence anyone was looking for him?

Lakerman's seen a few pictures of this former researcher pre-breakdown and disappointingly for him the man had failed to exhibit wild eyes, a matted beard, or a neck draped in a Newton's cradle of beads. Instead the fifty eight year old male was relatively non descript with brown hair cropped close to the skull. His sole distinguishing feature is a large Adam's apple that Lakerman imagines bobbing up and down the man's throat like the puck of an old test your strength machine. He'd seen one of those contraptions in a cartoon they'd studied in history class and the image had stayed with him. Doctor Marker's Adam's apple though wasn't even freakishly large, only noteworthy at best.

Lakerman can't square the dull image of the man with the manifesto he'd written and disseminated across the alternet. He opens a copy, applies analytic algorithms to the text and lets the a.i program sort through and pull out a few representative quotes. He swipes through them on his palm with an interest that has some qualitative effect on his eyes. The writing is rapturous and paranoid, and at times so insistent in the earnestness of its claims regarding the possibility of spiritual fulfillment that Lakerman feels compelled to believe in Marker's sincerity, if not the veracity of his claims.

Jesus, he thinks, what's gotten into me.

HOW I KILLED THE UNIVERSAL MAN

Doctor Marker had taken to calling the drug Noumenon in his writing though obviously most in the drug trade referred to it as N. Lakerman didn't know what to make of the name though his initial feeling was that it was self consciously clever and a total misunderstanding of the concept and therefore totally indicative of yada yada yada. Still, these aspects of the story, of a scientist apparently seduced into a loss of objectivity by their own invention, wanted by the police, and gone missing after having madly believed in a meaning outside of the drug, that was somehow through the drug ... This was something Lakerman felt he could work with, render coldly elegant, identify some telling aspect of modern life in. It was unlikely though that Lakerman would be able to explore any of this in his article, the significance he saw in it not really tallying with *donkeyWolf's* purview. Still, maybe he could recycle it for something else, another publication.

Lakerman's been given/rewarded/punished with the job on the tacit understanding he'll test the drug himself and use the article to report back from the other side of its meaning. 'Given your history, it might even do you some good.' His commissioning editor had actually said that to him. At least the itinerary of the trip was concisely timetabled. He's to meet with one of the pharmaceutical researchers tonight having been, via some suspect finagling, legalised as a final participant in the trial. Then he's to spend the following day looking into the branching, unaffiliated, cult club scene building around the drug's apparently moldable high. All this in the shadow of Noumenon likely being classified as a fully prohibited substance, carrying a minimum 3 to 5 year jail term a week or two from now. He'd like to stick around to profile any arrests made once the inevitable verdict comes in, interview police and perp, but he's due to leave before the ruling.

Lakerman lifts the glass to his mouth and tips it upwards. There is pressure against the lips but no cold feeling in the throat. The glass in Lakerman's hand is conspicuously empty. The emptiness is emptying. That's Heidegger. The emptiness is close to him. Building dwelling thinking in him. Etcetera. Lakerman chooses a bathroom at random. He finds a bottle of Campari in the tank of the first toilet he looks in. He goes to the kitchen to make another Negroni. He runs a hand over the time resistant novelties of plastic clad gadgets. He notices a lot of the appliances are stained a watery red with vegetable juice and that the juicer's blades have been worked to within an inch of their life. He notes how the turmeric and iron supplements have been left out to gather dust on the side. Lakerman wonders how Patrick Diaz's Abuela died. He feels a pang of remorse for his attitude towards the apartment. He lifts the Negroni up to eye level in a toast but the drink is too serious a colour for the Miami sky.

He wanders back into one of the three adjacent living rooms. There are still a couple of hours to kill before Lakerman has to leave. He probably shouldn't drink anymore after this, he thinks. There are notes detailing the supposed claims around Noumenon's effects and possible contacts in the club scene he could look over but the idea of it is depressing the hell out of him. The story donkeyWolf wants is obviously trash, a joke meant to both ratify and demean the possibility of 'drug culture,' a joke he's sure will make everyone who reads it dumber or, at the very least, more powerlessly cynical. Lakerman's thought about it enough to know how unlikely it is that his work is helping his species in any way. It bugs him but whatever. What else was there to do? He's just a wrongly directed organism, a single blood cell in the bled out world. All he can do is work to fill the wound he's been collectively prescribed. And hell, it could be a lot worse. After all, what if he hadn't gotten drunk? That would have been terrible. Lakerman is distantly aware of the need to sober up. He could go for a swim. One more drink, he thinks.

Two drinks later and Lakerman is logging himself onto *donkeyWolf*. His last feature has gone live. It's part of a series interviewing former occupants of migrant camps and exploring survivors' guilt. He was unsparing in this last aspect, in the questions that he'd pose and the confessions he'd pursue. He'd got into journalism by learning how to make the hard sell of who he was, and how he'd got to be here, trace an inviting cross over simpleton hearts. Detailing the horrific in a powerfully neutral tone was his unique selling point. He'd elevated it to a style. His first published piece bore all the hallmarks of his work though in a manner that seems somewhat overstylised to him now. This piece took the form of a profile of himself and included himself hounding himself, posing questions to himself as if he was not himself. The whole piece remorseless in its judgements and line of questioning. Nevertheless, the article had impressed with its power, clarity, and well crafted appearance of unwavering honesty especially given the artificiality of its premise. Lakerman depicted himself as a person defined by erasure, part outline and part impenetrable shadow. The skeletal biography he provided sketched a man unable to experience pleasure, a person irrevocably marked by trauma. Lakerman writing of himself that 'He seems, in the affectless portrait of his internal "life," to believe he is merely language, an impoverished language uninhabited by being but still cognisant of its historical referents. Or as he would put it "a data leak," the leakage being his automatic sense of the world, his continued ability to pass through it while still considered a person.'

Adopted from Roscoff at eight by the British State and expected to fulfil part of its quota for the G.C.C.E.A. (global clean up citizenship exchange accord) Lakerman's IQ scores had ended up testing off the charts. He'd subsequently won a scholarship that saved him from a life dealing with obviously toxic waste and was legally adopted by a family of Cambridge academics, a fact which only exacerbated his guilt. The disappointment of his deep eco-phenomenologist step mother in his choice of career was marked, she said, by care. His stepfather was a mathematician who had suicided in the past year. The family had loved Lakerman as well as they could but Lakerman hadn't felt much towards them even as his behaviour fell within the acceptable remits of rebellion. His rebellion occurring in areas both academics had at least a little understanding of, or sense of proportion about, given they too had grown up in a time in which taboos regarding recreational use of substances and sex were being eased and loosened like a belt. Alcohol and drugs and sex though provided no access to the interiority of real feelings for Lakerman. They were a change of scenery and context and welcomed for that but he couldn't find anything about them to lose himself in, that would move through him in some form of permeating wave. Alterations of consciousness were just another, less tedious, abstraction. In the profile Lakerman detailed relationships that had become increasingly destructive in behaviour and was unsparing of his own flaws or culpability. The John Lakerman of the text frequently expressed a desire to die, stating it was a decision he felt he could take at any time and one that he could imagine would not necessarily be aroused by a sensation of pain or even depression. And yet, through what appeared to be a genuinely in the moment realisation, Lakerman had, with the aid of the interrogative narrator, come to realise he must still have faith in the possibility of finding some form of genuine pleasure in existence. Either that or that there was a pleasure beneath his awareness of it, for he was still pursuing something in the world. He continued to exist. The profile concludes in the vaguely optimistic speculation that Lakerman needed to serve this pleasure by remaining active in a world that largely repulsed him.

And what was it Lakerman was really looking for? What the article couldn't say was the last and most humiliating truth. Beauty. Lakerman wanted something beautiful. He'd heard of such a thing but had not encountered it. And besides the urge belonged several centuries in the past, if ever.

There are zero comments so far.

His latest series on the migrating world had been nominated for, though not won, some trade awards. This in spite of the negative reputation *donkeyWolf* had garnered in the field of serious journalism. It was obvious that *donkeyWolf* published the series solely for a veneer of authenticity. Lakermam's work was generally intended to distract from the fact that *DKW* accrued the majority of its revenue by creating original Attention Disordering Content. Lakerman's work salted the truth of that, lending the company the appearance of sincerity, of something at least trying to think. The commissioning editors and producers of the ADC, many of whom were talented professionals, sublimated the largely unspoken contradiction of their ability and its purpose into a house style of humour that was complexly stupid, crude, and snottily redolent of an 'ironically brandable' nihilism necessarily framed as thrillingly pointless. What they produced was genuinely terrible, Lakerman thought, real crap. Work not even pretending to be better. He didn't know if that was a good thing or not, the lack of pretence. His article for instance was posted directly next to *How to make a bong out of a coconut*, a video tutorial with an Eastern European stoner. It felt to Lakerman as if the majority of *donkeyWolf's* content believed the end of the world had already occurred and, judging by the hits accrued, they had tapped into something wildly popular. The view count for the coconut video alone had likely been seen by more people than had ever truly been happy in the history of the world.

There was a logic to all this that was easily conceived of in conspiratorial terms, Lakerman thinks. After all, *donkeyWolf's* provenance, who it belonged to, pretty much said: nothing matters, nothing you say matters. But the truth was, he thinks, that donkeyWolf *just was* modern confusion monetised. And while money, Lakerman was sure via Ursula K. Le Guin, was eventually going to go the way of kings, he still required it to live. Which meant he needed his articles to get attention. This particular article, given its content and his style, was bound to be popular. If it was popular he could maybe leverage some sort of freedom regarding his next assignment.

Which means he has to be able to write it. Which means he needs to sober up.

* * *

Lakerman is walking as if he's going to the building's gym but at its entry he takes a hard, if unbalanced, right. He enters a dark and empty courtyard across which the perfect rectangle of shimmering, underlit, water seems futuristic. The blue gel of the swimming pool at night. Perfectly electric. The sea couldn't move him here but the swimming pools were sublime. He imagined the blue was a portal to somewhere uncannily the same but beautiful. He jumps in. Underwater, life mounts his breath and skirts the ramp of his lungs as he pushes himself to the point where rising, rushing, shattering upon the surface registers as desperate need and he breaks through in that impossible rush of crossing borders with his mouth open and his eyes stretching across the vast pupil of the night. Lakerman feels his mind dilate and for a few moments that empty centre of himself is filled.

He floats on his back, eyes rolled into space. Everything up there was older than life. The space around him was older than life. All space. He floats on his back, drones studding the sky instead of stars. He's dimly aware he's crying when a security guard comes and orders him out the pool. The guard shouts some questions. Lakerman has to prove who he is, which is sobering enough.

* * *

Inside the apartment an alert sends a vibration through his skin. The trial is in an hour. Shit. Lakerman changes quickly. He spreads two fingers out across his left palm. A square of black enlarges underneath the push of his fingers until the centre of his palm is wholly inky and arrayed with a menu of light connected constellations. The known universe is pre-existent there, held in captive potential, and capable of being routed through his skin at a moment's asking. Who gives a fuck. Lakerman gives the address of the clinic, sends the map to the car in the garage, then lets his flesh show flesh again.

One of the benefits of working for a self consciously hipsterish media network owned by one of the worst and therefore richest companies in the world, is that the need for appearances facilitated the exchange of the immaterial for the material and vice versa. Lakerman knew a few freelancers who worked almost exclusively for tech, who made content in exchange for discounts and payment plans they'd work out with the parent companies of their infantilising employers. Lakerman had picked up his own skin-plant via a piece of off-the-books subliminal copywriting he'd done for a gambling website his editor had put him in contact with. He takes the 'elevator' to the carpark.

* * *

Outside the air has a texture and weight to it that clings a little desperately to his clothes. It is there in the lack of oxygen, the huddle of warm metal, the drama of breathless things. The car connects to his palm. The door slides open. The vehicle is a tank-lite thing that's unbelievably crass to the majority of the world but which seems, given the tremendous distance between things here, to make sense on some lonely, aggressively isolationist, scale.

Lakerman takes a deep breath, climbs inside. The car smells like microwaved carpet. The vehicle was a few years old and still fitted for non essential air con but Lakerman couldn't, out of habit, bring himself to turn it on. Florida was the last state to place regulations on Air conditioning and many of the older models had yet to be stripped of the capacity. All over the U.S People were dying in their cars. It was a period of adjustment, they'd been told.

The car starts up and pulls out of Coconut Grove, Lakerman going through the usual show of making it appear as if he was driving. Largely out of habit. The rental cars were by policy 90% self driving rendering Lakerman's input largely symbolic, requiring him at most to be minimally in contact with the wheel, to check in physically every five to ten minutes with the world around him. He's free to observe the road, the organisation of remaining life there, his brain streaming it all. The car passes a dead alligator laying at the side of the road, doomed by the sun, pitched on its back. Lakerman has read about Alligators increasingly being found near home pools, often dying at the edge of the tiling, exhausted and overheated, unequipped for the first time in however many thousands of years for the world as it was. These alligator corpses with their rubbery, mask-like, muscle-lubed flesh, appeared to Lakerman as something diminished and strangely outdated, as if their bodies' limited gestures had been animatronically controlled and their sudden mass deaths were just the revelation of this fact. A planned obsolescence.

In the distance a series of roads sign the air in brutalist bubble writing. Lakerman admires their smooth and soft seeming concrete, the uniformity of felt tip grey. Only here, he thinks, could concrete appear cartoonish.

There was another Miami of course, one he'd never access and which the auto car would seize up and all but refuse to enter. A Miami of block shaped universes, of horizons   physically and emotionally constructed by deprivation. A Miami of scalded flesh and keratoses, of babies crying with their mouths full of sun and the heat of their blood rising like an antique thermometer towards their brains.

Other than the security guard, Lakerman realises he hasn't seen an embodied human being for nearly three weeks. Granted for eleven days he'd been interred in the depths of a cargo boat bound from London, medically sedated and stored at a cellularly preserving temperature as per his contract. The port in Miami was totally automated and there had been no other passengers on any of the other boats. He had expected that. He had expected the streets to be empty in the morning when he arrived but it was evening now and the pavements everywhere were still abandoned. There was something monk-like about life in this moment, he thought, an avowed silence. The noise was all interior. It could be hard to take.

He checks the weather report. It tells him it is still too early for joggers and pedestrians to risk outside activity, that the danger of their reaching a critical temperature was too great. It didn't help of course that Miami hadn't been able to invest in Stomata beyond the minimal infrastructure the federal government had heavily subsidised and which just about stabilised the environment. The mayor of Miami at the time having put the majority of their budget into making the sea wall palatably invisible to the residents in an act of communally minded repression fifteen or so years ago.

HOW I KILLED THE UNIVERSAL MAN

Sold as the internet of plants, of life even, the emergent properties of Stomata as it multiplied seemed to take everybody by surprise even though this was what its corporation, UbIQ, had promised. Stomata was a programmable plant organism capable of being rapidly grown into nearly any form and which ate CO_2 at a prodigious rate. An organic computer able to form alloys with other materials and cell-laminate any existing object, Stomata could conduct and store electrical current, generating power from the carbon dioxide rich atmosphere. As Lakerman understood it, every Stomata plant was connected and capable of networking with other units via signals of odour and electrical frequency, a communication matrix largely based on trees and fungi but with added central processors, quantum computing, and a variety of compatibility seeking A.I. that allowed resources and effects to be transferred across the organisms. This had created what came to be known as 'An economy of air.' Areas in which stomata was concentrated, in tandem with the right algorithms and a.i intervention, allowed for the establishment of climate safe zones and since UbIQ's patented tree-top technology continued to explode in demand, it would have been anti-capitalist, therefore unpatriotic, not to charge a competitive rate for the survival of the planet, one that Miami had subsequently never been able to afford. UbIQ and their CEO Anthony Husk had grown god-tier rich via these formulations of privatised air and portable micro climates, localised weather. UbIQ's CEO was, Lakerman recalls, currently bidding to turn the moon into real estate, at least on social media. There was a surprising degree of agreement about his right to do this, on social media at least, although no one could tell if it was a joke or not.

Across the Rickenbacker Causeway Lakerman spots an abandoned sneaker fused to the pavement, melted into the tarmac until only the sun bleached tongue of it remained. The tongue waving a flag of submission at some non addressable entity, time itself perhaps. The skein of rubber was all spread out around its flap, sticky like gum and puddled, he thinks, in an abstract commentary on the toxic footprints human life memories in the earth.

Sun, concrete, technology and waste on fire. This was the first world now, its waxed edges. Lakerman takes a picture of it.

* * *

The research laboratory is clad in reflective glass and the explosive aura of its own architecture. Multi-tiered, domed and turreted, it was from a satellite view that the building must have made the most aesthetic sense. Distance made it comprehensible but up close it appeared to sit imposingly between dimensions. Whole floors jutted out from the tangential centre like possibility, bridges establishing gaps like choice. Lakerman hadn't been to any research facilities before but he was pretty sure this approach to design was unusual, that it spoke of a hidden need for identity, to impress a static difference upon time and space.

Lakerman swipes his hand at the entry to the north section. The building greets him and Lakerman quickly moves to mute it. He tries not to think about the fact that the voice still exists, is still there narrating and logging his movement, that his choice amounts only to a decision not to perceive.

An elevator takes him automatically to floor 19. Rooms open for him as he passes. Wafts of information waiting to be triggered hang in a generated field around him, the building spamming his muted body with information. He's led to the Lifepax wing by a thread of green lights and a warm glow in his hand. There's a door with a reality augmenting logo of a beautiful green field and a face he suddenly recognises as his own turning in the middle of it. The face has a smile that is both recognisable and suggestive of an excess of joy, an excess that has always been beyond him. The face is exactly how he imagined happiness might look, subtle and complex but unmistakable, and it takes Lakerman a moment to realise, even after all this time, how easy it must be to feed his likeness into a screen, to design the features of joy using his pre-existent musculature and available data. Half a beat more to realise of course the logo must change to reflect whoever entered. That the happiness changed.

The company's name unfurls across his image.

Lifepax- here to carry you when nature can't.

This was where the drug was routinely tested.

The door slides open.

* * *

The hum of air conditioning in the reception area is industrially present and ambiently real. The refrigerated air preserving the room and its contents on the edge of some imminent existence. There is an uncanny stillness to the room and its objects. The chairs, and the magazines, and the reception desk, the surface of which is augmented with a tub full of glazed candy and a little bear with a heart for a digestive system on it, all seem sterile and untouched. Nothing emanates, the atoms between things slur. The waiting room was a place of suspended possibility and it felt to Lakerman like Time and Space were a placeholder here, a semi colon in the mad, multiplying, clauses of being.

Lakerman sits on a chair. He assumes notifications of his arrival have been delivered to the chain of recipients either overseeing this little drama or taking part in it. The web. Ugh. He receives a message. An alert jumpstarting the air, ringing in his ear, pulsing not unpleasantly through the tips of his fingers. He can't check it. The tone of the alert meant it was a personal message, unrelated to work or his assignment. He can't handle that now and besides it was a hard thought to guess who would want to contact him. There was the remote possibility it was someone from his intimate past for example, one of those bruised shadows being brought into position by the obscure forces of nostalgia and concern, chance and repetition. By some genuine flaw in the pattern. It remained unlikely though, Lakerman having effectively amputated most of his social life over the last few years. Anyone who'd felt close enough to register their desires upon him had been let go of in his pursuit of some solitary pleasure. He'd tied his indifference so tightly around their care that they'd dropped off, fell aside, were in the past now shrivelled and bloodless. He accidentally scrolls through his memory archive, playing back the only saved message from his personal contacts. It's from his last relationship. Agatha. The one that had really gone toxic. He listens for a moment and then turns it off. Could it be her that had messaged him? Let it end there, he hopes, thinking again of the message. Like anything ended.

A doctor emerges from the doorway and stands behind the desk, changing the texture of the room. She begins to talk and the sound of manipulated air drops below a roar.

"That's better. I simply can't understand the need for such noise. It's for show really, for the investors, the aircon is 'eco friendly' if you believe that? I'm surprised they didn't go for dry ice. You must be John Lakerman. Now that I look at you, you actually do look like your profile. That's kind of rare. So, in case you don't know and haven't read the info pack we sent, I'm Doctor Andrea Christoff and I'm going to be your Wizard of Oz today."

"Excuse me?"

"It's terminology we borrowed from VR therapy. We're kind of the people behind your experience if that makes sense? We're managing the fantasy. Follow me."

Christoff is British, about 45 years old, and dressed in jeans, t-shirt, and a fashionable blazer. The notch of her collarbone is dappled with freckles. Lakerman's observing her intently as they walk down a series of short corridors while simultaneously trying to follow the various threads of her conversation as she pokes fun at the building, laughing at the light fittings and mood music which she says she can alter at will. There is something discomfiting about the rapidity of her speech, the way it forms a manic twin to the building's disembodied desire to please. And then, when they reach their destination and she turns to him to say this is it, this is the room, Lakerman is startled by the disjunction between her voice and face. Her speech has an unsynced quality, the voice full of confidence, the face increasingly a mask. He thinks he can see a desperation, physical and slowly borne, developing in the widening gap between them.

Doctor Christoff beckons towards a padded bed in the room. Lakerman sits on top of it and looks around. The room is a soft cell of untipped furniture, rounded edges and cleverly 'unobtrusive' electronics. She takes his blood pressure.

"Now, I take it that you understand this is a regulated 3 month dose?"

Lakerman's look is one of studied concentration, a leaning into this new piece of information.

"So you didn't read the legal waiver you signed before. Quelle surprise. Don't worry you won't undergo a continuous trip and if you don't activate the programs again, which i'm not going to give you the key for anyway, they won't umm be present."

"Present to what?"

"To you."

"Where are they when they're not present?"

She begins to fix pads to his lips, mouth, and throat. He's about to ask her what they're for when she shushes her fingers into his throat and answers him.

"We've known since the nineteen nineties that areas that are active when we speak out loud are active during inner speech, right? These pads measure the vibrations sent to the speech mechanisms in your throat, tongue, etc, and the A.I.. translates them into language. We figured if we could construct a way to measure and translate vibrations we could read and even implant ideas in order to help with the emotional augmentation of the drug. The biotech and this hardware theoretically allows us to build a psychological and chemical profile whereby the creation of new, non depressive, thoughts are materially possible."

"You're going to control what I think?"

She shakes her head and laughs though her mouth is only slightly parted.

"Not exactly, how can I put this? Ok. There are these small intelligent, biological computer programs inside the drug you're dissolving. Similar to stem cells in their potential. Anyway, they flow through your skin, your blood, map and monitor your brain. They'll test your hormone levels, track any synaptic firings like a bloodhound and and take notes of where your eyes go. They'll connect and cross reference this information with your external data production and once they've got a semi accurate model going re: likes, dislikes and emotional patterns and recognitions, they'll begin to offer alternative chemical settings for your experience which will, coupled with our guided therapy, provide you with the ability to choose optimised and exploratory emotional reactions to real time events. Now, what sort of implants do you have?"

"I have maps, universal control, a basic call and search function, this palm plant."

"That'll be fine but... it's a bit basic. The more apps you have the more data, the more data the more nuanced the experience. What you probably haven't been told is that the project was initially for the development of a whole new treatment for depression. It wasn't just about the drug. That was standard knowledge for all our participants."

Lakerman can't read what is happening. He feels he is being toyed with in some way, that he is the victim of some elaborate stunt. He decides to play it straight.

"I think before we start I'd like to ask you a few more questions about the development of the drug."

"I'm only authorised to run the trial as I would for any other applicant."

"So, consider me a particularly anxious patient and practise your bedside manner. I'm nervous, what can you tell me about Doctor Marker?"

"I'm not here to talk about Ken, in fact that is strictly off limits and you've likely turned the building into one big tattletale just by the sheer act of mentioning him here."

Her fingers are still pressed into his throat. He glances upwards, meets her eyes. "What he, Marker, posted online... I have this feeling that it wasn't actually from him. I'm not even sure how he could have disappeared. And if he hasn't disappeared then...y'know, where is he?"

Her fingers leave his throat.

"If you want me to continue with the trial," Dr Christoff says, glancing at his palm plant, "and my guess is you need this job, it would be wise to change the subject. What happened with Ken... it's not something any person could really claim to understand. He didn't know where or when he was. He abused his own supply. It was like time and space had fallen apart for him. Put in these lenses."

She passes him a pair of AR lenses. He slips them over his eyes. "These are a standard reality augmenting filter. Our use of it is going to be pretty subtle. No Pokemon."

She stands up and retrieves something from a draw in the desk behind her. She opens her left palm in front of Lakerman as if she was holding out a treat for a dog.

"You can ingest or inject." Her right hand sweeps over the two prizes held in the flat of her palm.

"I feel like they should be presented on little velvet cushions."

She doesn't laugh.

"What's the difference?"

"You strike me as someone who would know."

"That's an obviously memorable quote."

"It's going to be the least memorable thing you can imagine soon enough."

He rolls up his sleeve.

He scans the doctor's face for any trace of animosity as she turns his forearm over with her hands. No words pass between them as the tip of the syringe sinks into his arm in a quietly satisfying motion. The needle is greeted by skin, enveloped in the formalities of entry level wounding, and takes up residence in his flesh via the body's logic of acceptance. The metal integrated, sealed up in the border.

Lakerman's already totally transported by the time the syringe is half emptied. Thoughts and feelings rise from fields of neurons like crickets at sunset. And what will they devastate in this swarming oneness? The sense of time he is experiencing just hits space differently. It is not subjugated to distance and there are no words there and it is impossible to measure. Time turns recognisable *now* as the needle is, he notes, extracted out of his arm. The tip of it beaded like rain. Lakerman feels a lucid joy, one his consciousness keeps waking up in and noticing. He doesn't think this waking is associated with any kind of forgetting, as you might suppose, rather he's existing in a constant state of realisation. The total contains the possible, he thinks. Lakerman looks around and sees that the surface of each thing in the room contains its own glowing firmament, a sun and a sky given to giving out life. Dr Christoff is kneeling in front of him. He feels he is laughing uncontrollably and yet he is also aware that his expression remains calm and neutrally composed.

"So from what I can see on the screen you're well into phase one. We're taking a reading. I'm going to monitor you on this and I'm going to at times suggest images to you while altering the way the antidepressant works. Now, from what I understand you're an orphan with a significant experience of trauma?"

He tries to open his mouth but the world is already in there.

"Now, I'm going to... This experience, remember, is therapeutic. It's not really about pleasure. Let's see what we can pull up."

"I want to know that beauty is something my body can do."

He hadn't intended to say that.

"Unexpected. You're going to feel a lot of things now."

It's like he closes his eyes but it isn't that. Lakerman sees himself as a seven year old boy walking towards a barbed wire fence in the distance. There is refuse stacked waist high either side of him and a lake covered in mould the colours of a gasoline rainbow. The sensation for Lakerman is somewhere between memory and experience.

"Roscoff?" Andrea says but her voice is wind and sky.

Garbage Christ. A thirty foot geoglyph located on the far east side of Roscoff and collaged out of mounds of nappies, plastic bags and carefully sculpted cultures of mould and rot. Lakerman didn't know whether the symbol had been intended sincerely but it had quickly become the site of defiantly non-satiric worship. There were those who claimed its appearance was a miracle, nothing to do with the world of men. But God was in short supply at Roscoff and a certain disreputable air hung around the religious. Others thought the whole thing an elaborate psy-op intended to distract from the need for unified action. What else was there, what else. The thought trails off, loses velocity. Lakerman realises he's digressing, avoiding something. He tries to find his way back to the boy, to the logic of that feeling. It's like he closes his eyes again but that's not it.

A boy walks through a trench of shit. The smell must be unholy. The boy hasn't thought about that particularly. He is hungry. He is always hungry. There were rumours of rabbits at the edges of the camp, not far from here. It'd be a miracle if anything other than vermin could survive this. The boy knows that, but he's hungry enough to want to believe. He notices a dark shape slumped in the distance. It could be anything. Still, there is a quality to the shape that makes the boy want to examine it though he does not know what that quality is. Lakerman wants to tell the boy to stop, to turn back, to go somewhere else. He knows the boy is going to find a dead body. He knows the boy will find the dead body face-down, its torso twisted like an eerie tree. The skin becoming bark. The boy will have no idea how old or what sex the body is. He'll turn the atrophied thing over and look where the eyes should be and then what's there will take something irrevocable from him.

Lakerman watches the boy walking towards the body. He can't stop it. The body is lying face down in the gravel. The boy does not want to turn the body over but he feels compelled to do so. He places his hand on a bony shoulder and pulls the body onto its back. The corpse's face wears a racoon's mask of blood. The boy looks into the place where the eyes should be. He sees two squirming orbs of maggots rolling around shattered sockets in primordial orgasm. Feasting. The maggots a grotesque parody of an eye. The scene is horrific but something is different. Lakerman can stand to see it. He feels the sense of horror he had once felt about it slowly thaw itself, the thought relaxing into his inferred body. He realises it wasn't so much that something had been lost in the trauma as something other had been put in the place of his thought. That feeling is gone now. A gentle erasure of the erasure. Lakerman looks at the dead body with a sense of fraternity. He sees in the maggots not a reminder of life's conditional violence but instead a truth of interconnection, the interdependence of life. He sees there a sense of consistency that the world had lacked at the time. The boy begins to cry. Beautifully. He pours a handful of dirt over the body's torso. Then another and another. Lakerman finds the boy's emotions and the tone of his reactions to this world are differently peaked in ways that he's allowed to remember. Empathy makes the boy's heart slip out of his mouth and beat earnestly against the floor of the present past. The boy looks up and Garbage Christ is alive in the sunset. Masked with beauty. Had the sun been setting then or does it just feel appropriate, Lakerman thinks. The boy lays down next to the grave and closes his eyes. This is not a memory at all.

The camp dissolves as Lakerman's thoughts lose structure, language poorly subtitling the fluidity of images trafficking his mind. He thinks of the sun and plastic. Oil and water. Unstoppable fire, extinguished life. He sees a featureless woman and a man emerge from a light and stand in front of him in painfully obvious symbolism that he nevertheless cannot understand. Lakerman feels a penny appear in his hand. He tosses it towards the woman. It lands in her skin, scatters freckles across her collarbone. Lakerman cannot see the woman's face. All he can see are the freckles. He knows it is Andrea. The woman reaches out and touches his face. Lakerman experiences himself as the child he wasn't. Being held. Protected. Part of him wants to laugh at this but he's only dimly aware of that part. The feeling is something else. Good enough. He begins to cry ecstatically. He finds himself forgiving himself, forgiving the world, nature, people. Beauty is honestly there, it *is* there. He feels he knows this. He's not sure how long this will last but this is definitely something new, a new feeling for him, and he is all but ready to go mad at the truth of this *original* emotion he is experiencing when the intensity dials back, drops off, and he is again coming into being in the eyes of another. His identity reforming itself around Dr Christoff's sky grey iris.

"I think I'm in love with you."

She cocks her head.

"You are and it is real even if the agency you had in contracting that emotion wasn't totally manifest. Here's a spoiler: It's not so surprising given what I've linked myself with now. Call it an insurance policy."

"I think I felt it before this."

"You didn't feel anything, really, before this. Are you listening to me?"

Lakerman experiences a kind of being double. The words coming out of his mouth are resembling something he would say but he's not experiencing them at a thoughtful level. They're at the edges of what he's really thinking about and experiencing. And yet, when he does catch himself, when he hears himself on the periphery, then what he is saying seems important. He listens. Tries to will himself to remember it.

"I don't believe you were researching an antidepressant for one second."

"If you were a real journalist you could probably find that out."

"The answer is always money."

"There might be more to it than that but yeah, that has to be a part. But imagine being so rich you could buy a reality.'

"Who owns Lifepax?"

"If you think about it you already know but I'm not sure you'll be allowed to remember any of this. Still, I'm impressed you've the gumption to ask given the circumstances and state of your feeling. Now, I'm going to send you out into the night on a high. Maybe I'll see you out there."

"Wait, what?"

* * *

Everything but plastic was breaking down. Things were in a kind of reverse that wasn't simply an undoing. This was decomposition. The fever of the way we imagined ourselves rotting ourselves. It was there in the regression from language to image, from lines of movement to blocks of pure surface, to the image of an impossible laughter crying out in one blank faced abstraction, transmittable and accepted worldwide.

Lakerman's by the pool and still tightly wrapped in a state of becoming, a bud developing interior to its matter. He's been tripping ecstatically for nine hours and is only now dimly aware of his body as a thing locatable in the world. He thinks about Doctor Christoff. The penny in his hand and the spray of freckles across the well of a collarbone. He remembers human contact, the desire for it. In his mind he perfects it, imagines what it could be. Lakerman experiences a sense of creation in his reverie, that is, something that goes beyond him. A feeling that separates and excludes him.

There are times like this when the drug lets him feel Bone-sad, this permeating and marrowing sadness, depthless and unquantifiable in its connective poignancy. He recalls the message he'd received at the lab. He opens it up. The alert had been from his therapist. Asking when would he be back, how was he doing, was he safe? Lakerman wanted to tell his therapist he was happy and that this happiness manifested itself as a kind of gravitational field holding all his other emotions in intricate and revolving patterns. He wanted to tell her this was what he had always imagined being really consciously alive felt like. A state of mind one could accept. But he knew his therapist would then ask him how he felt about himself, deep down, and how he imagines he will feel once this feeling has changed or left him, as he surely knows it must. And he'd have to answer that he imagined that he would still feel his emotions were just cunning acts of imagination, sat upon drives that only fascists could approve of, but the difference was he now knew that he could reorder those aspects of himself, that flow of desire, that he could recode the source at a practicable level.

And so Lakerman doesn't reply. Instead he composes a voicemail to donkeyWolf's editors to sound out the possibility of restructuring his contract. He tells donkeyWolf he's willing to sign an exclusivity contract with them but he wants to see what his tech options are. He tells them he's ready to make himself into an image for donkeyWolf, to become an image *of* donkeyWolf, if it means they'll kit him out. He tells them he'll provide a port of genuine connection that they'll be able to wad a whole market around. He sends the opening of his article along as a taster. The opening is a work of commercial art. A call to arms to allow the drug to flood the market, to go public. There's a slight revolutionary zeal pulsating under the language, one that is unquestionably waiting to be popularised. Memed into existence. After thirty minutes an alert shambles his skin. It's a ten year exclusivity contract. He'll write in exchange for having a subcutaneous layer of graphene implanted and connected through 90% of his body and a borderline starvation wage. Then he'll be totally modern. The tech will be upfront but recoverable in the advent of any accident or termination of the contract.

Lakerman stands up and looks at the orange spattered blue and the yellow brick road of the sun's illusion paving the water. The blue water glistening, waiting to be disturbed. He walks to the edge of the pool checking instinctively for alligators. Lakerman stretches at the edge. He counts to thirty. The transparent marquee filters the UV rays but the heat is still borderline unbearable. He had always wanted to be a robot. Lakerman dives into the pool, swims the length underwater. He's still holding his breath when he rises to the surface. He'd always wanted to be a machine.

CHAPTER 2

THE MOST CERTAIN POSSIBILITY

I t's 2.AM and Lakerman's taking an unlicensed taxi to a Rave. He'd sent out algorithms and code breaking programs to scour the alternet for any information regarding the drug. It hadn't been necessary. *Noumenal Nights: The countdown to illegality* was being held at *The border* between the dark ages and Miami. Loose ends, Lakerman thinks.

The border was a warehouse located on a grid of twenty by thirty blocks that separated Miami from its spiritual and material nothing, a stable marker in an area otherwise erratically ranged with intensity and disconnection. Lakerman's heard of the border, understands for a certain kind of hedonist it represented a rite of passage. There are other night spots, gambles, *moveable feasts* as they were known, circulating around this no man's land. Places where you might be cut off, chased down, outed as a tourist. Pop-up businesses run by waster clans claiming to be able to divine a party or gangs of art school kids trying to symbolise an edge. Nothing had lasted like the border.

Lakerman's drumming on his leg in the backseat. His consciousness experiencing itself as a wave and what the wave rises from. In separate moments of clarity Lakerman wonders how long this high is supposed to last and how he will recognise himself when it ends. He at least has the impression he's acting normally. The driver, after all, hasn't looked at him once since he entered the car. The driver instead staring fixedly into the road, into the night, his eyes a repetition of concrete and the glare of headlights, all these colliding temporalities. In order to anchor himself, Lakerman orders the driver into a set of perceptions:

(1) The driver is a young man who looks old.
(2) He is clearly dying.
(3) Of cancer, probably.
(4) His face is a clearing for ghosts.
(5) The eyes are so hollow the light doesn't hold to them.
(6) He's at least six years younger than Lakerman.
(7) South American too.

The driver's eyes meet Lakerman's in the rearview mirror. Lakerman feels so connected to the driver in this moment that he thinks he can read his mind. What the driver is really thinking doesn't bear repeating. Lakerman's thought recoils.

"This is it."

The car pulls up in front of *the border*. Lakerman watches people staggering towards it like heal me, i'm sick. *The border* is augmented with a hologram of a gothic church. The towering buttresses and gargoyles flicker and glitch to reveal the dense, squat, cuboid of the warehouse beneath. Lakerman watches light tremble with bass, weightless forms and heavy sounds colliding. Lakerman gets out of the car. As he scans his ticket an automated voice informs him that *the border* consists of three floors or 'moods.' The first floor of the club is *The Threshold*. The second *Inner Space*. The third: *The New Liminal*.

* * *

Lakerman's surrounded by bodies and trying to make sense of *The Threshold*, warbled with beats as his mind is. Everyone's dancing, their sense of themselves as selves all bent and quivering around a grain of finitude, bodies signing time around the temporary becoming of beats. Mad drums. Each body's a flickering set of coordinates alternating under metallic lights that map, in real inconstant time, velocities of emergence and change. Lakerman watches the hard surfaces of light gleam around tranced out skulls, their neon eyes polished by sweat, concavities of cheeks armoured with shine.

He heads to the bar and orders a vodka tonic that arrives lukewarm. He moves through the room, navigating the clustered bodies. There are cryptic messages in the heat packed air, information in the rendered sweat. From what he can make out, each body was expressing that:

> What they might see meant everything.
> What they could see was possibility.
> What they would see was another matter.

For a while it wouldn't even seem like a disappointment, Lakerman thinks. To be what they were in their becoming. That would require reflection. He takes the stairs to the second floor, enters *Inner Space.*

* * *

Inner Space was filled with people who looked like they were doing ableist Stevie Wonder impressions as they massaged one another. There was zero irony in the room. A club rat approaches Lakerman. Leads him to a corner. The club rat stops and looks at Lakerman very earnestly in the face. She is a young woman covered in neon glitter. Lakerman feels a tremendous surge of empathic warmth towards her. The young woman opens her mouth.

"It's the drug you know."

"What is?"

"Whatever you're feeling or thinking or imagining this is. The room has a particular frequency of transmission if you get what I'm saying."

"How do you know I'm feeling anything?"

35

The club rat looks at the ground. Smiles at it, shrugs. Applies some lip gloss. She looks up again at Lakerman with concentrated sincerity, her eyes manically glittering.

"Listen, I'm out of money, I want to score and you look like you need to soon."

"What can you get?"

"Everything from N to N."

"You can get Noumenon?"

"What do you think we're here for?"

"I'll buy it if you let me interview you."

"Interview... I don't think."

"I'll use a fake name."

"All my names are fake. Interview for who?"

"For donkeyWolf."

"No shit, donkeyWolf? Ok, yeah. Drugs first though, I'll be more interesting then."

He wants to deny what she said but he doesn't. She looks at him vaguely impressed.

"The vibe of Inner Space makes it pretty easy to fleece people once you've got a hold of its mechanisms but really, I can get stuff."

She leads him over to another club rat, a terminally sullen looking young man (even when doused in glitter, Lakerman notes.) The young man's pupils have collapsed into two concentrated points crushing the world in front of them. His brain maybe wanted the world to be as understandably complex and recognisably beautiful as a diamond, Lakerman thought. Scratch that. Delete. Lakerman 'trashes' the note. That would never make it past the line editor.

The girl lowers her head in front of the young man.

"This guy is going to buy for us."

The young man doesn't say anything.

"Now I'm buying for all three of us? This isn't the dealer?"

"This is my boyfriend. I can't take you to the dealer for reasons that should be obvious. You can wait with him, though. Just transfer me the money through gladhand."

"How do I know you're going to come back? That this is even your boyfriend?"

"I'm still high enough to feel compelled to. And he is my boyfriend and he's wonderful. You should listen to him."

She puts out her hand. Lakerman shakes it. He notices a leopard print of freckles on her exposed shoulder. The last of his expenses are transferred. The girl leaves and Lakerman finds his arm involuntarily rising towards the space she has just occupied. Weird.

Lakerman sits in front of the young man. Lights a joint, offers it. No response. The young man hasn't acknowledged Lakerman's existence enough for this to count as a rejection. Apart from his eyes the rest of the young man's face is unexceptionally there. Unshaped, though not gormless. Not even that. Lakerman didn't think it was possible to be so expressionless. It's almost shocking. It has something to do with the lack of relationship between eyes and face, he supposes. Lakerman is imagining snapping his fingers in front of the vacant face when a warm voice, rich in feeling, begins to speak through the young man's body.

"I suppose you've heard the theory that we're living in a simulation, that we're the conscious scenarios of our future ancestor's past? The maths is solid. My take: we're an attempt to work out what the fuck happened. Disaster world numero whatever."

Lakerman maintains eye contact with the blank face out of which this ventriloquized   voice speeds. There's no recognition of his presence.

"I find this idea totally romantic and meaningful. What went wrong? How could things have been different? What if this were the simulation where things worked out? And we happen upon ideas and technology that our future ancestors don't know about? What if we could retroactively save the planet, life? Imagine a world that isn't hell. I heard a scientist say that if you rewound and played back time then evolution wouldn't happen the same way twice. Is that what we are? A recording subject to change? I hope this is a simulation. The idea of a simulation lets me believe in the future and Free will as a

37

determined variable. Which is something I need. It makes me feel like my life means something even if it is a total wreck. I exist. I contribute to existence. I'm worth as much as a rock at least. Though my father would say 'Little difference'. Listen, I know you're out there. Here's something you should know: I've always loved drugs, for as long as I could love. As long as I remembered it: love. As long as I remember. To think that could mean something...imagine. The point is I don't love drugs anymore, I love this and it's different."

The young man shuts down, his intensity shrinking to a hard dot. Lakerman takes another hit and finishes the flat vodka tonic. Ten minutes later and the girlfriend is back and grinning. She pulls a small folded triangle out of her back pocket. The young man's head turns towards her. She begins to speak to Lakerman, the boy, herself, no one.

"Did you ever learn about the fortune tellers children used to make? You know the one, You remember? The one where someone would tell your future by lifting up the flaps from a paper triangle... and doesn't it strike you this is just an adult version of that?"

Lakerman doesn't respond, he wants to see the contents. She unfolds the paper to reveal two thin squares of translucent paper. One is missing a corner.

The young man sticks out his tongue. It just hangs there. The girl looks at him, smiles.

"We split it equally. Want to start with quarters? We should hang out. Become covalent bonds."

"They only had tabs?"

"How else does it come?"

"I used a needle before but the tabs I saw were way thicker than this."

"Holy shit, a needle?"

"What?"

"Nothing. Just holy shit. Since it is very few people's deeply held fantasy to be a lying piece of shit, I'll ask you straight out. Were you part of the original trials?"

"Technically. It was an assignment."

"You should be upstairs."

"What's upstairs?"

"The doc, the doc and a whole bunch of pharma grade N."

*

"I wondered if you might find your way here. You realise you can't write about my being here, that you can't even suggest it?"

The New Liminal was just an extension of *Inner Space* via a rooftop stamped with sky. There was a bar and a curiously roped off, and immaculately black, shed in the centre. A few muscular bouncers stood fast in front of the shed. Christoff, evidently seeing him on some camera, gave him clearance.

"And why is that?"

"Check the waiver you signed."

"What are you doing?"

"Working."

"According to the crowd downstairs you have a duty of care to the trialists."

"It's not a duty. It's a discount. Listen, are you going to try to put any of this together soon or not?"

"What do you mean?"

"Why are you here?"

"I'd like to buy a couple more doses."

"You don't need that. Activating the program is as easy as sending you a text. Here."

Lakerman's skin trembles with information. He opens a long series of code. He just has to verify it. He has a minute left.

"Obviously I won't be able to direct it, so it may not be as therapeutic as our earlier session."

"Was our earlier session therapeutic?"

"I thought so."

"I may need several points of comparison. Can I buy more, to have later?"

"It'll be illegal later so I can't answer that really."

"Can I buy more needles now?"

Doctor Christoff smiles.

"Why not?"

The club rats are outside. Lakerman passes them one of the needles, tells them to share. He hears himself telling them to email him their experiences. "That's the late capitalist price i'm putting on this 'gift' yeah?"

Lakerman walks to the threshold, the light painting his face, his heart warping into sync with the bass. He begins to dance.

* * *

Three weeks and one long and heavily sedated boat ride later, and Lakerman's back in a safely gentrified part of London interviewing an artist for a profile about their work when a report of a shooting in Miami pops up in his news feed. Six dead. The quaintness of a non-global catastrophe showing up there strikes Lakerman as unusual. Usually his feed was just apocalyptic/eco facts and niche philosophy memes. He opens the link. The artist is telling Lakerman that every aspect of the show was made out of plastic, that the particular plastic they had used would take longer to degrade than the human race has existed, that's over two hundred thousand years. It's practically impossible to melt too, the artist says, it'd take a sustained stream of flamethrower fire, forty to fifty seconds at least of gouted flame, to even begin to make the curvatures lose resolution. Lakerman nods. The artist says each object label in the exhibition bears the same title. Each piece is called 'Mass Production Continues.' The artist looks expectantly at Lakerman.

"I thought you couldn't make this plastic anymore."

"You can't, legally. But it's still out there. It continues. It's not going away and there's already too much of it. How very human, I thought. We've already outlasted ourselves. We could have been the last generation you know? Certainly, one of the last. This exhibition is a monument to our colossal stupidity and ego at both a personal and international level."

Lakerman continues to nod away as he looks at the article. The shooting is a two paragraph story, tucked away on what appears to be an exceptionally low budget regional news site. Lakerman scans the article trying to figure out what glitch in the algorithm could have produced this, could have reasoned he'd want this? Lakerman visibly reacting when he notices one *Andrea Christoff* identified as being among the victims. None of the other dead are named. No other information is given about Christoff, no identifiable reason why her name would be singled out. She is not even referred to as a Doctor.

The artist asks him if he is ok, more annoyed than concerned.

Lakerman asks if he can view the entrance way's sculpture. He stands by the words *'hubris-nihilism.'* written in eight foot, fuschia pink, all but immortal cursive. Lakerman's bowling pin shadow transforming the piece into *hubris-nihilism!*

Lakerman looks at his shadow. He makes a note. The artist asks him what he is making a note of. Lakerman tells them. The shadow of the mortal. The artist thinks the phrase is about their work. They think it will be about their show. They're only slightly right. The artist grins, slaps Lakerman on the back.

"I knew I was lucky to get you."

*

In the cramped, boxed, crawl space of his modern apartment Lakerman searches for mentions of Andrea Christoff online. There's nothing. She's not even on social media. Or at least not on any accessible platform. On a hunch he searches for funeral services in the area of the shooting, clicks monotonously through them. Forty five minutes have passed when he feels something barely imagined come sharply into focus. The club rat's image windowed in front of him. He scrolls down. There are details of a Catholic service planned for next Tuesday. A message board beneath that. Most of the messages were people he could tell were old acquaintances, school friends who had likely cut ties with the girl once she'd rejected their lifestyle. These were people whose love of the past had evidently been rekindled by the loss of a future. The messages showcasing atomised hearts and poor spelling.

A few comments stood out in their anger and recrimination. It was through them that Lakerman pieced together a narrative. The boyfriend had been the shooter. He'd shot her and Andrea and two others at random before turning the gun on himself. It happened at a health food store in Wynwood. It was such a well-worn scenario with the usual cast: Male-protagonist, Female victim, bystanders- tragic, that it brooked little to no surprise. Everything is neat except for the coincidences, Lakerman thinks.

For instance, they are dead and Lakerman knows about it. This is strange and interesting enough that his heartbeat, paranoia, and curiosity can't work out the nature of their relations.

He tries to brush it off.

Can't. He leans back against the wall. There's no way those club rats could afford to even pretend to be healthy, Lakerman thinks. He tries to remember the things that the doctor had told him. How he'd felt about her at the time. They were all over the place, his feelings. He couldn't piece them into the world. There was a feeling there but it was closer to an echo i.e totally removed from the substance that produced it. He knows he had loved her for a moment but it scarcely seemed credible. Where was the scar? He shudders. He felt washed out. Coming down. There's something attached to the feeling's waning, a secondary memory tagged there. The thought seems to suggest itself: how rich would you have to be to own a reality? God Tier Rich, Lakerman thinks. He orders a Negation Burger from his favourite eco-junk food dispensary and begins to look for information on Lifepax's owners. There isn't much of substance. Lifepax forms a recently purchased part of the Weber pharmaceutical group which is a subsidiary of Ulti/Multi a corporation involved in the production and retailing of electricity which in turn, Lakerman sees, was controlled by a holding company residing in the abstraction of some likely submerged Cayman island. The holding company is called '@lantis. Inc' which felt like a fuck you to the world on every conceivable level.

He turns back to Weber. He learns that, before the acquisition of Lifepax, Weber's had previously been a generic pharmaceutical company rather than one with any significant ties to research and development. Weber's was the world's biggest generic pharma group, hoovering up expired patents at an unsurpassed rate and able to heavily market meds to the lower middle class while retaining a kind of aspirational level of basic quality to the working poor. The medicine they produced generally working as far as such medicine worked. Lifepax had been a total outlier in terms of Weber's affiliated business model, focusing as it did on research, and Lakerman is struggling to see the logic behind it. Other than the work on N, known here catchily as: LPX 08 09 11 20 21 13, the chemical division of Lifepax had been relatively inactive since the takeover. Lakerman finds a few trials for drugs conducted and financed and currently under FDA consideration, all of them predating their acquisition by Weber, as well as a host of research grants and about a dozen citations on academic papers issued and referenced since. The majority of papers were with titles such as:

Impulse thought and exo-muscular potentials for amputees and paraplegics

Neuro-language imaging for hardware syncopathy

Transferable Optics: transversal image potential for paraplegic communication

Massaging trauma networks:Emotional algorithm therapy for PTSD Veterans

Intercepted Brain Messaging - exploring the possibility of multi-sensorial and reproducible experiences in different brains

The research grants post acquisition appeared largely to correspond to the papers and marked a significant shift from pharmaceutical to biotech at its most speculative. One research grant was for something called *Hiktum - BVR* which had been licensed to the chemical division of Lifepax. He'd noticed it because it had been the only research grant given out in that division other than Noumenon since the acquisition and subsequent shift into tech. Hiktum, Lakerman notes, had evidently been a huge failure for the company, not even making it to trial and seemingly having been discontinued weeks after funding. Lakerman clicks on it. He's surprised to be taken to another website.

Experience the latest in OpenWorld technology. Navigate Victorian society as one of the New Women on the eve of a rupturing event in space and time. How I Killed The Universal Man employs a unique reality engine and self learning algorithms to create greater realism and psychological acuity. With this latest release Phenom Games is set to revolutionise the medium of gaming.

Lakerman stares at the screen. He needs to know how a pharmaceutical company and a video game software startup are connected. He experiences a morbid excitement. Lakerman believed corporations as entities possessed an unconscious and he couldn't help but feel this one was beginning to talk through its speculative dreams of the future. The excitement gives way to self-loathing.

A buzz of skin and the cartoon sounds of a bomb whew-ing through the air inform him his food is arriving. Outside his door the night sky is ahum with delivery drones. The sky swarmed with lights. His food drifts down in a compostable parachute. Lakerman closes the door and sits on the floor in front of the computer. He pushes the wall. A section pops open. He extracts a plate from the draw. He pushes the wall back into position. He unwraps his food. The packaging of the burger tells Lakerman that this burger negates 0.04 metric tonnes of CO_2. The packaging encourages him to buy more. To never stop eating. He takes a bite of a greasy plant based burger. The burger 'bleeds,' pink juice spattering the white of his top. He rubs the t-shirt between his thumb and forefinger absentmindedly.

The juice was engineered not to stain. He puts the burger on the plate and the plate on the floor.

There's very little online about Phenom Games. It had been registered for about five years as an independent company and was disbanded shortly after being bought by Lifepax. The head developer was listed under the punkish sounding moniker of Trevor Orschach, a name which Lakerman immediately assumes is a pseudonym. Phenom Games had released a couple of retro, text based, adventure games as well as a Virtual Reality Therapy Simulator that Lakerman dimly recalls a controversy around. He finds a semi-successful limited streaming docu-series entitled 'Emotional Terrorism: how a small, experimental games company destroyed my family' about it and scrolls through the episodes at six times their recorded speed. Someone is talking about a suicide and Lakerman suddenly remembers the game's famously perverse premise. In the game you played a therapist tasked with keeping a patient, who was invariably a mirror image of the IRL player, from committing suicide. The patient wasn't only physically modelled on the player. The patient's biography, psychological issues, kinks and photo guided memories were gleaned or approximated from the hacked data of the player's digital portrait. The patient encountered in the game was wracked with a sense that their lives, which were those of the player/therapist, were worthless and that there was nothing in, or outside of life, that could give life meaning. To 'win' the game one had to argue oneself out of suicide which was apparently impossible.

The game, Lakerman remembers, had been found in breach of the national ethics committee for the violation of a series of privacy consent laws and had largely disappeared into the viral market under a tide of lawsuits and bans. That ought to have been it for Phenom games and Orschach but, having been bought by Weber's, a large swathe of the lawsuits against them had apparently been dropped despite the death toll and whispers of blackmail.

Phenomenal Games. Noumenal Drugs. Maybe Marker had been leaving some kind of cryptic clue when he named it, Lakerman thinks, unlikely as that may be. He takes another bite of the burger. Same outcome re: his shirt except this time the 'blood' makes him queasy. That it'll disappear makes him curiously depressed. The whole world had become uncanny a long time ago, he thinks.

Lakerman closes the computer, rolls a responsibly sourced, low water consumption Joint, and mixes a Negroni. He doesn't stand up once. About five minutes after exhaling it occurs again to Lakerman that Lifepax and donkeyWolf have some form of relationship. Ergo the trial. It's probably nothing. Still, the thought is unsettling enough for Lakerman to obsess about. It's nothing, he thinks. There had likely been a report on the Doctor Marker controversy at a lower/local tier of media. Niche. Peer reviewed perhaps. donkeyWolf's research algorithm must have divined something in those bones. Then the editorial team would have put in the preliminary work, spotted the angle, rubber stamped it, and contacted Lifepax. Most likely they sold the story as a P.R move and negotiated Lakerman's place on the medical trial as a good will gesture. A place on a trial for a drug that was due to be criminalised, he thinks. It was the kind of thing donkeyWolf did as part of their brand, i.e. tiresomely shocking and ethically reprehensible. The M.O. was already in place. No need for his intrigue. This was purely symptomatic, he thought. The problem with an attention economy, he thought, is that no one was equipped to do anything with this exchange except render it crass.

Anyway, he's not really concerned with any overt conflict of interest between donkeyWolf and Lifepax/Weber. After all, donkeyWolf media are owned by *the infant food company* and the CEO of that still largely 'family' owned company was of the God Tier Rich variety and therefore singularly independent, untouchable and in strategic relation to anything they didn't outright own. Lakerman was aware the IFC's own ties with the media were historic and constituted a shadow history of Latin America. This was common knowledge. It turned out that even a connected society couldn't choose to care.

He reopens the computer. The tint of the light is a balm to his eyes. The cursor on the screen in front of him is blinking at Lakerman like the Cheshire cat gone dead pan. He googles *The Infant Food*

Company, clicking on a site he knows is probably a red flag on his browser history. It's all there. Founded in the eighteen hundreds as a way of providing synthetic baby food as a response to a high infant mortality rate, *the infant food compan*y had radically diversified over time to honour its existential motive of profit. When medical evidence and an improvement in social conditions solved the problem of infant mortality and demonstrated the self-sufficiency of nature, the company moved into the production of ice cream and cocoa based snacks. The IFC's association with Freud's cousin Edward Bernays revolved in part around this transition into the snack industry. Bernays had told them this change would align them with a larger transformation in the West, namely that of need to pleasure. At the same time as repositioning the IFC in the Western world Bernay's brief was to help the Company coordinate a guerrilla marketing campaign for their surplus original products in 'third world' countries. The deliberate disinformation campaign was dispersed through government issued warnings, old fashioned sale samples, entertainment, naive doctors, bribed doctors, amongst other dubious and hard to verify methods. The campaign helping to preserve a facsimile of their original target market outside of the tiresome notion of human rights to the extent that they kept producing the obsolete. Then, following Bernay's suggestion, the IFC acquired the most popular national brands of cereals and other food stuffs in each Latin country, added sweetener or msg, and reduced the size of the products by 4-5% in order to further insert themselves into a communal history, to monetise nostalgia while tainting reality. To the first generation the disappointment of the product offered a poignant reflection on a childhood memory impossible without the renewable sense of loss each foodstuff brought. To the next it didn't matter.

Factor in the IFC's buying of land and the jobs they provided, another form of indentureship, and *The infant food company* might have been said to have a sizable impact on South America as a continent. In the 1980s *The infant food company* had continued to expand by building large scale, environmentally unfriendly, factory farms on amazonian land in order to supply themselves with milk and meat byproducts while investing in bottled water stocks and pushing for the privatisation of water supplies around the world. Then in the 90s they covertly founded a chain of health food shops cornering the 'organic' and 'sustainable' market and even fostering a certain antagonism between the 'ethical' chain companies and the visible behemoth of *the infant food company*. This established the organic as ideological yet privileged and the public face of *the infant food company* as the immoveable state of things in general. Thus the IFC had established a monopoly on both privileged hope, the salve of the middle class as Lakerman in his more negative moments conceived it, as well as the generalised nihilism that played in the background of mainstream, consumer oriented, life. A state of affairs that in the early 2000s became exhaustingly referenced in an ad campaign designed to reduce the impact of the association. During the shift from print to digital, writing to video, and thanks to the companies act of 1922 and corporate personhood the infant food company covertly acquired and absorbed Externacore media group who, buoyed by the financial doping of the IFC, added a number of startups to their burgeoning portfolio.

And thus donkeyWolf was incorporated.

Ice clatters against Lakerman's front teeth. He is disappointed to find he has finished his Negroni. He looks at the joint in the ashtray and feels faintly parodic. He tries to clear his head. He's still anxious but at least now that anxiety could be anything, could just be the world. Lifepax and donkeyWolf, he thinks, any connection was tenuous at best. He closes the computer, lays down. Rolls into his sleep space.

What am I doing, he thinks.

* * *

It's 3pm, he's barely slept, and Lakerman's forgotten to remove his augmented reality lenses. He's finally drifting into r.e.m sleep when a message begins to aggressively and repeatedly explode in digitised confetti against the interior of his eyelids. He turns on his side to dismiss it. It will not be dismissed. The message is really a question. The question accesses his calendar. The calendar is bright white, numbers written in pale green font, each square reassuringly empty as a Buddhist. There is a measure of calm and then the question rewrites itself in flashing red on today's date. Lakerman palms the lenses out of his eyes. An alarm begins to sound on his computer. Fuck it, ok, he thinks. He opens the alert. The moment he understands what he is seeing he can't believe it. Lakerman's being asked to confirm an appointment for 7pm with an installation artist who is going to implant his graphene hypo-net. The appointment he's been given is with UbIQ at their flagship clinic in Kings Cross and what they were offering clearly exceeded the terms of his contract. He had offered his career to donkeyWolf for a fraction of this and from what he understood he was way down the waiting list for any operation, six months at least. He figures someone at UbIQ's public relations department must have been monitoring his work, reasoned Lakerman would likely write a complimentary piece about the implant, and thought it would be good publicity for them. He reads a message from donkeyWolf informing him of the changes but that his contract still stands. UbIQ had paid the difference on top of what they had offered. The move was therefore optimally structured. Everyone won. UbIQ got publicity at minimum expenditure, donkeyWolf maintained their hold on Lakerman's career and Lakerman was lucky enough to hit the lottery tech wise. It made sense. After all, Lakerman's in the midst of a cultural moment. His article on Noumenon had been an unqualified success. It was being alleged in various territories of the alternet that his work had initiated a conversation that was taking place outside the culture war's bracketed enclosure of the social. He'd arrived in the UK, a week after the piece had gone live, to find it being widely shared and frequently employed as a front for people's online personas.

The appeal of the article, Lakerman believed, was likely to do with the alternative to modern life he portrayed Noumenon and biotech as offering. Everyone, he had written, knew identity was incoherent, reductive and fundamentally unstable, a series of nodal points in a complex and interrelated network the scope of which was too fraught to ever really cohere or integrate enough into an 'individual.' And yet everyone was still taught to individualise. This created powerless individuals addicted to the system of individualisation, a lobotomised self. You, by dint of loss. It had been this castrated individualisation that had led to the burnt nerve ending of the earth, environmental collapse, commodified nihilism. People knew this in their hearts, he wrote, knew that they had suffered a profound loss. Lakerman depicted Noumenon as offering a promise of intense personal realisation coupled with a release from identity's overly adhesive properties. An opportunity to really be able to choose. To be conscious. To not have to encounter oneself or another self in any funhouse mirror of representation but instead learn to be the mirror, this was the dream, Lakerman had written. Reappropriating disassociation, he called it. A campaign to legalise Noumenon, to bring it under review, had subsequently started up in earnest. A million signatures and counting. Lifepax had yet to comment.

He has accepted the appointment of course, and is calculating the fastest route to the clinic. He makes a list as he applies sunscreen. First, the implant then the article campaign, eventually emancipation. That's the plan, he thinks. Lakerman's long term goal is to get out of his donkeyWolf contract while retaining the merch. He thinks that if he can subtly engineer public favour around the right to augmentation then donkeyWolf might be forced to renegotiate their draconian demands on his intellectual property. He already had an angle for this that he thought seemed promising. There were no official numbers regarding the number of Hyponet users available to the public but he figured there couldn't be more than a few hundred thousand. The price was prohibitive, something to mortgage a future against, and the idea of an implant like this was still relatively niche so his guess was that the majority of implants were either corporately or militarily sponsored with all the usual manner of privacy violations such support constituted along the way. Lakerman was going to contact as many users as he could and give an unsparing account of the financial subjugation and exploitation his hunch told him they were suffering under. This social critique would be intertwined with an argument to make the technology cheaper, a right like the internet. He'd argue that the only way to fight exploitation was to devalue its means by giving everyone access. How he'll get any of that past the editors he's not sure but he could leak work if necessary, write anonymously in parallel to his donkeyWolf work, he thinks.

Lakerman picks up the UV umbrella. He repeats: First, the implant. Then, the article. Eventually, emancipation. In between step one and two he'll shoot the last syringe of Noumenon and try to detail the difference in promised intensity and what that might mean for him. Christoff had said the more tech you were fitted with the more effective Noumenon could be, it still hadn't clicked how. And then, for the first time that morning, he remembers the shooting, Andrea, the feelings he'd had about her that he reflexively thought rendered her inaccessible and totally unknowable, even if it doesn't feel like that to him now. He experiences a sharp body shot of emotion that he just kind of absorbs, ambiguity and all. Lakerman keeping it all on the internal.

He leaves the flat.

* * *

Three hundred years ago the pavement in Kings Cross had been cobbled and cracked, breaking out of the city's skin like some Victorian STD. Now though, the concrete was smooth and unlined, the street resolutely sexless in its uniformity. Lakerman looks around. The entirety of Kings Cross had been recast by soft power ventures and embroidered by talent convertible to taste. Very few residential buildings remained and much of the new architecture appeared to be a brutalist take on ecological thought. Nature was muscle in this economy and was compartmentalised and flexed as such in powerfully isolated quadrants of Life.

The streets though are lifeless and empty and Lakerman's shadow spoons across the concrete towards *The Tree Of Life*, a bio-genetic sculpture created in collaboration between the artist TOR and UbIQ's engineers. Its position officially marking the entry to the UbIQ-owned tech quarter. According to the plaque it had been created by the artist to celebrate the anniversary of the great global climb back. Apparently the world wasn't getting any hotter. Not that you'd know it, Lakerman thinks. Still, he's aware the air around him is noticeably fresher here, that there is moisture in the air that seems to clean away the sweat of his body. Up close, the tree makes him gasp.

The *Tree Of Life* is leafed with an astounding variety of type: Coy Vine, delicate Cherry Blossom, Autumnal Maple, Yellow Gingko, Big Hearted Catalpa, and more that Lakerman can't identify and is too tired to image search. These are all enfolded and arranged together into a harmonious whole. The effect is one of both convexity and concavity, an outward force of life and inner field of home. The two shifting and alternating in front of his gaze, never settling.

Yellow, hypoallergenic, pollen dusts the tree of life's upper leaves and branches, lending the tree a golden hue, a crown of light. Every two hours, an automatic message states, the tree releases the pollen and a curved swirl of mist envelopes the tree and graphically streaks the surrounding ground, coating everything for a moment in a radiant fallout of beauty. After a few minutes the pollen sterilely disintegrates into nothing and the tree resets itself.

Walking closer, Lakerman notices the trunk of the tree has a fascinating if unnatural seeming whorl in its trunk. The whorl in the trunk, positioned at eye level, resembles a gnarly oak, though its lines are concentrically perfect and etched into the body of a sequoia rising fifty feet into the air. He walks up to the tree, reaches out, his hand caressing the whorl which he notices reveals a portion of heartwood at its centre. The heartwood is the colour of dried blood. The heartwood is exposed but not vulnerable. He circles the tree. There are no ants, caterpillars or spiders. No beetles or flies. No bugs anywhere, Lakerman thinks. There are no nests in the branches that he can see and Lakerman's willing to bet the Cancer Foxes don't fuck with the tree at night. The absence of stains or piss smell is revealing, he thinks. Life here, Lakerman thinks, is censored by beauty.

The *TOL* is, of course, technically not a tree but rather a Stomata plant fashioned into a talented rendering of a tree. Leaving the shade of this *biological machine,* an advert informs Lakerman that for a small fee he can manufacture a cloud to shade him as he walks around. He declines. The advert doesn't quit. It projects a small, unskippable, guerrilla holovert. Lakerman watches a blonde white woman and her child flicker into existence. The woman opens her purse and a cloud floats out. The cloud is light grey with an idea of rain forming in its centre. The woman hands the child a thin wand shaped object with which he seems able to hold the cloud like a string attached to a balloon. The holovert expertly exploiting nostalgia for a lost past. Lakerman's eyes well up involuntarily. He shakes his head, rolls his eyes. The woman and child disappear. Behind him pollen streaks the ground golden. Lakerman puts the route to the clinic on audible. He listens to the global positioning system, following its orders and descriptions of the world, vaguely comforted by the neutrality and accuracy of its totally externalised and therefore limited voice.

Just ahead. You have arrived.

* * *

The clinic is birch tree silver with weaved walls of Stomata polished into a slick, almost reflective surface. The building is tunnel shaped and its curved walls appear to expand and contract, gently yawning into the blue. Lakerman places his hand against the building's surface and feels the calm, measured, pulse of an alive thing. He observes his breath and heartbeat slow and sync with the building in vascular empathy. The building is active and organic, intimately involved with matters of light and oxygen.

Entering he finds that the interior is single floored, open plan, hangar-like. The majority of the space though is cast in an artificial darkness. There are no employees and he can see only a small area of light ahead of him, drawing the dark around itself like a candle. A genderless voice invites him to enter the waiting room, to browse UbIQ's range of ecologically driven products. Lakerman frowns, says "I have an appointment."

"Of course Mr Lakerman. Someone will be with you shortly. Meanwhile, please enjoy the waiting room, you may find something else of interest here."

The light in the waiting room is tastefully curated and heavy with poignancy. It is as if the magic hour were following you around. *Every* surface is burnished amber with artificial sunlight, every *thing* sacredly aflame. The layout of the floor is outlined by a complex Stomatar vine wiring the space into geometric forms of useful emptiness. Every room is a blueprint of a room. He watches one retract and reform, change purpose. The vine's growth pattern is controlled, endlessly modifiable, and managed by UbIQ's *natural programming* technology. Enslaved nature, Lakerman notes, curated space.

There are maybe ten other customers occupying the waiting room. The public, unofficially known as tourists among the 'culture' of the company Lakerman has read, browse the merchandise that emerges, unobtrusively, in coronas of light and delicately arranged garlands within each 'idea space'. Each outline of a room has a product embedded in its centre, offering its hidden gifts once someone enters. Lakerman watches a middle aged woman entering a room/idea-space. The space is empty but for a table covered in soil. The woman touches something on the table and a Stomata seedling grows into what appears to be a modest dolls house replete with furnishings. The final addition to the diorama, a doll, stumbles forward in awkward animation towards the woman and opens its palm. In the centre of the doll's palm is a new Stomata seed.

Lakerman watches the Woman mouth the word reset. The doll's house immediately begins to compost. The house and doll rapidly collapse into waste that becomes soil for the new seed. Lakerman watches the woman say something he can't quite work out. A new house, smaller than before, begins to structure itself into existence.

54

Lakerman realises she is designing a home.

"Mr Lakerman, please make your way to the Pharmakon to speak to one of our artists."

He looks around. At the edge of the waiting room there is only darkness. A section of Stomata splits and forms a pathway for Lakerman that leads past the exhibition rooms and three or four metres into the inky black. Flower buds, spaced at mathematically satisfying intervals along the vine, open and close and pulse gently fluorescent, changing pastel candied colour every few seconds. This variation of Stomata likely spliced with a Jellyfish protein, Lakerman thinks. It's an old trick, a little dated. He follows the pathway to where it stops in front of a wall of darkness. Lakerman looks around. The pathway behind him no longer glows and the waiting room is no longer visible. He is suspended in space.

"Please step forward and enter the Pharmakon Mr Lakerman."

He reaches his arm out. He cannot see it. He steps forward, passing through the darkness and into a white and totally illuminated space. There are maybe one hundred people here. The same genderless voice invites him to take a seat and to address any questions he might have to one of the screens in front of him. He sits on one of the transparent benches planted into the building. As he opens his mouth the screen responds in the voice of the building.

"It is a dark light John. An opaque hologram."

"And why do you do it?"

"To preserve the uniqueness of each experience UbIQ provides."

"How did you know I was going to ask about that?"

"Let's call it a guess."

Lakerman shakes his head at this coy attempt to unnerve him via implicit deindividuation. They have no idea what he dreams about, he thinks. Lakerman looks around. The Pharmakon is a fantasy of minimalism graffitied by commodified notions of cool. Gallery white, but partitioned with benches via the golden ratio, the whole aesthetic is both Ancient Greece and indicative of a neurotic, modern, hygiene masking itself as futurism. There is a space in the centre of the spiral hallway where sculptures of DNA and the biological sign for life are rendered in classical marble as decoration. The room itself is circular and low walled. Like a giant Petri Dish, Lakerman thinks.

An announcement is made informing the public that "the first wave of Artists will be entering the Pharmakon shortly."

"Jesus" Lakerman says. The monitor in front of him says "Cynicism is old world, sarcasm the lowest form of wit and everyone is trying their best."

"Mute."

The screen turns white. Lakerman's surprised to look up and see a garishly coloured rainbow maned unicorn emerging from the centre of the spiral and trotting towards, and then patiently addressing, an old age pensioner. The old age pensioner is holding a broken tablet that has been obsolete for at least five years. The unicorn rears up on two legs, begins to explain something about warranties. The next employee that emerges is a six foot stick figure with his right arm apparently on fire. The stick figure's mouth is a dark, permanently open, black pit. It forms an empty syllable, a silent scream. Lakerman googles the image. It used to be used on boxes of matches next to the phrase 'Danger of Children being burnt.' The burning stick man walks up to a teenager who has a glazed expression and hands stitched with decorative circuitry. They nod at each other. They are friends perhaps, Lakerman speculates. More employees arrive, faster now. They are all using avatars, perhaps to preserve their identities from any particular threat, perhaps to tap into some psychological profile of the clients. Lakerman watches the general public interacting with unicorns, emoticons, glowing blue lizards. Almost everyone is being seen now and he's about to ask the monitor about his appointment when he is greeted by an employee presenting as a canvas of skin with the wound of a famous cartoon Mouse cut into it.

"Hi, I'm Goofy." The mouse says. "But you can call me Donald huh huh." The wound moves slightly as the person talks, an animated musculature moving under the 'surface' of the skin. The voice is similarly copyrighted, an octave beyond the human. Lakerman rubs his temple. UbIQ had recently bought controlling shares in the company who owned the mouse. Allowing this kind of bastardisation was probably the corporate equivalent of eating your enemies hearts, Lakerman thinks.

"I'm going to be your installation artist today huh huh. I see you're getting the works. I'm impressed. I haven't had a chance to do one of these that wasn't your standard employee issue for a while huhu. Before we start I have a few a questions we need to run through but first I'll have to ask you to sign our standard waiver/terms and conditions."

"How long is it?"

"Like you're not going to sign? Huh huh."

Lakerman looks up at the canvas of skin.

"I'd like to read it all the same."

"Scroll through the mail I've just sent you."

"You don't have a print copy?"

"Huh huh."

"You're going to stand there the whole time?"

"I have to."

"Couldn't I just ask the machine?"

"Maybe, but you'd probably need to hear it from me."

Lakerman's only really scanning the waiver. He's buying time.

"You said something about an employee issued... Do you have a graphene implant?"

"Everyone who works here does huhu."

"Can you deepen the voice a touch,   give yourself an octave or two?"

"Certainly."

"Is the implant you have the same as I'm getting?"

"Not exactly. I mean you've paid for full APPS and have a subscription to UbIQ's Beta testing trials. Ours has limited functionality in and outside of work."

"So, my body is new territory and yours is... China?"

Lakerman thinks he can detect something real stiffen behind the avatar.

"That's not how I meant it sir. I'm very lucky to have this job and the implant. I'm very fortunate to be working for UbIQ and I'm not really sure what you mean by saying China."

"I get it, your sincerity has convinced me. I truly mean that."

"Is there a problem sir?"

"So, other than work is the hyponet..." Lakerman doesn't know how to finish his question. Ending it with fun would depress and deflate him, ending it with important seems ...vulnerable somehow?

"Is it useful?"

"Of course."

"What do you like most about the implant?"

"The Games, the games are the best."

"Oh."

"There's all kinds now."

"Right."

Something in the terms and conditions catches Lakerman's attention.

"What does 'I hereby grant bio-chem access to all UbIQ affiliated health apps mean?"

"It's basically allowing an advanced biometrics wellness program and early health warning system to collate and test your readings. Your data only gets used by the app itself and anonymously for research into diseases."

"Into curing diseases?"

"I don't follow."

"The research would be to find cures to diseases I assume. This is an assumption you're encouraging me to make?"

"I'm almost certain that would be the case given UbiQ's mission statement."

"Do you know where I could find out who was involved in this research?"

"I don't have that information available to me but I'm sure if you contact..."

"Ok, Ok. What can you tell me about the apps that are being used?"

"The LitFit, AyDoctor!, and GentleThought Apps employ an algorithm based on an intensive and ongoing quantification of the organism that is you at both a neuro, enviro and microbiological level."

"Could you be both more specific and generalised so I can understand?"

"Think of your body as an unknown territory, an undiscovered ecosystem. Turns out each man *is* an island. The implant is your ultimate explorer. It's mapping you. It's learning you. The implant measures everything from rates of synaptic fire, chemical balances, serotonin levels etc to your level of hydration and posture. It registers how much you cry, when you cry, and at what. It'll calculate how much sleep you get, how much R.E.M sleep you get, what neural pathways get reinforced and which ones are dimmering over time. It'll use your location data to have a sense of any environmental issues at play, what and who is around. Air quality. It uses the IP addresses of everyone you come into contact with in order to establish certain effects of your relationships and theirs. It'll calculate your attention span and, if you're using augmented reality lenses, what you look at. The big data of your perception and biology et al gets cross referenced with your neurochemical framework to produce better algorithms allowing the LitFiT, AYDoctor!, and GentleThought Apps to offer tailored exercise routines, diets, pre-emptive medical care and self care suggestions."

"Can I turn that off?"

"You can but it's a hassle and what if you then got a tumour? Or the first signs of skin cancer?"

"You know if that's actually happened? I mean statistically it's possible but it sounds like alarmist bullshit."

"It happens. It happens *a lot*. Plus you need all three if you want to make the most of the beta testing subscrip. They've released one recently, Opscions, that sounds incredible."

"This isn't what I imagined."

"Listen, numbers don't define you or what you'll become with this."

"I don't want an identity."

"Then share absolutely everything. Be totally known."

Lakerman signs the waiver. The wound of the mouse appears to be healing into a scar, the red lines fading into pink.

"Can I ask you a question?"

"Of course, that is why I am here."

"Do you always use an avatar or is it only for work?"

"Always for here. It's a requirement, part of the culture, but I like it. Outside of work, not so much although there are a fair few who are into it."

"You don't find it demeaning?"

"In what way?"

"In that you can choose to be anything but yourself?"

"Not at all. I mean, identity *is* an avatar."

"An avatar for what?'

"For whatever hasn't appeared."

Lakerman takes a note.

"Would you mind if I used that?"

The musculature 'under' the wound tightens.

"I think it would be best if we went straight to the operating theatre, from what I've observed we can waive the psychological questionnaires for now."

*

The operating theatre resembles a stock photo of an 1980s L.A tattoo parlour. It's a total time capsule of hoary cliches remarkably inoculated against irony. A half empty bottle of Jack Daniels sits in front of a problematic calendar and a neon sign that reads PARTY in hot pink. The mahogany liquid of the bottle slicked oceanically metal with the reflection of neon. The Installation Artist seems more relaxed in this environment, Lakerman notes, the carved lines of the mouse scar slackening slightly. Lakerman sits down on a hydraulic chair, the shape of which is comfortably humanoid. He swivels around to face a large mirror. The Y of the PARTY sign flickers out. In the mirror the reflection TЯAꟼ makes Lakerman smile.

"Do you like this? If you don't we can change it. We're expected as employees to make certain guesses about customer preference based on the data we receive. I mean the implant has predictions but they still want us to act on intuition for some reason. I'm actually getting pretty good."

"And you thought I would like this?"

"I thought you'd like disliking it and that after I explained you'd probably be happy to keep it as a kind of warning against, I don't know, your own confirmation bias?"

"I feel personally attacked."

"But we can be anywhere you want. This is all hologram based anyway. The only thing I'd have to physically remove is that chair and these."

He pulls on what looks like glow in the dark rubber bones. He hands to Lakerman what Lakerman recognises now as a model of a child's spinal column and rib cage. Lakerman runs it through his fingers, hoops his hands around the pliant bone.

"You know what these are?"

Indestructible plastic spines discontinued, Lakerman imagines, due to the speculative horror of an uninhabitable world filled with Halloween skeletons. The exact point evolution became dated by the process of Anti-fossilisation. This resistance to change that had characterised the human species race to the cliff.

"Nope."

"NeuroProsthetics. Discontinued. A former UbIQ competitor if you can imagine such a thing. Bought up and disbanded. Officially they were for people with spinal injuries. They were kind of mind-modelled, joypad configured, electrically rechargeable bionic limbs. Unofficially they were one of a series of body parts funded in a bid to create an indestructible body. For real."

"Is that right?"

"They're just the kind of trash our owner is inexplicably obsessed with. These are de rigueur for every operating theatre. Company directive."

"Any idea why?"

"He just loves this shit."

Lakerman looks at the employee, narrows his eyes comically.

"What's with the performative swearing? Are you running a script on me? Is this part of the sales pitch?"

"Nothing like that. I don't have to be as formal here. This room isn't a camera. My body isn't under any regulatory system. Everything here is disabled because of the secrecy around 'the process.' I wish you hadn't asked me those fucking questions outside though man. My post-op debrief is going to be such a hassle now."

"Sorry."

"Don't mention it."

Lakerman's thumb runs over the rubber of the bones. He feels a set of raised letterings on the inside of the third rib. He turns it over to look and see @lantis corp. That's familiar, he thinks. Atlantis, he thinks. He's interrupted by the appearance of a small plastic case hovering in front of the Avatar.

"Have you taken any drugs in the past three months?"

A syringe has been added to the Mouse Scar's avatar. The large needle sticking out of the now animate gloved hand of the wound further distracting Lakerman from his thoughts.

"A little weed."

"Nothing else?"

"Nothing else."

The gash of a smile opens across the mouse's flesh.

"Liar."

"And if I had?"

"Worst case scenario is the bots would try to rebuild the chemical from the traces in your system. You won't die, probably, but you shouldn't operate heavy machinery."

"How does this work?"

"You ever seen when a tennis court or area of play or something gets covered by Tarpaulin? Maybe the sun is too hard or it's going to rain? Then all those bodies rush out holding onto the fabric to make sure it all gets covered?"

"Yeah."

"This is like that. The little Xenobots in here are all tasked with covering your interior in Graphene, unfurling it and installing the apps."

"So what do you do?"

"What every artist does. I create solutions for your body. I monitor, I adjust, I pilot. If there are any stray robotics in your system we'll talk and maybe collaborate."

"Stray?"

"These things are like plastic now. They're in everything. "

The mouse scar stretches itself towards him, the musculature assembling and disassembling through a refined pattern of mechanisms like a physical lock.

"Do you want the injection in your head or foot? In the foot means more discomfort while they assemble. In the head means you go pretty numb straight away but, y'know, it's in your head huhuh."

"Head."

"That's what I figured. 2 for 2 today."

The mouse scar tilts the chair back. Lakerman can't see how the mouse is manipulating the needle. How its body would render that concealment. There's the slightest of stinging sensations and then the swab of cotton upon which Lakerman sees a dot of blood, tiny as a pixel, as it sticks to the flesh of the mouse wound. The swab disappears into the skin, forms a little lump there. Fades away. Shouldn't that be put in the bin, Lakerman thinks.

"It should start taking effect in just a few minutes. You're *the* John Lakerman right?"

"I suppose so."

"That's how I knew you were lying about the drugs, I didn't need the app for that. I read your article on N and all your blogs. I didn't really understand the fuss but then I remembered you're a tourist writing for other tourists. You're an ambassador, or something. I know some programmers who would love to contact you. Actually, when they heard you were coming in they asked me to give you something."

"What?"

"A gift."

"I only got the appointment a few hours ago."

"I don't think so, they've had you down for months."

"I don't understand."

Lakerman's body is going numb. He can't feel anything. The Mouse's wound begins to drip blood.

"About the present," the mouse says, "I'll just leave it inside huhuh."

* * *

CHAPTER 3

EQUIPMENTAL BEING

Lakerman's attention is an arpeggio and Reality has certain possibilities of cadence. Lakerman is sat cross legged on the floor of his flat, halfway through a glass of chocolate flavoured oat milk and with his mouth full of vegan cookies, when he becomes conscious of himself as a thing localised in space and time. For the past five hours perception and reality have shifted sweetly through possible positions, surprising interchanges, ascending and descending in a complement of difference, undoing the glacial idea of any uniform moment. Fuck holism, Lakerman has thought in the better moments of whatever this is. It arrives to Lakerman's attention that he does not know how he got home or where these cookies have come from. He is not in the habit of buying cookies or drinking chocolate milk. Lakerman is, however, newly aware that the tradition of pairing milk and cookies at Christmas in the U.S dates back to the great depression and that this tradition has its roots in Norse Mythology and an attempt to curry favour with Odin via the leaving of species specific treats for his eight legged horse. He frowns. Lakerman realising in this moment that he does know how he came home: On public transport, quite normally, ears plugged with music, outwardly secure while internally hallucinating Santa riding a spider horse and holding a depression era pitch fork as a wikipedia article on the origins of cookies and cream (disambiguation) was read out in a monotone by the ghost of his step father done up in period garb. He knows this is how he got home but he has no memory of it even if there are images attached to the thought. He'd also had a conversation with his editor at donkeyWolf regarding a meeting tomorrow the content of which he can't remember. Then he'd gone to the supermarket where he'd bought an enormous amount of food and drink. He can't explain it. It was like his existence had been radically split, one half compressed and edited into highlights, the other visualised data guided by impulse. As if the self had been in two places at once. Evidently, he thinks, there has been a reaction between the residual Noumenon in his system and the implant, resulting in some kind of associative fritzing that's fucking with his temporality.

To the right of Lakerman a brand name bottle of Gin he can't afford is chilling in a bowl of perma-ice. He reaches to look at its label. Something stops him. If he wants to stay here, he realises, he has to concentrate. He reaches again for the Gin but, grasping it, he's already gone.

Lakerman stands behind a bar in Italy over two centuries ago. That's just the environment, a referential caption, preloaded knowledge, an unquestioned given. There's wood and peasants for period detail and that's it. A military man of high social ranking asks for a cocktail, a Milano-Torino or *Americano*. Lakerman is about to add soda water when the soldiers' hand stops him. "Più forte," the soldier says. Something stronger. Lakerman picks up a bottle of gin. Like this, Lakerman learns, the Negroni is born.

Something stronger.

He is in the room again. The cookies have been finished, crumbs vacuumed. The oatmeal glass is gone, rinsed clean in the sink behind him. At his feet is a sepia coloured Negroni with a pornographic amount of condensation wetting the glass. He takes a sip. It's bitter like the past and yet some syrupy aspect coats his mouth thick with promise. Lakerman is watching a standup routine on YouTube, and has been for the last half an hour. Surprisingly, he can recall it all despite his hallucinatory history lesson. The comic delivers a show written by A.I.'s attempt to mimic the comic's own observational style. That was the throughline joke: The disjunction between one grasping, off kilter, view of the world and another. The comic was skilled if generally banal and Lakerman guessed the audience's secure laughter might morph into something more taxing, revealing a trough to its peak and the possibility of falling forever. One could hope. Quite likely the comedian would offer some commentary on the A.I.'s standup only to reveal that this had in its turn been scripted by the A.I. putting into question, the comedian would note, whether the absurdity of the previous 'mistakes' had been intentional or not.

"Now, of course this part was not in the script. Or was it?"

At the end, Lakerman imagines the A.I. would turn out to be profound though crucially unconscious of its own meaning, while the human would be absurdly meaningless and exhaustingly self aware. He concentrates on the stand up. Everything happens just as he imagined. I'm on some kind of delay, he thinks.

Lakerman takes another mouthful of his drink. He notices the gin bottle is three quarters empty but he does not feel drunk. If only every poison was as medicinal seeming as a Negroni, he thinks. He lifts the glass to eye level. The colour is a strong mood. He wants to think about Miami, to remember it all in sequence but Lakerman is lost in colour now. Forms and theory. Collaborations of light and evolution. Histories of venal trade and venal value. He's learning about cochineal, a small insect used to create red dye. The surface of his hand approximates the weight and texture of a pestle and mortar. He grinds hundreds of cochineals into a powder, and adds a little water. The red is vibrant, slightly coppered, it looks like his Negroni. He wants to lick it. An indigenous woman stops him.

Lakerman wakes up to himself in his bathroom. He is scrubbing the sink and the toilet has been recently bleached. The cubicle around him blooms with chemical flowers. There are cultures of life in the cracks of his wall and he feels their blind struggle and the satisfied discharge of their energy expended in replication. Lakerman scrubs so hard a bubble escapes the brush. He pushes his finger into the soap bubble. It indents then floats away. He thinks: Surface tension equals non violent resistance. Gandhi appears in the reflection of the tap. He polishes Gandhi's glasses. The hot tap. H for Heidegger. Images of Gandhi intermingle with footage of Heidegger.

Lakerman deep fakes his own imagination, begins to put together what he imagines is shareable content. He calls it:

'When Gandhi met Heidegger'

Gandhi tells Heidegger It's obvious Nazism is latent in Heidegger's thought. Heidegger wants to protest. It's a possibility of his thought, he concedes, but not intended and certainly not obvious or a consequence of it. "Ask for forgiveness," Gandhi says.

"I can't," replies Heidegger, "I'm dead. I'm no longer being in the world."

"Also, you were, like, really a Nazi." Gandhi says. "For realsies."

"That was the *me* of the *they*. I should never have entered the marketplace. I belonged in the mountains with the peasants, living beyond politics. Look at what I could think, what I did think."

"You overrate both beauty and its proof. You might have been kinder but you were an arrogant prick. It doesn't matter what you romanticise, only that you do romanticise. Romanticising is the death of an-other."

"Fuck off Gandhi."

Lakerman gains consciousness next to his mini oven. His eyes widen in fear. There are strange shapes and unknown textures in his mouth. His mouth is full and lubricated. He spits out whatever is in there in a panic. Yellow and red things stain the floor. He has evidently been eating a potato dish rich with vegan Ghee. A half finished bowl sits atop the counter. He stands up. Oil has separated from the sauce and moves in globules on the surface of the dish. Lakerman bursts into tears in relief. When he has recollected himself Lakerman feels a little racist by association, he hopes the choice of food had nothing to do with the hallucination of Gandhi. He looks down at the food spattered on the floor. His stomach cramps. He notices other boxes of food and highly sugared vegan gummy sweets brightly arrayed around the room.

Lakerman is beginning to feel nauseous. There are many voices inside of him now. What identifies itself as his own voice is detectable only by its disjunction, a noticeably off note in the swell of possibility.

The other voices keep whispering options, statistics, outcomes and desires but nothing feels tangible enough to fill the blindspot where 'he' ought to be. Lakerman feels a mounting panic. An impulse that isn't his commands his body to breathe and his body responds. Lakerman is breathing slowly and deeply and his attention is with his breath, his existence in this moment. He is breathing as if in a meditation but Lakerman is not in a meditation and among the settling calm and the alteration of his detuning brain waves a panic, only able to state itself, skates atop the deepening peace. His thoughts feel taxidermied, detangled and glazed, the language he used to articulate the world around him a kind of phantom limb, a referential memory he can only experience in absentia. He struggles against the tide of wellness, the release of serotonin, the jags of optimism.

Lakerman begins to worry that he has become a living memorial to himself, a fully mathematisable thing syphoned into another, larger, and unknowable thing within which he'll accrete in the saddest of ways. He is telling himself he is worrying but he cannot experience this worry physiologically. He thinks this intervention on the part of the implant chances a partial corruption of his thought, that he won't be able to remember his real thoughts, the original fading from this denaturing exposure, and that after a while his thoughts would come to occupy a kind of flattened terrain as they lost their architecture, leaving him alone with experiences deboned and frameless, so that the sense of self embodied in them would become haunted, lost in the limitlessness of their flat distribution.

Lakerman forces himself to cry and the room trembles with a strangely insincere weeping. His computer turns itself on, a hologram beaming out of the port.

"Hi, my name is Jane. I'm a UbIQ customer service A.I. and I am here to help. Now I see that this was an implant directed call regarding some emotional distress after your recent installation, please could you state the exact nature of your problem?

Lakerman doesn't respond.

"I see, So you're hearing voices and feel that your emotions are no longer your own? You've tested positive for substances that do not occur unaided within the body and which have led to a destabilisation of both your perception of reality and self. Your attention has been partially liberated from language, your conscious and unconscious have uncoupled. You have become unpredictable. As a safety precaution your implant has thus defaulted to the Gentle Mind App mood inducement protocol. Yes sir, I will deactivate that for you soon but Right now I'm acting as a focus for your sense of self and your resistance. Entry into the network made available by your implant can be a little disorientating at first and any substances you may have taken can exacerbate this shift. Added to this sir I can see you are a new user and therefore we don't have enough refined data to form a resettable core for your identity. Therefore it is best if we begin by asking you to think differently, to understand you have the choice of what to think. Let me give you some information. You'll have noticed no doubt your craving for sugar and fat. The organic robots require the energy to complete the installation, this is all normal. Please rest assured all this is temporary and that your vital organs are all functioning fine. We have two options moving forward. Either you allow the mood to subsume your thoughts or we can induce a state of rest while the installation completes itself. Please choose one sir, Option A: Allow yourself to be calm or Option B: eight to ten hours of sleep?

Lakerman does not say anything.

"Excellent. Please find a comfortable place to lay down and rest assured that you will still wake up as you. Tomorrow morning a tutorial will be made available to you on how to maximise your hypo-suit and what chemicals you ought to avoid."

* * *

Lakerman feels like shit. His body feels weird, thin and spiny. Brittle. He feels delicately boned like a bird and just as easily crushed. Heart-thumbed. A bird in the hand, two crushed skulls in the dust. He doesn't know what he's thinking. He's had no recollectable dreams, his sleep taking place at the edge of oblivion, a sleep unconscious of unconsciousness and its forms. For this reason, it is ten to fifteen minutes after Lakerman wakes that the nightmarish memory of a scarred outline of a mouse saying something about leaving a gift inside his body, pushes itself to the forefront of his horrified consciousness.

He's calling UbIQ. He wants to know what the fuck is going on.

"The mouse. I want to talk to the employee wearing the mouse Avatar."

"We have four: Mighty, Jerry, Pinky and the Brain, and Speedy."

"That's five."

"Pinky and the Brain are a single unit."

"This one was *the mouse*. It was the mouse but carved into a back."

"Carved into a back? Like a Wound?"

"More like a scarification. It's sort of an appropriated tribalistic..."

"So he was a canvas of skin with an animated wound as an avatar."

"Yes."

"I'm sorry sir no employees here fit that description and from what you've described such an Avatar would be at odds with the Stomata brand and mission statement. Frankly, there's no way an employee would be allowed to wear such a multiform to work. They'd be sacked on the spot."

"He told me I'd been booked for an appointment months ago."

"I'm sorry sir but that is simply not the case. We have no record of any appointment for you."

"I was there. Check your cameras."

"I'm sorry sir as part of our commitment to your privacy all video footage is wiped and IP information is cleared. We have the receipts of course but ...do you have a digital receipt?"

"Listen, I had the location turned on. I'm going to send you the data now to show you I was there."

Lakerman checks activity™. He'd apparently been asleep all day. He checks his emails for the one he'd received from donkeyWolf. There's no trace of it there. Lakerman slumps to the floor. He closes his eyes. Behind his eyes there are icons dimly blended into the orangey black of his eyelids. One of them hops slightly, shakes itself invitingly. Lakerman ignores it.

"We do have evidence of an interaction between you and one of our customer service A.I.'s and, umm, a full recording and transcript of your interaction and a timestamp. Unfortunately we can't discern the reason for your interaction whatsoever..."

"What? "

"It appears that neither of you spoke. The entire call was silent and... For what would you be getting a tutorial for?"

"For my implant."

"You don't have any implants sir, and you are not registered on any of our records. Our A.I.'s also publish their thought processes for inspection. The A.I. Jane that you 'interacted' with was entirely blank. Frankly, we are worried she has some kind of virus, it should have been impossible for you to contact her and we are currently investigating how such a mistake might have occurred..."

"Is there any way I could talk with her again?"

"I'm afraid not sir, interaction with our specialised help team is for customers only. And you didn't talk the first time. Were you drinking last night?"

Lakerman hangs up, slumps to the sofa. Food debris hops into the air. The effect reminds him of anime but it's not kawaii at all. Lakerman closes his eyes. One of the icons brightens there. The icon shimmies and shakes without a hint of seduction. The icon is of a polka dotted box tied with a bright yellow bow. Lakerman consents to opening it with an imagined nod in its direction.

You've received an invitation!

Is spelt out in fireworks and the pale smoke fireworks leave behind, that mournful scaffolding fading across the cut scene of his eyelids. A virtual flier unfolds. White on black writing. The invitation archives itself upon his reading:

'How I Killed The Universal Man (Ultra Rare N. edition). April 15th. Miami. Wynwood 602 West Avenue 24/7. Codeword EVOLVELOVE'

The mouse scar had said something about games. The invitation had to be the present, or part of it at least. The date was five weeks from now. He'd have time to take a cruise but on whose money and what pretext? Lakerman's skin is chafing from the inside. Maybe he could make a pitch to donkeyWolf to allow him to follow up the criminalisation of N in Miami? He could leverage his popularity, argue that a sequel article, however uncool would prove commercially smart. He gets a reminder about his meeting with donkeyWolf today. He doesn't know what it's about. He guesses it's something to do with his implant. Something's been botched. He wipes his staticky tongue across his teeth and feels a stiff crumb of sugar coating their walls. Lakerman insides feel cured and dried out. There's something half full about the last breath he took, like it didn't take in oxygen. He has an intimation that his body has gotten away from him. He doesn't act on it immediately and a moment later there's a fountain of vomit flowing from his mouth to his lap. He wipes his mouth, wriggles towards the shower hole. There's just enough water to rinse off the sick. He sits down under the dry shower head shivering.

ACTIVATE OPSCIONS?

Lakerman rubs his eyes, they are wet with tears. He's too confused to care. A voice internal to him but not identical to thought, i.e mercifully maintaining the distance of his attention, goes ahead and explains anyway.

Opscions is the new UbIQ app available for beta testing to subscribers. It analyses data from all available programs and uses a rapid learning a.i to produce dialogue trees, gestural reproducibility, and probabilities of outcome in regard to your stated and pre-assessed aims. It also contextually studies the available data on anyone within your field of attention to guarantee access to a variety of potential povs and cross referential morality takes.

Go on?

What is Gestural Reproducibility, Lakerman thinks. He's surprised to discover he already knows. Gestural reproducibility is the capturing and/or designing of facial expressions, both your own and others. These expressions are then calibrated in real time via zonal skin gridding and UbIQ's patented internal modelling technology that provides muscle markers for your face to move into and hold. The implant confirms whether you succeeded in recreating the expression accurately and how normal the transitions into it had been (calculated by speed and fluidity). Once the patterns are accurately established, and the transitions recorded at an agreed upon level of 'naturalness', the hyponet can send organic robots into the musculature in order to reproduce certain gestures or tones of voice at will. The dialogue trees allow for the clarification of choice and probabilities.

This must have been what Christoff had meant, Lakerman thinks, about the link between the technology and the drug. The neuro-apps being designed by UbIQ were so conceptually compatible with his experience of noumenon that the relation between them felt like serendipity. Is there a link? He touches the spot on his head where he remembers the needle going in. There's nothing there. He feels sick. His body seems rubbery and dumb to him. He feels his rib. Lakerman remembers the rubber bones at the office, how they had @lantis in raised lettering written across them. He checks his search history. Atlantis was the name of the offshore account that owned Webers and thus Lifepax. If there was any connection between UbIQ and Lifepax then there's a possibility the implant and noumenon were developed under the same corporate umbrella, he thinks. If that were the case then why would they be kept so far apart, and what about that invitation?

INSTALL Y/N?

* * *

donkeyWolf didn't have permanent offices and so meetings of importance generally took place in rentable workspaces. Lakerman already knows donkeyWolf's treatment of this temporary space will be gaudily and obnoxiously on brand and he's bracing himself for an ill-judged lack of discretion on the part of his employers as he arrives at the 4EVERWORK4U space. Curiously the meeting is just him and his editor, Gem. Gem had phoned him while Lakerman was in the midst of his split screen hallucination and booked in today's emergency meeting without providing any real basis for it though Lakerman figures it has to have something to do with his implant and the subsequent confusion around its registration. Gem is an alcoholic, post op, non-binary, gender fluid individual whose pronouns are they, them their and XE. XE is three years younger than Lakerman and about four times as cynical, and while they'd both broadly agree on the veracity of that statement each would be at pains to point out just how unquantifiable the assertion is. Which is to say they're not exactly friends but can usually stand a few hours in each other's real time locality.

As expected the rented office is mostly an exercise in the gestural power of empty space and an ironic joke about the cost of transparency. Lakerman doesn't have to discern this last point, 'an ironic joke about the cost of transparency' is printed in frosted lettering on the glass walls of the large, and largely empty, office. In the middle of the office Gem is kneeling at a Table-pad. The room is pretty much otherwise bare and minimalist in a way that seems tawdry. donkeyWolf have rented at least three quarters of the available floor space, literally marginalising the four startups two of which, Lakerman notes, appear to be some no-mark content producers. He raps on the glass, has to do it several times to get Gem's attention. Eventually he's buzzed in.

Gem's leaning over the tablescreen seemingly inspecting its surface when Lakerman enters. There's a ¾'s empty bottle of white wine and a full highball glass stationed in front of Gem. Lakerman spots another three wine bottles in the bin and guesses there's a bottle of vodka playing hide and go drink inside the retro drawers of their desk. Vodka and white wine mixed at a forty/sixty ratio being Gem's drink of choice. XE's term for this mixture is hard wine.

"Take a seat."

There's a bowl of fruit on the chair where Lakerman should be sitting. He stares at it.

"Oh, I forgot... we're interviewing for your job," Gem says. They cross their legs and lean back into the ergonomic cushions.

Lakerman picks up a piece of fruit. He thinks it is a mango. He's not sure. He sniffs it as if that would make a difference but then the fruit actually has a smell. It's subtle, not too pungent and somehow appropriate for the object. A sign of the so-called naturally occurring. Lakerman's impressed, against his better judgement. More by the gratuitousness of the fruit's presence here than its existence.

"Probably you're used to people coming in here," Lakerman begins, "and asking you 'Is this a real piece of fruit?' and then being all impressed when you tell them it's grown outdoors. That it was something Sun ripened instead of Sun-killed. What they don't understand is that the kneejerk assumption that this is more real than, I don't know, the mango flavoured sweets melted into my pocket lining or some genetically modified corn crop, falls into the trap of thinking its possible for anything to be unnatural, that we are some kind of god like species able to act and create outside of nature and that, my friend, is some Westernised passivity inducing bullshit."

Lakerman makes out he's about to hurl the mango across the room but instead, at the last second, gently rolls it across the T-pad and into the Editor's lap, He puts the bowl of fruit on the floor and takes the seat. Gem looks down at the mango in their lap and places their hands around it. They are holding it like an American football, if the person holding the American football was deeply suspicious of both the presence and function of actual physical objects. XE looks up at Lakerman.

"Drink?"

"That depends, is that regular or hard wine? Good or bad news?" Lakerman asks.

"Why don't you try it and see?"

"I'm not sure I'm that thirsty yet. Why do you drink that? You can afford so much better."

"If I don't deserve it, I don't drink it. This I deserve. Here, it's pre-mixed."

They slide a tumbler across the table. Lakerman is ninety percent sure Gem has watched videos on how to slide drinks across tables on YouTube. Gem's search history suddenly becomes available to Lakerman. Out of respect he refuses to look.

"Thanks," Lakerman says.

Gem takes a long look at him as he reaches for the glass. Lakerman feels as if he is being weighed, sized up, appraised for initiation or rejection in some way. What he is uncertain about is the degree to which any and all of those effects may be sincerely or ironically intended. Lakerman finds himself memorising XE's facial expression as an image for reference. It is now, he realises, completely accessible to him, reproducible, a thing that he can extract data from, tag thoughts to. He's suddenly cognisant of the ratios of distance between Gem's lip curl and nostrils, the names of each activated muscle of their cheeks. Opscions. Lakerman superimposes the editor's expression over his own, wraps his skin around it. He moves his lips, clenches his jaw slightly. An internal buzz tells him whether he is closer or further away from replicating the look.

"What on earth are you doing? Are you taking the piss?"

"Nothing," Lakerman says, relaxing his face and taking a sip of the hard wine which screws it up again. "I don't know how you drink this. It's impressive. "

Gem smiles.

"You know what I like about you, Lakerman?" they say finishing their glass and removing something from their desk. "You respect alcoholism as an addiction. You know the work that goes into it. With drugs the addiction is baked in. They're definitely fun at some point and for most people. Where's the challenge? Alcohol on the other hand is some primitive shit. Pure diluted poison. It's proletarian. It takes work and real desperation to form a need. And it's unpredictable. That's why I got this job, I think. They know I'll put in the extra work to get where I need to go. To become combustible."

Lakerman nods along. Gem is drunk and while Gem is always drinking this is the first time Lakerman has seen them visibly affected by alcohol. Lakerman remembers Gem saying once that XE took drugs to sober up from the alcohol.

"What did you want to see me for that couldn't be an email?"

"You're a Negroni guy, right? It's 'your' drink. It's kind of a joke that you drink that, don't you think? Do you think it's cool? When I was a kid if someone did something too obvious we'd say 'chose' as in, it was obvious you chose to do this and it's lame. You've made a drink into something memorable about yourself. Chose. Total chose. Lord Jesus, I need a straightener." The editor tweezers a small baggie out of their breast pocket and flicks it provocatively at Lakerman. "Hey, do you want some smart coke? I like it but I'm *just not addicted to it.*"

"Chose. Where's all this memorable talk coming from? Also, this coming from you and your hard wine is peak bullshit."

"Hard wine is all about merging assets, altering boundaries and what I like to call party efficiencies. It's an innovation in streamlining resources."

"I actually wanted to ask you something. Other than why I'm here,"

"Oh the big questions. You'll be disappointed to know I have it on good authority that there were some genitals involved at some point in the process. A fact often forgotten by your type..."

"Hilarious. Have you heard anything about my implant and the point of this meeting?"

"They have the same answer."

Gem activates the mirror app on the T-Pad and starts chopping up three chunky looking lines on its newly reflective surface. Gem looks up from the desk at Lakerman and their expression is composed and cautiously alert, sober seeming and in hi-def. This is in direct contrast to the sloppiness Lakerman thought he'd detected earlier.

"That's what I have to tell you. We've been told we can't do it for you. Naturally, you're released from the exclusivity clause etc etc So, off the record, maybe you've dodged a career shaped bullet there. The way things are going. I mean how much more entertaining can we be? Last week our top Jewish comic Sleazy E was crucified live on every major app the company owns. In Jerusalem. By an Italian. Who was a Pilates teacher named Pontious. It was huge and now it's forgotten. Anyway, we can't do the installation. They're criminalising PayTech policies as of next week, arguing that it threatens the social economy, that it doesn't take into account the necessary/unnecessary flows of currency. They're scared of the new barter economy cause they don't know how to tax it. The government's ineffectually draconian as fuck. I'm writing a piece about that. The return of the bartering economy. Obviously I won't publish. It would be insane. Maybe you write it. The point is we want to keep you. You're a valuable asset to donkeyWolf media, always have been, and even more so now. We're prepared to offer you a raise and support your loan application for the tech you want. You won't be exclusive to donkeyWolf but we will expect you to regularly publish with us."

Gem sits back in their chair and then violently hurls the mango at the glass wall. The walls shudder causing a fashionable looking intern's hairstyle to glitch in the tessellated space around the office. The intern's real hair is shaved close to the skull as opposed to the rainbow serpent nest camouflaging it.

"That's my boyfriend," Gem says.

(a) Say nothing
(b) Your boyfriend?
(c) Tell him something strange is going on here.
(d) Tell him the truth about the implant

"Who am I kidding? Obviously right now we'd have you writing the whole damn site if we could. You're a star kid. BTW, if you don't say something with respect to my outrageous flattery soon I'm going to be very offended."

"You're telling me I'm not getting an installation from donkeyWolf and the contract is null?"

"Listen, you're disappointed. I understand. We're going to do what we can. That's our nice side. The carrot at the end of the stick. The stick itself though is all kinds of nasty. It's wrapped in barbed wire and steel wool. The stick's there to make the carrot, which is obviously just a fucking carrot, look good but if the stick wasn't a real option on the part of the stick carrier why have the carrot at all? So the stick owner would advise against you taking this up with any lawyers. Obviously, we are going to look after you..."

Lakerman is trying to make his confusion read as appropriately upset but he's feeling increasingly out of control. He's reminded of the Gentlemind App. He becomes aware of his breath. He feels his heart slow, his muscles relax. Lakerman begins to feel his conscious self is but a port in an infinite ocean. He enters the ocean, assumes its limitlessness briefly then comes back to himself. A small alert lets him know that he's achieved '*condensed meditation*' and unlocked '*journey to inner peace.*'

He says "Ok."

"It's settled?"

"I guess. I need to think."

"Ok. That we can work with. Meanwhile, I've got two assignments for you. You get the second on the condition of accepting the first."

Lakerman is barely listening. He just needs to get through this meeting and find a place to think everything through.

(A) Ask "What's the first assignment?" in an ambiguously grudging
   fashion
(B) Drink more hard wine and wait to see what happens
(C) Tell Gem about the Implant

Lakerman assumes an ironically weary position.

The editor smiles. There's some sense of relief in there. Lakerman can tell by the way the skin of Gem's face is held back, immobilised, by the smile. A slight, bio-electric, flutter travelling through the sail of their cheek. Lakerman can see it. Possibilities regarding the meaning of this spasm branch out, intersect, form narratives receding into the distance. Lakerman is aware of the choices present to him, sees them clearly defined as choices for the first time in his life.

"Ok, then. Excellent. Assignment one. A doctor at this no mark, dependably underfunded, general hospital has been caught data-mining the deaths of her patients, measuring chemical releases, hormones, recording brain function, wave frequencies et al and selling them on the alternet. Apparently there's a whole market for these recordings. People bid medical bill sized amounts on this stuff. You could call it," the editor makes punctuating spotlights of their hands, "Data mining the deceased: Grave Robbing in the age of biomechanics." Come on, that's good."

Lakerman nods politely, takes a sip of the hard wine and almost unconsciously reconsiders the offer of Smart Coke. The editor sees him eyeing the lines and pushes it towards him. At the window a different intern takes the first by the arm, points inside the cube and makes a piously horrified face.

"Aren't you worried about..." Lakerman gestures towards the window.

"Them? I'm supposed to act like this. I'm on brand."

'What do the people buy them for?"

"What?"

"The death tapes."

"Don't be naive. They Jerk off to them. Probably. Why else would you? It has to be sexual."

"Can't we leave that idea behind?"

"What idea?"

"That everything is about sex except sex which is about everything else etc, ad infinitum. Wouldn't it be more interesting if what they wanted was something else?"

"We're not all as evolved as you, though that's probably why they want you for the story. For your particular species hating slant."

"Who wants me for the story?"

"The algorithms, of course. I'm a largely symbolic figurehead you know."

Lakerman is still looking at the lines of smart coke.

"What do you mean?"

"What are you waiting for, just have one. There's something else I want to..."

"I shouldn't."

Gem's eyes narrow into two little darts.

"Why not? What have you been up to?"

"Nothing."

"And what meaningful thing have you got to do?"

" I've no meaningful things to do, this morbid assignment aside."

"Then why are you waiting? Won't this make work more fun? Isn't it part of the story? Let your pleasure centres sing."

Lakerman licks his index finger and dabs it into one of the lines. He lifts it up at the editor and then rubs it into his eyes.

He looks up at Gem. Lakerman is not blinking at all.

"There is something I want," Lakerman says, his expression already buckling under the high "I want to go back to Miami, I've been researching..."

"Let me stop you there. The second assignment."

"I'll just do it. Whatever it is. But I want to go back to Miami, that's my condition, and it has to be by next week."

"And if you go back then everything between you and the company is sorted?"

"Yes."

"The second assignment is in Miami. Marker, the missing pharmacologist, has resurfaced. He's been arrested. We want you to get an interview with him, cover the trial. You leave in a couple of days. No take backs. So this is a yes?"

Lakerman chooses to nod.

"Ok, now about the first assignment, it's a little odd. You'll have to transplant your IP, effectively go offline."

* * *

The taxi noses through a thin static of hot rain. Lakerman grinds his teeth unconsciously in the backseat. He blinks and becomes aware of the sound of his jaw. He forgets what he was thinking about. He relaxes his mouth slightly and feels a little calmer. The coke's paranoid edge is being brake-parachuted by little, time released, fist bumps of serotonin and dopamine. Smart Coke. He looks at the screen on the back of the seat and remembers that he was researching Opscions via alternet video boards. He's scrolled through obscure subreddits dedicated to detailing outrightly bizarre, possibly faked, interactions. The app by consensus is fatally riddled with bugs and laughably glitchy. Behind the bitter comedy of failure though there existed other, more interesting, possibilities for the app and the glitches would eventually be resolved in a way reality couldn't, he thought. He figured the more people encountered each other with OpScions enabled the more they would be reminded of choice and the less bound to themselves they would be.

He looks up and watches the approaching city collect in the windscreen. He counts railway stations as they increase in frequency, their shelters stockinged in dim shadow and aglow with phosphorus tags of graffiti. Somewhere in those creative gestures, Lakerman thinks, amid the interlinking patterns of spray paint – and lost in each busy entanglement of colour – were the amino acids of some other possible existence coded onto the world. He feels he can take apart the overlayed images like a sigil and find the rearranged wish underlying them. They'll all say roughly the same thing, he thinks.

He leans forward towards the front seat, forearms pressing into thighs, wrists crossed between his knees. He looks at the driver in the mirror and asks what time they will be arriving. Lakerman is eager to arrive at his destination as soon as possible, which is of course only natural, but the desire feels especially pronounced and meaningful to him in this instance. The driver glances at Lakerman in the rear view mirror before continuing to fix his eyes on the road. It seems to Lakerman that it is taking a long time for the driver to reply and so he repeats the question regarding their estimated time of arrival in a more authoritative tone. When the driver finally does respond his reply is irritated and sharp sounding and stands in marked contrast to the actual content of his speech, which is vague and imprecise. Lakerman leans back, runs his tongue over his suddenly icy teeth. Twenty minutes to an hour. It doesn't matter. It's probably for the best. Lakerman drums on his knees, tries to enjoy the drive.

They enter the city proper and Lakerman notes the driver sweating profusely. The bones of the driver's knuckles are bulging under his skin causing deportations of blood, comets of white to appear there. It is as if the skin of his hand were coughing up its bones. There has been an increase in traffic but not of a magnitude that would justify the driver's reaction, Lakerman thinks. He looks out at the ballet of cars, Lakerman temporarily losing himself in admiration at the speed and organisation of space and matter. The lack of ego. Each lane of traffic is a puzzle of interchanging positions, an intricate flow of co-operative need, of desire and distribution. Each car's A.I. is so finely calculating the space of the moment and adjusting to it, that the entire process strikes Lakerman as a truly aesthetic expression. Here every car was enmeshed in simultaneous relations with an amorphous, shapeshifting ... it wasn't whole, how could it be whole and change? It was instead a machine that produced change. The traffic is profoundly alive, Lakerman thinks.

A sign flashes to remind everyone that manual driving is not permitted. The driver's hazard lights are on and he has taken to the emergency lane. Lakerman realises that the driver must feel himself to be under tremendous pressure and this pressure likely accounts for the somewhat strained relations between them. To escape the automated alarm and avoid recognition the driver is required to follow the protocol of every broken down A.I and hold a straight line, at a recognised speed, with an extremely small variation in either speed or verticality certain to trigger detection. The bearing of such pressurised, skill based, mental states is likely arduous in a way Lakerman figures he isn't best placed to understand.

Except Lakerman also doesn't understand why he would take this taxi, it's not clear to him at all. This is a taxi that would have to be sourced, specified, primed for possible illegalities and... Lakerman realises he doesn't remember anything about the meeting with Gem after learning Marker had turned up. His high suddenly pulls out like the tide gone Catholic, revealing the cosmic desert beneath. Lakerman's au fait with this kind of soul hollowing moment and at least smart coke's trademark comedown response would be sure to render even the most brutal dose of anxiety and self hate manageable. Still, something is realer, ergo more frightening than usual, about the sensation. He tries to call Gem. Can't. Something is just not there. Lakerman realises he is totally offline. He is sweating. His hands run over his body. No knife wounds, no surgical scars. In his pocket he finds a note. It's handwritten in cursive so it looks fake like a movie prop.

We've forgotten how to remember.

He supposes Gem wrote it though neither the handwriting nor the tone seem congruent to what Lakerman understands about the editor's identity. Still writing does strange things to a person's ability to represent themselves, he thinks. The statement itself doesn't strike Lakerman as a particularly enigmatic or interesting comment on 'modern life' which he assumes it is trying to be. It was both trite and overwrought with meaning. And it is this sensation of dismissal that triggers his recall. Gem had told Lakerman it might be hard to remember, that going offline tended to result in these little amnesiac episodes...plus the coke probably wouldn't help. Although now Lakerman is wondering if the coke hadn't been a deliberate ploy on the part of the editor to get him onboard. It was hard enough when connected to get into the habit of recollection and not just the impression left behind, he thought. Consequently, going offline exacerbated this problem and often led to a sense of disorientation and bewilderment. A sense of being stranded in a future without a past. The note had been designed to produce a knee jerk reaction in Lakerman that would stimulate his recall if he could ground the memory to the sensation. This arrogant, judgmental, sense of superiority was what Gem and he had agreed on as the emotion Lakerman was most likely to produce in a given moment.

"I'm a dick," Lakerman thinks.

This thought was the second necessary trigger. Everything comes back. Lakerman breathes through it.

It turned out The Doctor Death Tapes story had a more complex angle. Doctor Mary Trustin was claiming to be a whistleblower. She said she had evidence a potential health crisis was being covered up. Gem thought it was probably bullshit but still worth checking out. At least that's what the algorithm was strongly suggesting. Even if it was bullshit, Gem said, the act of profiling the fake conspiracy, and the desperate mind behind it, could be an article by itself. The conditions Doctor Death Tapes had stipulated in return for the information were total disconnect, analogue interactions only, Lakerman was to leave no unintended data behind. donkeyWolf had gone as far as having someone act as a surrogate for his life. Which meant Gem was either knowingly lying about it being bullshit or hoping that the algorithms had fucked up in their budget allocation which would allow Gem to maybe wrest some editorial autonomy back.

The surrogate was probably in his house at the moment. Sleeping or conforming to Lakerman's internet history. Drinking a Negroni. Surrogates were both illegal and largely below the law. They copied lives. Finding them, and finding people willing to be them, to act out another's life and negate their own, was a covert operation in exploiting the vulnerable and about as morally tangled in the politics of self owned desire as one could get. He didn't feel good about this but at least it was only a short lease on life.

The doctor had asked that Lakerman identify himself as Joe Vale. Despite being offline Lakerman still has to pass as a citizen and so Joe Vale is carrying empty profiles, self selecting algorithms, locked kingdoms of a hastily generated subjectivity. Data with its precise approximations of a life. The camouflage would be enough to pass any brief check into Joe Vale's recognised existence but it wouldn't stand up to any half serious deep dive should, for any reason, the authorities' interest in his activity cross the perfunctory.

Lakerman reviews the charges and coverage of the story. Dr Mary Trustin was accused of selling people's intimate biological data, and keys to understanding that data, at the point of death. To record a death outside of government sponsored research was prohibited by law and the invasive nature of the doctor's alleged business was unprecedented. The narrative around the doctor, such as it was, had already hardened into the ghoulish and the moral, often at the same time and as the same thing. The doctor's existence was supposed to tell society something about its voyeurism, its desire to see, the lack of privacy. That was wrong, Lakerman thought. This wasn't some Medusa to be defeated by the shielding mirror of art. It doesn't explain the thoroughness. The depth of the violation wasn't equivalent to the patterns of mass fantasy, even abstractly. They didn't match in a way Lakerman found credible.

Though you might, he thought, construct a sexual fantasy from the meaning of the numbers, or the idea of precision, or even invasiveness as a *thing*, the numbers themselves were never strictly necessary. And these recordings and the data they left behind were raw, unprocessed, exacting and meaningless to Lakerman. Ten point zero three could be high, low, death or happiness etc as far as he knows. The names and language around them was jargon heavy, cryptic and totally compressed. The significance of everything remained inert without the requisite expertise. The people who bought these, there was a fantasy there of course, but it wasn't sexual, or at least the sexual couldn't be the dominant note, he thought. It's about a certain authentic limit, he thinks, about the finite, i.e what is, transitioning into the infinite namely what isn't. Lakerman reads the list of alleged violations that constitute the charge. They include a vibratory read out and analysis of activity in Broca's area. The doctor had also timed and monitored various chemical and hormonal balances in the body leading up to each individual death. She had provided in depth nerve and neurological mappings of the mind-body death, and sent recordings of the synaptic light shows playing out in the empty planetarium of the skull. Shows culminating in the anticlimactic organ darkness of the eternal goodbye, the forever sudden end, the non transitory moment in which the improbable logic of life gets worn out and found fallacious. Lakerman coughs. Once, twice. A trickle down the throat. The cough becomes a retch. He begins to dry heave in the backseat, bending over his lap. He is struggling to swallow but he also does not know why he is trying to swallow. Lakerman begins to feel he cannot breath and when he catches the taxi driver's eye the sense of anger and disgust he finds there feels like a confirmation of the person Lakerman is. He doesn't understand what's happening in his life right now. He tries to think about the assignment. All of it. What puzzled him the most is why Mary Trustin would choose donkeyWolf with something so sensitive if it isn't total bullshit? He makes a note of it. The note reads WTF.

* * *

The facility where the doctor worked is not modern. Lakerman notes the discolouration of brick, the bubbled paint, the steady growth of not-thereness in its finishings. The building was neglected, looked poor and dying like the social class flocking to it. That Mary Trustin was still working here as a doctor despite being under arrest for gross, in every sense, malpractice told you everything you needed to know about the kind of work being done here. Lakerman refastens his face mask as he enters.

The hospital is full of people. The doors are manually operated. People's phones are *objects they hold* and the internet connection is weak. He looks around. He is totally unregarded. The people here appear shelled by their situation and everyone carries their own force field of pain. Space is pregnant with shock. There is no privacy and yet everyone is alone. No one moves well. Everything is sad and heavy and insular. Lakerman laughs joylessly and then begins to cry. There is a minimal transition between the physicality of the two states. Fortunately Lakerman is in the right place for such a display to avoid warranting much attention. His emotions are a virtual sinkhole collapsing the connect of his body, he is crying uncontrollably into the non-space. Deep down he knows this has little and everything to do with something specific. This must be another side effect of taking a body offline, he tells himself. A strangely unattuned sensitivity. A sensitivity that ranged over the world but never quite communicated anything stable back to the user. Lakerman carrying the unmediated world as a scar. Non-surgical. Rough. Wonky.

He asks a nurse if she knows where Doctor Trustin is.

"You must be Valentino Vale's son. The Doctor is in 5C."

* * *

The name badge reads 'Mary Trustin" but the doctor resembles a highclass forgery of Andrea Christoff, right down to the distribution of freckles across the dipped notch of her collarbone. *Like a handful of pennies scattered at the bottom of a wishing well*, Lakerman thinks. Mary's twenty or so years younger than Christoff and maybe a kilo or two lighter but the similarities between them should be impossible at a structural level. She could be her daughter, Lakerman thinks, if it was possible for a daughter to be uncannily *identical* to her mother. Her eyes, in particular, are fucking Lakerman up. He can't get past the sense they're more than evocative, that they're not referential so much as repeated. He hasn't completely ruled out that the perceived likeness might be symptomatic of his own technology assisted trauma, a hallucination, a projection of desire reheated and loaded with virus-causing bacteria. But then, when she speaks, her voice chimes with Lakerman's memory in a way that disarms his poise, makes him want to stumble forward, arms out, his neural pathways napalmed with desire. He hasn't even registered the body in the bed.

"Hi, You must be Joe Vale?"

"Yes" I must look like shit, he thinks.

"I'm Doctor Trustin. Pleased to meet you. We don't have long," she says gesturing to the patient on the bed. "Your father, here..."

The man on the bed is barely old enough to be his father, Lakerman thinks. Maybe if Lakerman had been sired by a thirteen year old. It was possible. Lakerman refuses to think anymore about his parents. Their absence is obviously expanding within the present but it's not like he's about to root around in that particular hollow for any truffles of grief. Lakerman observes the body on the bed. The man's breathing is shallow and rapid. He is covered in tattoos.

"Is he going to die?"

"Yes, in about ten minutes more or less. All we can do, if we're given the chance, is mitigate the pain, clear up, and then have you sign a release form consenting to his body being used for research. If anyone asks the line we're supposed to give them is 'this is standard practice now.' We're not in the remotest equipped to deal with what we're seeing. Technically you shouldn't be here, but I need you to see him die. The people we've had come in with this particular... problem...don't tend to have many people caring about them. Valentino's different enough that we need some authentication however faked. You just need to see."

She has told him he is going to watch a man die. He observes in himself how this complicates his attraction to her, makes it more diffuse and prone to perverse shapes. In the migrant camp he had seen bodies. He had seen people beaten and shot and had supposed they died. He had seen the huddled masses, yearning to break free, use women and children as a human shield. The age old insignia of their vulnerable, sentimentalised bodies, adorning the horror. The huddled masses pitching their beauty against the hearts of soldiers and barbed wire. Lakerman had seen the bodies the next day strained through the mesh like pulped tomatoes. Regardless, he had happened upon all these deaths. Intruded. No one had asked him. Being asked, given permission, didn't make it any better. Death then, Lakerman thought, was a moment without intimacy one way or another. Lakerman looks at her and notices for the first time the pallor of her skin. How the paleness is complicated by the slight sheen of moisture emerging from beneath its surface. It's not that she seems unwell exactly, he thinks, it's more like a spritz of unwellness. As if her proximity to death had made her body take on some ephemeral aspect, a nearly-thing unable to hold form.

"Hey, what's wrong with you?" Mary Trustin is frowning angrily. "I can't have you nodding out like that. Are you cogent, can you be trusted to remember, to record this?"

Two options present themselves to Lakerman with an unusual clarity:

(a) "Remembering and recording are fundamentally different activities. I'll do better than both, I'll get to the shareable truth of things. If this is such a coverup how am I able to be here?
(b) "What's wrong with him?"

"That's not a bad question" she replies, "though it's still a waste of time. I've been tampering with the data, fudging the prognosis. Your visit will be an error in judgement but not so suspicious that anyone might have to kill me. I hope. This will just look like a close call you see? They won't know you've seen. Just don't fuck up and leave exactly when I tell you to."

"What's wrong with him?"

"He's undergoing an RCT: Rapid Cellular Transmutation."

"Is that similar to any of the diseases I might be familiar with? You said it was a virus? Is there anything you could compare it to for me?"

"There's no equivalency. He's about to grow a new body part and either the strain of this expenditure of energy or the dramatic change in the area this event takes place in will cause his death. This is the fifth case in the last month."

Lakerman frowns at her.

"How is that even possible?"

"We don't know exactly, we only have correlations. Before Valentino here all of the afflicted have had full body implants. Largely corporate, some military, all low rung. People who hadn't received much love... They'd all hacked their implants despite the possible jail time they'd incur. Valentino here is something of an outlier in that regard... Most of his tech is burner."

"I don't understand the link."

"The truth is we don't know either... A new cancer, possibly. It's possible we may have discovered something hyper-carcinogenic and environmentally organised."

"What makes you think that?"

"We've noticed a spike in Valentino's PRO-count during his stay here that is off the chart."

"PRO-count?"

"Programmed robotic organisms. Many of them are self-replicating but dormant, many of them fulfil a singular, one use, function then float around waiting to be expelled. You know they are in every human body now? Even people without any implants have a PRO count in the thousands. Like plastic in fish, the way everything has a little capitalism mixed in. You know the nursery rhyme 'There was an old lady that swallowed a fly?"

"I can't say I'm familiar."

"She eats a spider to catch the fly and then a bird to catch the spider etc etc. Plastic, pollution, Climate change...these were the flies and spiders. We built tech to solve tech's problems and now that tech is everywhere. Everyone is fastened to the network from the inside. Each PRO is connected or has the potential to connect with the field however weak the signal. There's a whole network to draw power from. They lay dormant everywhere. It's not that everything is connected but that everything can be connected. I mean PRO's are generally considered to be totally harmless and environmentally benign but if that turns out not to be the case then we're all in trouble. As I said, all the other cases were people with heavy duty implants, so I thought maybe there's some time but Valentino's numbers tally with those of someone with implants. It might be a coincidence but..."

"What are you suggesting?"

"I think the disease transmits something to the organisms dormant in and around the body, that it signals to other PROS to collect, gather, form an assemblage and alter the structure of the body. An implant is basically an intensive colony and production plant for PROs. Implants monitor, determine the activities, and create the conditions of reproduction for the organisms. It's feasible they could cause growths but if that behaviour is contractible without an implant, we have to know what's triggering it."

"Wait... you think it's a non biological cancer?"

"I'm not even sure cancer is the right word. It's an error code maybe. Something's rewriting this body's genome, carrying out instructions that aren't in the DNA. Do you see how intimate this is? This is operating at a cellular level. Whatever is causing it has to be able to communicate at that level. I can't see any other way that's possible. Wait, it's happening."

She points over at the bed. Valentino Vale has sat up. He is looking towards Lakerman and Mary but it is clear he cannot see them. Mary presses something on her phone. The lights of the room warp in and out then settle into some low rent version of themselves. Valentino opens his mouth to scream but Lakerman can see that his throat is full of skin and new muscle. He apparently cannot close his mouth. Lakerman watches a vertebrae form and harden where his tonsils should be. Bone starts forming and gobbling up mouth space. Tufts of hair thread out of his eyes. The nose is elevated into an inbred snobbery. His jaw breaks, reverses itself, pulls a 180°, completely unhinged by what appears to be the rump of a head. The body thrashes around on the bed then goes limp.

Doctor Trustin turns him over. Where the back of his head should be there is another face. A clumsy Janus. A pair of eyes. A chin. A nose shattered by the skull it tried to break through. Even through the slathering gore Lakerman can tell the eyes are identical to the doctor's but that it is his own mouth that greets them. It is as if this face were the monstrous offspring of his desire.

"That's new" she says, "that's not... unintentional."

Lakerman vomits.

"Fuck."

"You have to get out of here now. Go to the desk and sign the consent form. Anyone asks you how your father is on the way out, you say 'Same as ever.' I organised the power cut to hide the time of death. Go. Meet me at the ruined chapel in an hour. No one can know you saw this." Lakerman walks out in a daze. He can regulate his voice but not the sweat as he signs the release form. He can only hope his shock reads appropriately.

* * *

It is a few hours now after sundown and the streets are a little busier, the distances between bodies a little less remote. Disconnected sounds, it is too early to call them music or voices (the distance having weakened their relations), begin to coalesce searching for communion and exchange. Drunks stumble out into the night from basement bars, pupils pulled like executioner's hoods over the dusk. Twilight hums with the promise of commerce and dissipation. Corner stores and synthetic fish and chip shops pull open their shutters and the warm, fluorescent, smell of the working poor floods into an abandoned world. The twilight setting the table for the nocturnal. All who would eat. After leaving the hospital Lakerman in his shock had found several bumps of cocaine secreted around his person and happened upon a speakeasy he was familiar with. He'd needed something to stiffen his resolve.

Long rumoured for gentrification, artists had begun to move here over the last few years to accelerate the area's transformation from bloody rags to unethical riches. This was part of London's evolution under capitalism, not so much a life cycle as a death spiral, decay and exclusion, promise and implication, a terminal logic of self cannibalism. Artists were like these unsuspecting pathogens, Lakerman thought, infectious agents of capital, inadvertently killing the poor, cocooning them in impossible pleasure and debt. The counter culture that made the culture structurally possible. Lakerman knows this area by reputation, one or two blurred 'evenings' out, and the shame of his continued desire to move here, but finding the chapel has proven harder than expected. Lakerman watches a cornershop open. He waits for the display of canned food to be replenished before crossing the street and entering.

An old man and a teenager stand in contrasting poses of defiance behind the till. The old man is wearing a long white robe of obviously religious import. The teenager is in athleisure wear and headphones. The primary difference between their clothing is in the fabric and stitching. Lakerman buys a coke and asks them if they know how to get to the ruins. The older man tells him to get out. Lakerman tries to show them his press ID. The teenager takes the time to read it, to verify text and image. The old man is shouting at the younger man not to be so naive. Lakerman leaves, considers where to ask next. The teenager catches up to Lakerman and gives him directions. I love your work, he says, I don't want to be human either.

* * *

Woody thickets of sun bleached bark and branch obscure the ruined chapel from the street. The dead vegetation is rigid and brittle and abundant. It is as if death had established its own negative circuit, one that drew the world through itself, generating not power, or emptiness but remains. Above the overgrowth, the tower remains intact and visible though from where Lakerman stands the clear, unflanked, space around it exudes a sense of erasure. The clear sky on either side, asterisked by distant street lamps, appears cleansed, however superficially, of human time. It is clear the chapel has sunk into ruin. Lakerman can relate. He can't tell if he is in shock, or hungover, or coming down, or in the throes of some post operative ache, but he feels like an exposed nerve in a freshly gaped space.

The chapel is only fifty feet from the main road and yet everything is different, Lakerman thinks. There's enough unsightly refuse caught in the roughly hacked pathway to the church to ward off any attempt to view the relation between overgrowth and destination in a fairytale light, whatever the perma-fat tramp snoring under one of the less thorny tangles of bush might ironically invoke. Sleeping beauty. Lakerman sighs, he is sick of himself and his reflexive bullshit. He feels his way through the undergrowth, his eyes trained on the ground for discarded needles, bodily waste, confrontational sex acts. Fifty or more years ago this place used to double as a music venue. Rock Bands, Electronic musicians, folk and psychedelia groups, orchestral interpretations of Aphex Twin, and Afro Futuristic Jazz ensembles all played here. Lakerman tries to imagine the old chords, strains of music, the hushed reverence, and pleading expectation of the crowd as an artform tried to act as a placeholder for religion. The music attempting to appropriate religion's architecturally situated awe, its communal import of place, the delirium of its proportions. It's not religion that was lost but Churches, Lakerman thinks.

In the forecourt a group of children, ages nine to thirteen years old he guesses, stand around a buckled chunk of stone and either side of a gate without walls. The free standing gate reduced to a strangely menacing symbol. A rag is passed between them and each child clasps it to their face breathing it in like its oxygen and they're the first mammals to transition to lungs.

"What the fuck are you doing here? I'm the daddy of this estate, know your role," one of the older children shouts at him.

"I'm here to meet a friend."

"Who?"

"Her name's Mary."

"Magdalene?"

"That would make sense."

"What's your name?"

96

Lakerman pauses for a moment.

"Joe Vale."

The children nod as if they had been expecting him. They insist he enter through the gate while they walk around the outside of it. They snigger to themselves as they lead him inside the memory of a building.

"Why are you laughing?" Lakerman asks the boy nearest to him. "It's nothing," the boy says, "It's just when we were young we thought that if you chose to walk through the gate you'd lose your soul."

"When you were young?"

"Mister, do you even know the life expectancy rates around here? Time is relative, yeah? I'm probably your age in a lot of ways. Probably had more too."

"More what?"

The boy rolls his eyes and shuffles his way to the front of the group.

Inside the ground and air are snowy with the ash of bonfires sunk into ember. They walk over broken tiles, crumbled brick. On either side of the entrance partial walls cast in the shape of graphs prophesying profound economic and spiritual recovery rise up to some fabled point and then disappear pointlessly into heaven. A flying buttress with nothing to exchange support with creaks like a tap above a taped off space. All the children bar the youngest circle around it unconsciously. The youngest child walks and stands beneath it. The rest of the children stop and watch silently. Ten to fifteen seconds pass before the youngest walks out of the zone and rejoins the group. Lakerman has the sensation he has just witnessed some ritualistic prayer.

There are tents pitched and shadowed with bodies on either side of the aisle walkway as well as several rows of pews, rotted and bent inwards towards the navel of the earth. A wind seems to flow permanently eastward. Almost everything and everyone within the ruins has faded, Lakerman thinks. The only colour he can see other than twinkling fire and the pale, washed out clothes of the people is a

97

stained glass window and the patch of light it casts at the altar. The illuminated altar is topped with a bunch of carrots being grown in a glass box. The carrot tops an eyelash of green shadowed with orange. The soil is dark and rich and a few of the carrots' taproots are visible through the soil. He looks around the church. Lakerman imagines this is how a desert forms. The gradual falling away of life with some surviving potential for beauty reshaped or discovered by the movements of time and place against it. It is at this moment that Mary appears at the altar. She is bathed in light and holding a battered tin watering can. She bends over the carrots. Was this the process of adaptation, metamorphosis? Even the desert had butterflies, he thinks. Lakerman looks around and finds many people have appeared to observe the watering of the carrots or else stopped what they were doing to watch. And then it occurs to Lakerman that the permeability of the ruins form, the malleable traces of its former connections, the empty narcotic hunger of the crowd, this display by Mary, it all reminds him of the Stomata showroom. He looks at Mary with the watering can and these carrots and thinks of the Stomata doll emerging from the spun house, the seed of the new in the core of its destruction. Life, basically.

* * *

Mary Trustin puts the watering can down and sits on a small deckchair that one of the children pulls up for her. The glass tank of carrots is to her left. The crowd has dispersed. Lakerman stands in front of her and lights a cigarette as another child passes her a book, a plastic baggie, a pencil case and some foil. The slanting light of the stained glass window and the moisture of her skin create shifting planes of light and shadow. The ambient sheen of her body changes colour from red to yellow as the sun descends. The light from the stained glass window is a kind of ancient neon, Lakerman thinks and then he's back at the *Borderline*. The club rat is looking at him with a manic intensity, glittering eyes. The empathy he feels for her in this moment has genuine force. A week from now, he realises, she will be dead.

"It's good that you remembered to refer to yourself as Joe Vale. You haven't totally lost it. That's impressive." The voice is from another place. What is going on, he thinks.

"It's the drug you know" the club rat says. "Whatever you're feeling, it's that." He's not sure she's right. He wants to let her know he can't help her, he's sorry. He reaches his arm out for her but she has already gone. Lakerman experiences the club rat's death in this moment as a death, as a subtraction from the possible world, a source of grief, for the first time.

"Hey, where are you?" Lakerman feels Mary's gaze digging through his features. "I'm just a little in shock," he replies.

"You must have a lot of questions," Mary Trustin says, folding a piece of foil into a small canoe shape and crumbling powder into its crease. "I'm an old fashioned girl so you'll have to go ahead and ask them. The order is pretty important and how much time we have while I can still remember, record, or 'find the usable truth', or however you put it, is obviously hanging in the balance. I kid. I'm usually coherent. I'm functional. This is Pure function" She gestures at the heroin. She places the canoe on the large book on her legs and takes a lighter and glass straw from the pencil case. She places the glass straw in her mouth, pinches one end of the foil and then runs the lighter back and forth beneath the crease of it. The powder sizzles, bubbles, grows as gooey as a good cookie, and then lets out a thin stream of smoke. She leans forward and chases the tail as it rises from the aluminium.

She lifts her head back. He waits a few minutes out of respect for the high before gesturing that he's ready to talk.

"Thank you," she says "I appreciate your patience. I'm ready now." Her voice seems to mimic the surroundings somehow: caved in and yet opened up in its collapse, a voice reminiscent of something complete. Lakerman looks around. The children, along with a set of teenagers, are stationed around like sentries.

"Why are we here?"

"This is my home."

"It's where you're from?"

"It's my home. I'm safe here."

"It seems lovely."

"We all look after each other.'

He waits to see if she offers him some of her heroin and then when she doesn't he sits down on a pile of bricks a few feet from the carrots and lights another cigarette. He takes out a pen and notebook and regards the weight of them in his hand, how unpracticed his fingers are at holding the pen, how unusual the relations between his hand and the paper appear to him.

"Go ahead," she says.

"Are the accusations against you linked to what happened back there? It doesn't seem to have affected your stand in the..." he looks around "community."

"I've been framed and around here no one cares about any of that stuff. It's not real to them."

"So you didn't make or sell those recordings?"

"No, the data on the deaths *I* sent were intended for other researchers."

There's something slight and italic on the emphasis of the I, even under her freshly fogged voice, that makes Lakerman continue to scrutinise her face rather than offer any of the expected emotional reacts.

She stops.

"Listen, it's true that the hospital has, in the last few years, engaged in selling intimate information around individuals at the time of death. The money it made was always for the hospital. To help there. Technically it's a legal grey area. Everyone signs a release form that donates their info to research. Selling it privately is obviously scandalous but it's the only way this place can keep going. The defence would be: How do you define research? And the community needs this hospital. Look around. I sent out that data because better equipped, better funded hospitals have a better chance of figuring out what's going on. Obviously those places are either compromised or the messages were intercepted."

"So you've never personally sold death data?"

Mary's hands finger the bag with the powder.

"A few times. But I wasn't doing that now. I was asking for help. I was set up."

"Who was buying?"

"The first expiration data I recorded...I'd been approached by a colleague higher up... Sounded out... After that... I'd get the occasional alert about who to record. I never had any direct contact with a buyer. The transactions were supposed to be anonymous but I was curious and managed to find a couple through the hospital records."

"Individuals?"

"Supposedly. I visited one. It was in Scotland. It was a thirteen hour drive. I found a fifteen year old. She was living alone as the lighthouse keeper there. A Sammy Malone apparently. She didn't have a hint of identity about her. She was perfectly lucid, capable but if I asked her anything about her situation it was like talking to an automated response that didn't want anything from you. I made up a story about why I was there. Said I was from the council and needed to inspect her living conditions. In her bathroom I found medication, a lot of medication. Experimental stuff, things I didn't recognise."

"Any branded?"

"The medicine itself was unbranded. Trialled. But in the wastebasket I found the directions for use and a piece of mail. No return address but a stamp from abroad and three letters: LPX. The instructions too were for LPX, I ran a search and there were a couple of matches but the one that stood out was for..."

"Life Pax?"

"Yes... you're familiar with them?"

"Getting more familiar all the time. Who was the girl?"

She begins to load a new line into the foil. Lakerman can tell by the ease of her movements that this is a case of prep for later, a subtle rather than definitive signal of the finite nature of their time. Her high must have started wearing off just enough for the first thought of the next hit to suggest itself and she's sufficiently practised, Lakerman thinks, to anticipate and avoid the desperation of the moment.

"She was a surrogate. I'm sure of it. Maybe she had some terminal disease or maybe someone she knew did. My guess is all those early purchases were made through surrogates."

"Early?"

"The hospital sells death on a larger scale now. It used to be done through individuals just here and there, now there are these dark money organisations who purchase it. It's almost an industry. I'd be surprised if it wasn't common practice in a lot of places."

"You said you had correlations but that Vale didn't correspond. Do you know anything else about him?"

"From his personal effects, I'd say he was a dealer."

"What kind of thing?"

"I can't be sure but if I had to guess I'd say it was drug tech, GRD's."

"Guided response drugs? Why do you say that?"

"For one he wasn't selling the stuff being used around here, otherwise we'd know him. Secondly, it would explain the burner tech he was kitted out with. Thirdly, it's the only thing that could connect him to the others. They were all gamers."

"I thought GRD's were just a novelty. Some shitty augmented reality visuals and a lumbering a.i trying to figure out your kink and then whisper it back to you."

"They've evolved. They're more like experiences now, not all of them pornographic."

Lakerman looks up at her. She's barely focused on him. She is leaning forward and running a frond of the carrot's leaf through her fingers.

"I used to play when I still had an implant," she says. "A lot of us here did."

"You had an implant?"

The sun has begun to set and Lakerman watches as a child, no older than ten, grinds his teeth while handing out candles and trying to sell psilocybin mushrooms. The child's head moves like a crippled bird on his neck, dragged and whirring, flapping from side to side. From what Lakerman can see his face is brittle and hatchet-like, skin so tight as to be almost transparent. The child's untamed hair is white and Lakerman can make out prices and weights and nonsense amid the snatches of sound he hears. Lakerman looks away. In the declining light the stained glass window is wine and silver coloured and the carrots look older than they should. All these details fall on and oppress Lakerman. The grey ash is becoming briefly luminous. Death floats gracefully through the air where his question lumpenly remains.

"You'll have to leave soon" Mary tells him. "So you better finish up your questions and start to figure out what you're going to do about this."

"You said they were gamers... what do you mean by that?"

"We don't know what they played but we know they logged significant hours on the Alternet's VR sites. Our autopsies showed a correlation between drug use and game time."

"You said you'd played, you had an implant?"

"As a student I'd received a sponsorship from a prestigious private hospital.. I received an early model implant as part of the sponsorship. At university we experimented. I took it too far, got caught."

"What sort of things did you... play?"

"The one that I liked the most... You'd start out as a light sensing amoeba... nearly all your other faculties were shut down. You were conscious but not thinking. I was just consciousness and a vessel for pulsing light. A warmth that was purely physical and an emptiness that could be filled, charged with sun. The relation between life and death was established in sensation not in the mind. There was no fear. Imagine that. Gradually I became other things: a droplet of water joining a river, a leaf eating light, a baby, a mother, until finally I was this series of stars exploding in what was the end and the beginning of time. I mean, it's almost impossible for me to remember how it felt or to find the language for it...rationally, I can reduce it by comparison...

Like it was akin to a near lethal dose of MDMA married to extremely high spec visuals after a systematic dismantling of my preconceptions via a series of DMT bombs and some high class poetry."

"I don't understand how it works."

"You'd have the VR link and the substances themselves were on a time release and able to regulate their digestion through triggers in visual and emotional reactions. The idea being certain narratives would correlate and interact with the drugs. As the drugs became smarter the GRD's became more complex and then when VR programming became more accessible people started sort of djing their experiences. Playing with release times, scenarios. Some went pro became Wo.oz'.s Occasionally, when we couldn't find a W.O.Oz..."

"A WOOz?"

"A Wizard of Oz. If we couldn't find one we'd borrow a world-template and let one another playlist emotions or ramble through some raggedly constructed, self penned, bVr narrative but– while the experience was always enjoyable and kind of interpersonally enlightening, albeit in a seriously mediated fashion– there was nothing quite like a heavily repped W.O.Oz for a night, weekend if we could afford it of incredible and profound experiences that would enrich our memories, lives and emotional palettes."

"When did you stop?"

"When they shut down my implant. I failed a drug test and lost my sponsorship. I was suspended from studying for two years but I wasn't blacklisted and my credits were still valid so I finished my training and took a residency at a general hospital. Don't you think it's strange that none of the articles about me mentioned I'd lost a prestigious sponsorship due to drug use? It's easily accessible information. Why would they do that?

"They don't want it to be part of the story."

"Wouldn't the general logic of the news dictate that mentioning my addictions would be newsworthy or at the very least salacious. If you actually write this thing, wouldn't you include it?"

"Of course."

"So, you see what i'm saying. We have gamers, a pharmaceutical company involved in buying illegal data through third parties, implants, governments turning a blind eye and a media disinterested in a scandal they'd usually eat up. What the fuck is going on?"

"Does the phrase How I Killed the Universal Man mean anything to you?"

"Not a thing, why?"

"Lifepax had invested in a game of that name. The inventor, one Trevor Orshach, has a history of creating subversive 'games', I'd be interested to know if there's any crossover with his work."

Her eyes widen and the freckles across her neck seem to glow like embers skated over by wind. She draws back.

"You know him?"

"He's from here."

She points to a large mural on the eastside of the church. At first the range of disparate styles and cultural references disguises the careful composition of the piece. Taken as a whole the image appears garishly disparate, the work of successive authors with little concern or care for one another. Classical wildstyle graffiti is overlapped with pervert Anime that abruptly clashes with impressionistically lit bodies whose dappled form appears carelessly stencilled over with nightmarish figures straight up lifted from Hieronymus Bosch. This heap sits heavily above some new age techno-religious nostalgia, divine robotics, the silicone east.

These apparently disharmonious aesthetics eventually coalesce through a set of suggestively interiorised relations that corral the chaos into some articulable meaning, a patterned thing. A narrative. The top half of the image depicts a wire frame mesh that dips like a gravity well, such as you might see in a geometry lesson about planets. The well is filled with bodies squirming against one another or else brutally compacted into stratas of flesh and bone. These sedimentary layers are rendered in anime's ecstasy of cute brutality and erotically ambiguous victimhood, flushed faces and lolling tongues stuffed with their own entrails form territories through which Boschian demons tunnel, their pitchforks throwing up Renoir-esque

105

self lighting gore. Partial bodies as Partial objects fucked with accordingly.

An arrow is painted over one demon and in the right margin of the wall the same demon is enlarged with statistics and a more detailed mark up of its face.

This demon is capitalism.

Special Ability: Ravenous hunger.

Beneath the lowest point of the massed abyss a small shower of bodies that have slipped through the gridded mesh fall into a cable. The cable seems to attract them from the air. The cable's jacket is printed with the words *Nirvana*. Its interior is swirled like the milky way and plugs into the navel of a robotic figure sat benignly in the pose of the buddha. This figure absorbing the cable is giant and genderless and pregnant. In one hand they hold a piece of ginger and in the other an egg. Next to them is an upended tree, its roots exposed to the sky, its trunk cut open and the rings arranged into an infinity sign.

Allegorical Futures is written underneath the image and signed T.OR.

Lakerman frowns. He is trying to remember where else he has seen T.OR before. The tree of life. That must have been Orschach too. Orschach in collaboration with UbIQ. Noumenon and how I killed the universal man connect Trevor to lifepax as well, he remembers. Orschach, Lifepax and UbIQ. Games, drugs, and tech. The party in Miami. Who wants him to go?

He looks again at the mural. The whole again refuses to balance in his mind. It was as if the mural resisted sense, as if Orschach had tapped into some method of organisation that scrambled the connection between the micro and macro. It was impossible to see the relations of image without first entering into those relations which then obscured the free floating totality of the image, its unrealised possibility. You couldn't see anything there until you did and while this forgetting in order to focus was a normal aspect of consciousness, Lakerman thought, the explicit revelation of the impossibility of seeing, the impossibility of retro-engineering a whole from pieces or pieces from a whole was the piece's real innovation. Somehow Orschach had managed to separate form and content, appearance and reality. Neither existed except as possibilities for the other.

"Trevor Orschach...it's not a pseudonym?"

"It's his tag name. No one who would know his real name is still around."

"What's his reputation like?"

"Runs the gamut of cult like figure, local boy done good, to total sellout. I don't think anyone but the fanboys really know what he does now."

"He ever come back?"

"Not directly. Every now and then a new painting appears. I suspect it's made by remote drone though there are those who believe he comes in person, prince and pauper etc or sometimes supplies appear from the sky in little parachutes that are branded with his artwork. And then occasionally something like this turns up..."

She gestures to the glass encased carrots. Under the grape purple of a still sunstained sky the case is like a relic of some holy tableaux.

"... these strange objects that get poured over for meaning, endlessly interpreted."

"What's everyone saying these mean?"

Mary begins to look around. Shift in her seat.

"That life grows in secret. The case is supposed to represent how fragile our privacy is, the soil is how lifegiving. You can understand the dark gives people ideas." She looks at him, sober and concentrated reminding him of her manner in the hospital.

"How safe it is for you here now is a rapidly closing window."

"I only have a couple more questions."

"Ok."

"Did you or anyone you work with try to contact anyone about this? Who else knows?"

"The only people who know about these cases are me, the Neurology Consultant, our endocrinologist and the senior medical director of the hospital. Of course we contacted the relevant organisational bodies immediately after the first case. The message we received from them was to send them samples and burn the bodies and to do all this in secret so as to avoid a panic. So, that's what we did. It didn't sound right. It didn't feel right. But they sent us paperwork. Lots of paperwork and we'd gone through all the official channels. After the next case arrived we contacted them again. It took us about a month before we realised we were talking to different A.I.'s. The hospital had been totally hacked, emails and phone calls redirected, vast swathes of data expropriated. The kind of data so sensitive that you're liable for its protection. We realised we were totally cut off. We tried sending emails to each other. They arrived but the content was differently stylised and subtly changed. Passive voices became active. If we wanted to talk to anyone about this, we realised, we'd actually have to talk to someone in the flesh. That's when it started to seem like we were being individually targeted. Anybody who seemed to even suggest trying to share air with another organisation were quickly driven out."

"Driven out how?"

"Shortly after the second case. Pretty much *as* the Medical director was talking about who we ought to contact next, and how, the director's search history started circulating in a chain email to everyone in the hospital contacts list. You didn't know if it was true or faked or a hybrid of the two but it spoke to something about the person in question. There was a certain psychological acuity in the accusations contained in their expression of desire, just enough to make you think it could be real. It made everyone real paranoid. The director denied it of course but he was in an untenable position. He told us again that we had to take the news public, to one of the big three media groups. After he said this other emails and videos started to leak. These were worse. The doctor said the videos were fakes that had been planted in his computer, but it didn't seem to matter. They'd been sent to everyone, everyone who had ever given their email to the hospital. The police became involved. He told us he wouldn't say anything, he'd lost credibility as a witness but wanted us to clear his name. He was sure he would be able to show that the videos were tampered with, deep faked. That left me, the neurologist, and the endocrinologist. After a few more cases Jason, the neurologist, disappeared. The last thing he told me is that he intended to go national. He wanted someone to know in case anything happened. He told me he hadn't left any data trail. Hadn't googled anything. Hadn't lingered over anything that might betray his thought process. He told me he was going to contact the news and the police... He would tell them he was culpable in a cover up. And later I thought of course he was going to do that, it fit. It was too obvious. He was a deeply moral person...I don't think he even knew about the data bundles the hospital sold."

"Disappeared? Is that even possible?"

"His IP says he's in China but he doesn't respond to any messages, his profiles are all abandoned. I went to the police, they were more concerned he'd escaped because of a possible connection with the director. That's when it struck me that China seems suspicious enough for any authority to wrangle a useful narrative out of. He defected, he was kidnapped, he escaped the law etc. I'd say it counts as a disappearance. As for the endocrinologist, it's true what they say about them."

"What do they say?"

"Nothing. And she's not saying anything ever either, trust me. She's looking for a way out. She'd hate that I'm talking like this with you but she'd never be seen dead here. It feels like every attempt to expose this thing has been predicted."

"Is that why you chose donkeyWolf? You're betting our reputation and your identity against an algorithm?"

"Not exactly that but also, yes. I barely had any idea your publication existed. I've never read anything except for once, over someone's shoulder, I caught a page of an article you'd written. I remembered your name because I liked the way it sounded."

"What was the article? Was it about drugs?"

"No. It was an interview. A woman, a survivor from the camps, who had ended up homeless and living with the cancer foxes. You didn't let up once."

"You felt sympathy for her?"

"Because of how relentless you were. Was it necessary?"

"I think necessary is a strong word. There was a point to it. If you felt sympathy for her then you admitted her existence, her choices, as a possibility for yourself. I wanted you to feel sympathy because I wanted you to condemn yourself."

"That didn't really come across."

"It doesn't matter. Why you? Why are you getting these cases and not ..."

"Like I said, so far it's poor people whose tech is conditional. They can't go anywhere else and they might as well be invisible to whatever functioning network excludes them. So, there's that and maybe we just happen to be the centre of the outbreak. It has to be somewhere right? That's one possibility. Another is the patients are being sent to us deliberately because, as we've seen, the hospital is compromised enough to control. That could be true too but it seems a little clumsy and labour intensive. The third possibility, and the one I'd bet on, is that we're not the only ones seeing this and the silence can't hold for much longer. There's going to be a devastating spillage and it's all about who gets saddled with patient zero."

"Last question, have there been any survivors?"

"There has been one survivor but he took his own life shortly after."

"What happened to his body?"

"The growth he experienced was small and relatively uncomplicated."

"What was it?"

"He had developed a scrotum on his face."

"Specifically where?"

"On either side of the bridge of his nose."

"Two scrotums?"

"No, no, his nose... his nose kind of partitioned the... sack... at least in warm weather."

"And in cold?"

"Sort of dead centre just below the forehead. It was like a frozen pea then. You lived in fear of him sneezing."

"Is that a joke?"

"Only partly, unfortunately."

"What did he tell you, did he have any idea how he contracted the illness?"

"Nothing. He was admitted because his neighbour had heard him screaming. He continued screaming during his journey to the hospital and for the first few hours of his stay. Even after a strong sedative was applied he continued to scream. After several hours of this he'd totally destroyed his vocal cords. At the end his voice sounded like a piece of Velcro. Which was fitting because he looked like something was being torn via a thousand little hooks from his body. Then he just stopped. After the screaming he couldn't communicate anything. He just sat there, shrugging his shoulders. If he was anywhere it wasn't there. His body functioned perfectly well but it was like he had beamed out. He didn't do anything until three days later he killed himself."

Dialogue options unfold before Lakerman:

(a) Ask about relatives in Miami
(b)Tell her about your implant and declare love (Trust)
(c) Get going
(d) "Have we met before somewhere?"
(e) Are you a clone?

He thought he was supposed to be offline. A small hand throws glittering confetti then snaps its fingers in the upper left of his eyesight. A notification inside his head says:

You are offline but you have attained and harvested several kinetic trophies! Congratulations. You have successfully built a biological reserve of power! A charge that could last up to thirty minutes. This reserve is currently set to 'incognito' mode. Touch your eyelid to go public.

Lakerman stands to go. His eyes dart around the ruins for the safest exit. He turns back towards Mary.

"Do you have any relatives that live in Miami?" Lakerman says despite himself.

"Doesn't everyone have a relative in Miami?"

"No."

"Oh."

"You haven't answered the question?"

"Is it important?"

"Yes."

"I don't think so. Not to my knowledge."

"Why did you respond with 'doesn't everyone?' if..."

"I was giving a flippant answer to a stupid question. Take this."

She gives him a number and an antique phone. Lakerman shoves it awkwardly into his pocket.

"You can contact me forty times on this. Or we can talk for fifty minutes. The phone isn't traceable, isn't online. The telephone company is long defunct but the comms have been maintained. Don't wear any AR when you use this. Go."

* * *

Lakerman's flat is in cleaning mode as he enters, the appliances humming through their ablutions. Something small and dark scurries across the floor and away from the shafting light of the open door. It observes Lakerman with a look of beaten servitude from behind a futon.

Lakerman regrets buying the Kafka brand robovac.

He sits down on the futon. The place looks just as he would have left it. The disorder all part of a memory he might have made, that he can believe is his own. It had clearly been a comfortable night in. One of moderate debauchery and drug abstracted loneliness. His hand reaches out and claims the usual half smoked joint. He hadn't even needed to look for it.

He knows the surrogate is currently stored in his sleep space, lying in the recovery position, waiting for activation. In ten minutes Lakerman will open up the space and lay down next to them. Joe Vale will cease to exist. All that is data will melt into air. The surrogate and Lakerman will then sync. Then this other body that has shared his life will stand up and wordlessly leave like Peter Pan's unkissed shadow.

Ten minutes.

Lakerman takes out the clunky looking phone and struggles to flip it open. His thumbs mash the *raised* buttons. There are no neo-hieroglyphic emoticons to foreshorten his range of emotion, render his sentiments exchangeable. There are only words flattened, tamed, totally dimensionless. A digitised language. Both are shitty, he thinks.

He writes to Mary Trustin that he needs more evidence. More examples. Something other than Dicknose. There is something else he wants to write and cannot.The phone beeps almost immediately. She tells him not to waste his credit, that everything has been burned. He asks her for any photographic evidence. What kind of evidence is a photo these days? She writes. Stop wasting credit.

 Lakerman flips the phone shut. He checks the time. He googles 'T.OR artist.' There's a list of publicly commissioned works but no contacts page. He can find only one image of Orschach. A self portrait. In it the artist is curiously expressionless, his face photographed from the front against a bright orange background. It is only the suggestion of intentionality in the context, the knowledge that the piece is art, that arrests the sensation of disquiet his face produces. It is similar to the mural, Lakerman thinks, in that the tension between logical impossibility and the experience of impossibility seems to neutralise one another, as if truth were a double backed mirror and reality only a thin layer of adhesive. The artist's look is so startling that Lakerman clearly recalls where he has encountered it before. The expressionless boy. The club rat's boyfriend. The shooter. Lakerman downloads the photo. He opens a sketch app. His implant connects.The app sketches, in photo realistic detail, the expressionless boy just as Lakerman remembered him. It is as if the implant has photographed his thought. Lakerman places a de-ageing filter over the image of Orschach. The similarity can't be dismissed. He runs a statistical analysis. It's a 94% match.

Lakerman searches through the obituary he'd saved and finds the image of the club rat. He copies Trustin's medical photo from the hospital website. He sketches Andrea Christoff. He lines up the Club rat, Mary Trustin and Andrea Christoff like the ascent of man.

He places an aging filter over the club rat and Trustin.

He resets.

He de-ages Trustin.

He resets.

In every iteration they were the same. Lakerman's alarm goes off. He pushes open the sleep space. The surrogate is there, fully masked and swamped in layers of gender neutral clothing. Lakerman lays down and the surrogate automatically rolls on top of him. The surrogate's body faces the ceiling, their arms and fingers aligning with those of Lakerman. The surrogate grasps the outside of Lakerman's hands and raises their four hands to the surrogate's throat. The surrogate pads Lakerman's hands against their throat. Lakerman begins to choke the surrogate. You had to choke a surrogate in order to reset them. The surrogate does not struggle but no amount of clothing can disguise the gristle and pop of the neck, the hard stuff collapsing in with the wet stuff. The surrogate's body goes totally limp. An alarm is supposed to let Lakerman know when to stop and so he doesn't stop. He knows that if the surrogate dies it wasn't murder, legally. Surrogacy itself was considered a kind of suicide to begin with and you'd be charged with hiring an illegal body which was serious in itself and you'd be liable financially for the destruction of said body but other than that... nada.

Lakerman stops. He hears the alarm. He's aware that he's not sure how long the alarm has been ringing.

The surrogate eventually gets up and leaves and Lakerman bursts into tears. He rolls out of the sleep space and lights a joint. He sends Mary Trustin a message.

* * *

CHAPTER 4

EGO DEATH FOR DUMMIES (LE PETITE MORT EDITION)

Lakerman's sitting in the lobby of London's Africa Hotel nursing a vodka tonic and wondering if he's about to destroy Mary Trustin's sense of herself. He checks the time on his wrist then shoves his hand into his pocket where he fingers the needle of noumenon he's sewn into his thigh. Donkey Wolf has him booked on the next WaterWarp cargo boat to Miami in an hour. The boat's designed to deliver trinkets from London to tourists all over the world though it's occasionally used to transport the dead or Upper Middle Class Economic Migrants to their new resting places. Lakerman has chosen the Safari hotel for their meeting both for its proximity to the Thames but also because he knew they'd be practically invisible here despite the milling crowds of tourists. The hotel was a vast kingdom of the blind and its occupants' smart VR would navigate their materiality with ease. With the collapse of commercial air travel twenty years ago tourism had become increasingly virtual. Generally 'Travel' was now conducted from large hotels dedicated to various continents. There was the European hotel, the African hotel and the Asian hotel in London alone. Going in person had given way to renting holograms and wandering round cities like a remote controlled ghost while a network of camera's constructed the cityscape for you and the hotel provided treadmills with complexly modelled terrains. Each hotel had floors or rooms dedicated to specific countries and activities to allow for backpacking, safari or surfing to name a few. If you wanted to eat out the app sent a signal to the hotel kitchen and the specialist chef of the regions on offer delivered an authentic version of the dish to you while you sat at Luigi's digitised cafe or wherever. The experience of shopping as a hologram allowed for the preservation of the awkward and possibly exploitative interactions with the locals and the mementos you bought would then be shipped to your home while a three dimensional print out of the object would act as a camouflaged substitute during your stay.

Lakerman feels in his pocket for the Juliet that Gem had sorted him out with for the trip. He takes the drug out and studies the design of the package. The blister features an unusually robust foil on which a white haired Grandfather is welcomed by a large family while the sun sets behind the sea in the background. It's a deliberately sentimental image for a drug that all but rendered you a zombie, Lakerman thinks. Pushing out the pill from its pack would all but obliterate the family scene in a way Lakerman knows he'll find quietly satisfying. Perhaps this was intended too, the destruction. All pleasures catered for. Juliets slowed the body's ageing, shutting down organ use and cutting essential processes down to a fraction of their output. This, coupled with a refrigerated compartment, meant up to a month of travel was reduced to a few hours of physical decay and brain ageing consciousness. He looks again at the single blister: *Travfreeze 5mg*. He didn't know why everyone called them Juliets.

Information unfurls in his mind:

The etymology of the Travfreeze drug slang "Juliets" is unclear though there are two strong contenders.

Meaning one: Juliet in French means 'youthful' according to baby name guides.

Meaning two: In the Shakespearean tragedy Romeo and Juliet, Juliet uses a potion to fake her own death so she can be reunited with Romeo. The deathly state the potion induces is somewhat similar to the effect of Travfreeze.

Juliets had become a celebrity drug. Child Stars, ageing film actors, and Korean Pop Stars under heavily incentivised and draconian seeming contracts were rumoured to use them in various doses between gigs to preserve their skin's marketability. It had of course also spread to human trafficking and sex work in ways so repulsive to think about that it made Lakerman feel psychotic to do so and so he did what nearly everyone did, which was simply to shut up, ignore it, and seriously engage with distraction in order to get away from the horror of the all too human dehumanisation. In his hand, right now the pill was just something that made his life easier. Full stop. He couldn't allow himself to feel responsible for the potential it held.

Mary Trustin arrives at the bar. Her pupils, he thinks, are like two fanged punctures in a corpse's neck i.e they retain a certain erotic suggestion but with the intimacy already turned out of them. She's high then, which might make it easier for him to ask her what he wants to know. Before he can say anything she hands him an envelope.

"We had another case."

"What happened?"

"A heart turned into a clitoris."

"They died happy?"

"I wish it were funny."

Lakerman peers into the envelope. "Is this a *printed* photo?"

"The only copy."

"What kind of evidence..."

"It's what you asked for. It's what I could get. The mutation is only one point of interest here. We'd have missed him totally if the body hadn't been discovered by the police and the post mortem hadn't turned up the...irregularity."

"The police discovered the body?"

"Take a look. It's a homicide. It's all going to come out soon."

Lakerman shakes out the photos. A headless, handless, footless corpse greets him along with a series of pictures of the figure's chest cracked and tented open. There's no clear way of identifying the body. Snaking out from under the armpit, though, Lakerman can make out something he initially thinks is a port wine birthmark.

"What's that?"

"Next picture."

The next picture shows two images of the victim's armpit side by side, shaved and unshaved. The shaved armpit reveals a tattoo in its hollow that causes Lakerman to start back in his seat.

"Why are we here?" Trustin asks. Lakerman's still studying the tattoo. The tattoo is of a scar in the shape of the mouse.

"I also have pictures."

Lakerman passes her a small stack of pictures that he's done up with string.

"This is like a very dark valentine," she says, undoing the bow, and looking at the first photo in her hand. The first photo has three images of her: Past, Present, and Future lined up in a deceptive chronology.

"Is that accurate? Did you look like that at seventeen?"

"Yeah, exactly. If it wasn't for the hair I'd think this was me. You used an app for this? Why is this one a drawing?"

Lakerman gestures for her to look at the next picture. As she does so her forehead tries to pass something to her eyes. It's an intensity they can't handle. The picture's a screenshot of the club rat's funeral service. Mary's own image subjected to the popular aesthetics of the living's nostalgia: A well lit death. Her face *un*real*ised* by the soft focus and softer Photoshop.

She flicks to the next image, it is the drawing of Andrea Christoff with everything that Lakerman knows about her written in. She looks at its back and front.

"What the fuck is this?"

"A dark valentine. I'm worried about you. One of them worked for lifepax."

Mary Trustin's mouth trembles with anger and disgust as she turns away from Lakerman. Lakerman though catches something in the fracturing speed of her gaze, a betrayal of unearthed interest, a counter force of will willing her to linger on him.

She turns back. Something has darkened inside her. The high still glowing enough around the edges of her perception to render her sensation of horror fuzzy though no less tragic.

"What are you trying to..."

"What family do you have? Were you adopted?"

"Stop."

"I think you're a clone. I think you're part of the reason the hospital is receiving..."

"Pictures don't prove anything and one of these is a drawing. A drawing for fucks sake. All recordings of the world are fundamentally untrustworthy. That's just a given."

"I've met these people. Shortly after I met them they were murdered."

"Murdered by who?"

"By Trevor Orschach or someone with his DNA."

"I don't have time for this."

"I'm worried you're in danger."

"I know that already. What worries me is how how careless you are."

"Says the Junkie."

Mary stands. She's leaving. She turns around.

"Why the fuck you?"

"Sorry, what?"

"It's a question you ought to ask yourself. For once it might not be egotistical to ask it."

She leaves. He remains at the bar. He doesn't want to think about what she said cause it's too late now. He orders another drink, pops the Juliet.

* * *

The water warp cargo boat is utilitarian grey, barely stickered by brands, and so boxy in form that it evokes the same machinic prehistory of the terminal now as insects and sharks. Only more basic than either of those, Lakerman thinks. This is a thing that floats, that blindly *hulks* through the sea, travelling from mass to mass, without will and unfathomed by desire. A successful thing whose lack of evolution testified to some prototypical and developmentally arresting success. Like a testicle, he thinks.

Lakerman notices a white middle class family waiting to board. A father and teenage son eye slunk and face-numbed on Juliets. The mother however is alert, radiating pain and worry. Lakerman's implant alerts him to the knots in her back. The pain they transmit lit like a map. He changes visualisation. He watches her back muscles, semi viscous and unfurling, stiffen into a landscape, her spine an evolutionary reading of the heart's seismic activity. She is holding her baby close to her chest, her gaze stopping and padding around Lakerman's skin like a safe breaker as he approaches. It's like she can't quite hear the click of his heart. It has been a while since Lakerman encountered something like this. He mirrors her expression with Opscions, his face becoming a star chart of hers photographed by the clench of his jaw. The mother shields her baby. There is a fear in her eyes. She doesn't recognise her gaze. There's something important in this, Lakerman thinks. He softens himself. He is amazed he can do this. She responds. He's vaguely sickened by her.

"Are you ok?"

"I mean I just can't believe they've done this. How could they be so selfish?"

She means the husband and son. She tells Lakerman Juliets aren't recommended for babies. No shit, he thinks. We're on a long haul trip, she says, and there'd been an agreement. To spend it together. Now look at what they've done.

"Are you?" She asks. Lakerman shakes his head. She nods. He can't tell if she's relieved or not, even with the implant.

"I took mine an hour ago." He says and as leaden as his voice is, Lakerman is aware that he can still feel his jaw, that his tongue moves zippily after his thoughts. It should kick in soon, he thinks.

The interior of the boat is an ark of tat. Antique plastic. Bundles of clothing and ash trays, the two by two of excess. He notices in the

121

corner a gaudy sculpture being tied down with Stomata. It's *'hubris-nihilism.'* Someone bought it. He got it now. The act of someone buying it made it into a better joke. The boat is totally automated but they've been accompanied onboard by a group of workmen holding tablets and placing the father and son in the automated wheelchairs. The mother is taken to a separate room.

"You're on a Juliet right?"

Lakerman nods and then he feels it sinking him. His body weighed with blood and bone. His breathing is slowing and will continue to fall. His heart is a planet whose gravity he collapses around. The workmen pour him into a wheelchair. The workman assigned to Lakerman is maybe fifteen years old. They reach the small room Lakerman's booked. The door reads Lakerman's ID. It won't open. The workman looks up at the family who are similarly having problems with their key. He checks the tablet. He swipes something at the door. It still won't open.

He beckons for his supervisor.

"Try switching them," he says pointing from Lakerman to the father and son. "Something has been up with the system since yesterday. It doesn't really matter for these matters of the flesh, they more or less know where they're going but it's been a total ball ache having to update the records with the merch. I'll bet they've just been switched."

"You want me to move him over there. And you'll move them over here?"

"Yes."

"Manually?"

"Yes. Use your body. Jesus."

"Seems weird. Will there even be space for those two in his room?"

"For two zombies, yeah. They don't make any rooms smaller than this."

The young workman tentatively holds the wheelchair's grips. Lakerman can feel the tension in the caress. He's identifying with this new body he's part of. He's something liquid bodied in metal. Then the hands become too rough and the wheelchair judders forward and halts.

"It's too weird touching things," the trainee replies.

The doors open as soon as Lakerman's six feet away. The room's structured like an eye.

A gossamer film coats the surfaces and floor of the room. Light from outside slides across the walls, broken up into an iris of rainbows. Lakerman watches gormlessly as the glazing on the walls retracts to a single square foot on the ceiling before constituting itself into a mitten shaped hand waving hello before dissolving and recollecting into an arrow pointing down into the centre of the room where a large derma foam cushion is set into the floor.

"That's new, when did they install that?" the younger workman says.

"I don't know. How's that other room?"

"A piece of shit in comparison. Did this guy ever luck out."

"Like it matters, they're totally fucked up right?"

"Right."

"What did the boy and father get?"

"A pillow and sleeping bag."

"That can't be what they paid for."

"They're not going to know."

"Till they wake up."

"Not our problem then."

They wheel him to the centre of the room. They tip him out into the cushion. The stomata gives a thumbs up. The younger workman is frowning at the hand.

"It must have been expensive, I don't get why it's here."

The older workman tells him it only looks impressive, that its A.I. is super basic. It's there in the room to spritz the body clean, to dust the reality from the dreaming body. To massage muscles at an appropriate rate. Check his vitals. Lakerman feels the world and his perception beginning to crystallise. The ceiling, in all its molecular streams, becomes the greatest painting ever composed. The door closes with a bang. No matter. Lakerman hears the outside world as a single sustained roar and everything in his conscious mind is just an eternity of him thinking OH and never reaching the end of that K.

* * *

Lakerman can't tell anything is wrong at first. He's not even himself yet. His body is conscious but there's nothing but darkness and the stew of emotions and a slurred internal voice like collected fat coming together out of the split of its fleshy internment. Electric meat fat orchestra. There are plays of orange from some outer source that help him locate his eyes. Now comes the panic. It comes with the awareness of his extension into space and limitless darkness. He can't move or see. Lakerman imagines he is totally paralysed. How long would it take for his voice to dissolve in his consciousness?

Lakerman directs all the will he can muster at his eyelid. It stutters open half an inch. There's the door window and a face behind it. It's Orschach, he thinks. He's trying to get in. Orschach's hair seems to grey and his face appears to be turning to putty with each effort to take down the door. Lakerman's hand flops around like a fish. He tries to scream. Can't. Something agonisingly painful is working its way through his urethra. He experiences a climax of pain and then he begins to piss himself. At first he thinks it's blood, then it is clear it's not. He must have passed the Juliet, he thinks. He doesn't understand. The hot stream of piss calls to attention the numbness of his legs. He moans or at least he thinks he does. The door is beginning to give way. Lakerman begins to rock his body. He hears the door shatter open and feet running towards him. He falls off the bed. His legs are pathetically inert behind him. He stops. No one has come forward. He hears the sound of a body hitting the floor. Lakerman manages to turn his head. The man is at least eighty years old but the trapped terror captured in the eyes belongs to a younger man. Lakerman can make out a mitten shaped bruise purpling grotesquely across the old man's neck. He passes out.

* * *

124

Lakerman wakes to the sound of wailing and the gasping sensation of lost time. He's so disorientated he doesn't even realise the old man's body has disappeared, that the door has been repaired. He staggers his way out of the room.

"It should have been you." The mother is screaming at him. Lakerman doesn't know what's going on. A police officer informs him the father and son have suffocated in their room. A ventilation failure. It had taken them days to asphyxiate. Lakerman remembers the man who tried to attack him. He thinks it must have been a dream. That's what he wants to believe at least. The officer is asking questions. Lakerman's executive functions haven't fully booted yet but Opscions has loaded and is parsing out various chains of affect that he's just about managing to stumble between. The officer asks him why a journalist has come *in person*. There's an accent on the word person that's ambiguous enough to linger.

The officer is waiting. He taps his foot.

(A) Continue to look confused and Juliet stoned only with an unquantifiable yet subtly perceptible degree of deception underpinning your expression (ignore)
(B) There was someone else on the ship
(C) Impress upon him the Importance of Embodied space to your personal brand
(D) More People will Die
(E) I'd like to call my Lawyer (intimidate)

"My brand niche is authenticity."

The police officer's emotions cycle through stunned, humiliated and furious. He stares at Lakerman.

"Part of what I do is be somewhere physically and then I sort of insist upon or explore the relevance of that to what I'm writing about."

As he's speaking Lakerman receives two alerts. The officer says something in reply then scans his details. He tells Lakerman they'll be in touch if they need him and confirms his address. Lakerman nods but the conversation is already fully automated and filed under junk and his attention is lost to scanning the content of his alerts. The first is a link to a business insider article. Real estate sale. The second he recognises as a tabloid newspaper.

Lakerman waves goodbye to the officer who frowns at him. Inside the auto-taxi he downloads the business article, discovers the chapel in Islington has been purchased and is expected to be renovated and serve as a new flagship Stomata clinic. He plays the short video accompanying it.

In the video Husk appears in his customary avatar of the five platonic solids, known colloquially as the UbIQ's cube. Each shape is contained in the cube and frames another in sequence, withdrawing from one another and extending out in accordioned folds of segmented space, so that at the logo's furthest point the icosahedron is partially nested in the dodecahedron which is partially nested in the octahedron which is partially nested in the tetrahedron all of which is fully contained in the cube. Each shape contains a letter of the company on one of its visible faces with the exception of the Tetrahedron and cube which share the letter U at an angle so it looms like a long shadow sucked into the horizon. The 'U' traversing the conical effect of the structure to provide further character to the intricate logo which struck Lakerman now as a kind of collapsed cathedral, some flat packed ghost of awesome space waiting to be pulled out, popped into existence. He knew that the disjunction in the mathematical sequence of the shapes' sides (20-8 -4 -4+2) had been nerdily poured over though Lakerman thought it was obviously a case of aesthetics being essentially unmathematisable and human psychology a bore. The cube, Lakerman realised, was there to act as a reassuring container, a compartment space or enclosure, a guarantee of inside out and out where the world was still exterior to UbIQ rather than interior to it. The thought strikes Lakerman as thematic.

Husk says in a Churchillian voice:

"We aim to be as respectful as we can to the history of this area and monument."

Husk stands aside to reveal Orschach's mural. A large mahogany looking egg vends itself from within Husk's Avatar and drops in front of the image of the egg in the KYBER-BUDDHA's hand. A wrecking ball then smashes through the hand of the buddha and cracks the mahogany egg in two. A veiny albumen and yolk of Stomata spills out onto the ruin and begins to bind with the dust. In a matter of moments a new wall is erected in which the image of the buddha's hand and the egg has been transformed into a terracotta looking embellishment. The stomata begins to slowly creep through the rest of the wall, simplifying the image into something ancient-seeming and prophetic, formatting the chaos into decoration.

Over this Husk intones:

"We aim to bridge the now, carry the past, transform the future."
The video cuts to locals in the area.
"Bloody Marvellous..."
"Everyone thinks this is good but they'll put the rent up now, we need to organise."
Lakerman closes the link. The second link is to a mainstream tabloid. The headline is "DEATH'S WHORE DOCTOR FOUND SWINGING" next to a noose and a face he refuses to recognise. He doesn't read any more. He flips open and turns on his antique phone. Waits. There's one message. It's a link that the phone obviously doesn't have the means to open though he recognises the domain. She's recorded her own death, is all he can think. She has recorded her own death and sent me the recording.

The taxi stops outside of the hotel and Lakerman pauses on the pavement. He waits a few moments before ordering a manual taxi and when it arrives he pays for it in Cash Money and gives Patrick Diaz's dead Abuela's address and looks around in some evolutionarily retained display of wariness even though he's pretty sure every threat is operating at a scale he can't comprehend.

* * *

THOMAS KENDALL

CHAPTER 5

CLOSED WORLDS

akerman's in the living room of Patrick Diaz's dead Abuela's house listening to water derive shape and trying to resist opening the link Mary has sent him. The situation he's found himself in isn't exactly optimal for analysing technological representations of death, he thinks. Patrick, unfortunately, had turned out to be home. He's currently in the bedroom with the bunk beds, showering in its ensuite with a girl who didn't give her name when Lakerman entered, though given the scene he'd encountered he understood why.

Lakerman had entered to find Patrick bouncing around on the sofa, his hands conducting a holo-controller while twelve men and eight women engaged in a variety of complex and contextually degrading sexual positions on his Dead Abuela's rug. It was difficult at first to tell that the bodies had no mass and it was only really the contrast between the literally faceless men and the Identical replications of the young woman that alerted him to the virtual nature of the orgy. It was then that Lakerman noticed the physical version of the hologirl in the corner of the room, to the side of the sofa, head to toe covered in medical electrodes and pressure sensors. Her body clad in flesh coloured plasters that creeped into and tiled the inside of her orifices, the cave of her mouth, the walls of her vagina, the muscle of her anus, all of her blood stress. He watched as she was guided through a repertoire of positions by the soft manacles and cords that attached her to the hexagonal pen she worked in. He noticed too, a small camera trained on her and focusing solely on her eyes which were wide open and unblinking, 'peeled' back, the two globes starkly revealed as if chipped out with a knife.

Patrick hadn't even minded the interruption. He'd thrown up his arms and positioned his avatar into a spectating position before walking unsteadily towards Lakerman. Patrick was so ecstatically drugged that his personality was like dark matter, Lakerman knew it had to be somewhere. Patrick gestured at the scene as he approached raising his eyebrows, his uneven leer seemingly imbalancing his head, creating a kind of falling momentum, so that he stumbled forward and into Lakerman's chest.

"I run a holo-tactile business," he'd said, looking up almost tenderly at Lakerman. "This is like a subscription event," Patrick's eyes rolled back in his head, "Thanks Abuela." He began to laugh.

Lakerman pointed to the girl in the corner. "She's having sex with everyone?"

"Sort of. There's a relay system at work here, everyone is hooked up in their fuck suits."

'Why is she staring like that?"

Patrick placed a clammy arm around Lakerman's neck.

"Someone paid a lot to have her eyes open the whole time and to see 'inside'. It's a simple electrical pulse, easy to configure. The hardest thing is to remember to apply eye drops regularly."

"Patrick, who is this, how..."

"That's my girlfriend man. This is our business."

"And the controller?"

"Some people want me to play their fuck for them. I pilot their orgasms. See this button is thrust, this is grab etc etc. This bar tells me if they're reaching a dangerous level of arousal etc etc."

Lakerman had tried to leave but Patrick insisted he stay, telling him that they'd be done in an hour and that then they could party in the flesh. It had felt a little like a threat. Lakerman had gone to the kitchen and mixed himself one drink, and then another and another. An hour later Patrick and the girl had gone into the bedroom with the bunk beds and an ensuite without acknowledging that he was still here. The fact Patrick had chosen the room with the bunk beds when so many others were available creeped Lakerman out for reasons he couldn't quite specify.

It's been half an hour since then and Lakerman can hear the hiss of the shower and the heavy silence moving through it. The outline of bodies stubbornly insisting upon their integrity as they change shapes to hold in pain, making themselves smaller, huddling around their core, forming a hearth for their flame. This thing that burns and lives in any touched thing and which was either dying or killing them, Lakerman thinks. Lakerman really can hear/see all this. The implant read the data from his ears, did the calculation, created a model of shapes that moved in the shifting of sound before him. *Situational quote app:*

"If we had a keen vision of all ordinary human life, it would be like hearing the grass grow and the squirrel's heart beat, and we should die of that roar which lies on the other side of silence." (George Eliot)

SAVE?

The longer thread of water stopping against the bathroom translates to Lakerman as the bodies have left the shower. Then the water stops entirely and a gentle sobbing pulses through the apartment. The girl comes out of the room to tell Lakerman that the party was off but that since he had come all this way he was welcome to crash for the night, since she figures he must have some reason for turning up unannounced. Her voice is so steady that it seems to right the room, to place the world back on its axis. Lakerman thanks her and she nods before going back into the room and closing the doors.

He switches off the lights and sits facing the sea. He receives an alert. *Knowledge Integration Complete.* He knows this means that the link between 'himself' and the implant is becoming more seamless, that knowledge would now become increasingly introjected into his consciousness, fired in the heart of twinkling synapses, fluidly coded along appropriate neural pathways. He frowns, had he consented to this or did the program just figure he would have?

Lakerman fixes his attention on the two files Mary had texted him. The first was:

DEATHMEGAMIX
(Durational Time Lord)
BY
BRKEN SANDBX
(Rec DOSE: A RORSCHACH BLOT)

The other file was called *MaryTrustin* accompanied by the dates of her birth and death, the date of recording (same) and what Lakerman guessed was her national insurance number. The first link was obviously the tech half of a Guided response drug, the other is what he expected. Both files had been marked as possessing content compatible with his implant. Games, she'd called them. He didn't know what he'd find, what aural, oral, visual, physical, mental sensations 'playing' them would induce. He's waiting until an appropriate time to find that out, though that time's a question of degree rather than certainty, he thinks. He takes a sip of his Negroni. Stories were being planted in his feed with the intention of directing his reporting. That much was obvious. He'd received an invitation, smuggled in a top range and unregistered implant, to return to Miami and play *How I Killed The Universal Man.* Who could have had the influence to arrange that? There were clones murdering clones and bodies stricken with mutation. There's a connection between Lifepax and UbiQ and all of that but nothing he's learned that would seemingly benefit any of them. Could it be Trevor Orschach?

Fuck it.

He turns his attention to the first link Mary sent him. Broken Sandbx must be the Wizard of Oz who had mixed the playlist and tried to control the tone of its accompanying hallucinations.

PLAYABLE CONTENT DETECTED!
Manufacture chemicals? Y/N?

HOW I KILLED THE UNIVERSAL MAN

Lakerman discovers that he knows that a *Rorschach Blot* could be generated in the body by having the organic bots mimic cellular behaviour, counterfeit genetic info and that since the Rorschach Blot was really a very strong sedative that shut down the language sections of the brain while activating a synaptic firing squad similar to dreaming, that he could produce it with minimal stress to his body.

Fuck it.
Play.

It starts with objects losing their shape. Lines warble, the distinction between things merge into gleams of intensity that dim naturally into nothing. There is a sudden roar of silence in his ears and then the numbed thud of something unanswered, an involuntary repetition, his heart washing up against a shore of bone. This feeling too becomes gradually muted until he has no sensation within his body whatsoever. He can't even locate his heart. There is only a void and his mind within it so that whatever he is, is a sky, an atmosphere.

And then it really begins.

Recordings of lost brain function and final chemical release, of hearts tracked until their last ambient beat and played out against some sad and strictly atonal infinity. His brain patterned in brief furies like an orchestra. His heartbeat mixing with theirs, his body producing theirs: The drowned. The slowed out. The let go. Lives strung through glitches of non existence, interlacing these flickering absences until what was left of that which lies between absences is hard to say, like lost time. And lower in the mix, creating depth, revolting against depth and in affirmation of itself, were even rarer recordings of lives suddenly and violently recalled into existence: depolarised hearts thumping with resurrected time. Hearts sparking minds. Resurrection. Electricity.

Lakerman is within all this. He can feel the pull of death sucking in the costume of his name and the rebirth after rebirth of each layered heartbeat, snapping back, a leashed engine of life, as migratory thought, randomly accessed memories, ranged over the territory of his brain opening up new connections, ladders of light. Things disappear and emerge. He can't tell the difference between awareness and experience. And then Lakerman feels the dropped beat of the heart, the cut out infinity of what is not, and there is nothing except his excitement straining to take shape, and as the formlessness becomes intolerable everything shrinks to a single heartbeat. His own. He feels his heartbeat rowing out of him and towards non-existence. He becomes only this gesture towards the world. There is a sort of ecstasy of relief. The heart beats, throbs, lets out a moan of blood and then it just doesn't. Come. Back...

Lakerman sits up gasping for air. Once he's caught his breath he begins to gag. He's shit on the chair. He waddles to the shower with a pillow case between his legs. Cleans himself and then rinses his underwear in the bath. He scans the bathroom medicine cabinet and a cleaning tutorial plays in his head. He mixes soap and baking soda. He scrubs and scrubs the boxers, plunging them again and again into the bath. Everything is done automatically and Lakerman watches himself going about these acts as if his body was some separate planet and his mind some defunct and barely operative satellite.

The sobbing in the apartment has stopped. He tiptoes to one of the other bedrooms. He doesn't choose the Abuela's. The link to Mary's death pulses in his mind. Laying in bed he opens it. He finds the file contains a number of other files. He opens her heartbeat, listens to its failure like it's trying to tell him something. While the beat throbs and washes against his blood, he inspects the rest of the data cache. He notices a file labelled Broca's Area. He opens it.

TRANSLATE? Y/N

It's his own voice taking up residence in his head but the garbled syntax and warping rhythm don't recall any recognisable language. The recording was either encrypted or gibberish. Or, more likely Lakerman thought, you couldn't translate anyone's thoughts to anyone else's throat, there was no universal alphabet of lettered movement. Then why record it, Lakerman thinks. The other files are strangely esoteric and include a short video of Mary reciting the alphabet in front of the stained glass window of the church.

Lakerman begins to imagine Mary. To remember her. He hears the sound of her voice. The way her jaw moved. The differences that separated her from the other clones. The Broca's area file begins to play again in the background. There's still something borderline Victorian about the spooky voice speaking in words where his embodied thought should be, the intimacy of her thought struggling to play across the twitches of his throat, but he's her mind now. At first it makes him want to claw out his eyes. The violation of it. The fixed volume of her thought, moving within his. The closeness of it.

I'm dying, she tells Lakerman, and I know it. I understand now. Can you feel this? I'm dying. Imagine this. There isn't much language to tell you that everything is ok even if it was. We only render what is observed and I'm entering possibility. Dying like this feels forever and nothing hurts. I can't tell you anything else. I'm not allowed. They'd find it. Her thoughts change tack, Lakerman no longer their subject. Wow, I'm really dying. I can't believe it. Just like this. It's not anything to worry about, unless...

These had been her last thoughts, he thinks. The last in language. He was slightly comforted by them but that was all. There wasn't anything in them that he could use other than the suggestion that she was being censored somehow. He scratches his aching thigh. The lump where the needle is feels bigger, swollen, potentially infected but he doesn't even care anymore.

* * *

He wakes at 5:30pm to find Patrick setting up a new hexagonal Sim Cage while his girlfriend takes her temperature and swigs what looks like glittery water from a silicone bottle. She is glaring every thirty seconds to a minute at Lakerman as he lingers in the doorway waiting to talk to Patrick.

Breakfast? Patrick asks, turning to him. Sure, Lakerman responds. Patrick points Lakerman to the Kitchen, walks with him, his hand guiding Lakerman's elbow. I've realised, he says, that you're not meant to be here. Lakerman nods. Now, I don't mind so much but Becky isn't so keen on strangers not paying their way, she has a thing about unexpected visitors. Childhood is a terrible thing. Well, you know that of course. Lakerman nods. There is a pause in the conversation. Lakerman offers to pay for the night and the rest of the week in advance. I'm only going to be here to sleep during the day, if then even. I won't get in your way. Excellent, excellent, Patrick says. I'm sure that will do the trick.

They scramble some vegan eggs, cook mushrooms and braise a piece of tofu and then arrange a plate.

A peace offering, Patrick says, entering the room and placing the plate in front of his girlfriend. Patrick leaves to make a call. Lakerman asks the girlfriend her name and she tells him he knows it already.

Intuition Alert. Nonchalance + interest in the taboo.

"How is the holo-tact business?" Lakerman asks.

"Fine. Today's my favourite client."

"How come he's your favourite."

"He wears my body like a straitjacket."

"How's that?"

"With this thing."

She points to a remarkably fine and translucent garment draped over the sofa.

"He bought that for me. Do you know what that is?"

Lakerman shakes his head. He knows but he doesn't want to risk spoiling the tentative conversation, fragile as it is. "It's woven graphene. The thread count is out of this world and it's like air on skin."

"What does it do?" Lakerman already knows of course, his implant connecting and combing through the history coursing and banked within the garment, written in its circuits.

"The fine hairs of my arm stand up on end and he knows. The timbre of my heartbeat, the temperature of my skin, the moisture and shine of my eyes. He'll sync with me as best he can. It'll register the echoing pain of a bruise or the implosive vacation of pleasure when I fuck."

"And his own body?"

"From what I understand he's voluntarily paralysed. He's into self suppressives."

"Rich, then?"

"You'd have to be. The really fucked up thing is that for all of this, it's not like he's even getting to feel what I'm feeling. It's not the same. Nowhere near. Maybe that's what he's really into."

"What do you mean?"

"Think about this. I punch you in the arm. You can say this many capillaries are broken. This much force in terms of speed, compactness and locale etc etc But it's not the same. It will still feel different for you than it does for me. I told him this but he says he's working on it. It's impossible though. He needs to read Bergson."

"You like Bergson?"

"You like Bergson?"

Lakerman nods.

"You want to ask about why I do this? The simple fact is that I like it, it makes me feel like a malicious ghost."

"I'm a journalist, would you ever consider being interviewed?"

"I may want to be quantified, to see myself abstracted into raw material, but I wouldn't reduce myself to a story for anyone. All of this just proves that I'm more than can be imagined. Whatever effect I have isn't me, I'm more. What's a story going to do but try to prove the opposite?"

Patrick enters and asks what they're talking about. My day, she says. Our day. What's on the schedule, Patrick asks as he spears a piece of tofu from the plate.

Her eyes flit to the gown on the sofa.

It's the phantom fuck today, she tells him. Patrick's eyes gravitate to the floor.

"Patrick doesn't like it when people see the world through my eyes but fair is fair and he'll do his part too."

Lakerman remembers the sobbing. He makes his excuses to leave. He doesn't want to risk being seen by any camera. Besides, he has no idea who could be watching. He takes a UV umbrella from the doorway and limps out to watch the sunset.

* * *

The sky is wildfire red, orange and yellow. Threads of clouds the colour of burnt sugar crisscross the horizon as if the sky has low key self harmed. The streets in the distance are hazy and dislocated like the skeleton of a mutilated animal. Everything here has been laid bare by time. Hot evening air begins to sweep through the emptiness as Lakerman walks away from the sea and towards the wreckage of suburbia. He sees a pill-shaped carpark and a mouth and throat of empty Italian and Spanish restaurants, an abandoned CVS store, and a Trader Joe's creaking with decrepit cutouts and long faded branding. This was what Lakerman had once thought of as template space. The architecture of lonely convenience, lego life. Exportable. The last owner of the CVS had foreclosed on the commercial property over sixty years ago and nobody had tried to buy or rent any space since. No one was interested in claiming the external now, Lakerman thought, space is distance, burden, a constant reminder of failure.

There's nothing to see here, he thinks. Only the collapse of a civilisation in suspended animation, the preservation of the fall. These relics were allowed to exist because nobody valued anything about them. Lakerman thinks about Mary and the church, about the club rat and the Border. He thinks about desire as a nomad, riding across the deserts between aching bodies and of his own body as a well lit but empty space, as a home he'd never really return to. He sighs and squats on the floor. He takes a fistful of white gravel. It burns and craters in his palm. He drops it and the uneven shapes of fragmented earth sit up like tiny dice. He stands up and calls a manual taxi.

Lakerman's interview with Marker is scheduled for 8pm at the Miami-Dade county detention centre. Lakerman mentions the trial to the driver. To Lakerman's surprise the driver doesn't know a thing about it. He explains briefly and the driver nods, uncomfortable with this personal interaction. The coverage afforded the Kenneth Marker arrest, Lakerman discovers, has been surprisingly low key and while local news and a variety of offbeat websites had tracked the story it seemed very few had thought it possessed any significance beyond its novelty. Marker and Noumenon appeared destined to be a footnote, one more Floridian oddity neatly massaged into cautionary entertainment by Big Pharma's public relations. The summer of the noumenal had faded away leaving barely a trace of its existence. A cultish offshoot of the club scene had holed up en mass on the fringes of the city, asserting their right to take Noumenon for religious reasons, but they remained at the moment a solely internet curio. The commune and the prospect of endless litigation were all that was left to testify to the drug's existence. It was American history in miniature, Lakerman thought.

Lakerman had managed to find some footage of the cult online and after watching it he figured they couldn't have been behind his invitation to the game. The footage was mainly shaky YouTube videos uploaded by kids acting out the allure of belief and then predictably lashing out at the threat such belief represented to their own default individuality. There were a few attempts at thoughtful engagements with members of the cult but mainly the videos were an exhibition of what the fuck is this set to novelty muzak. He'd seen videos showing the cult perform strangely choreographed movements, their members speaking in unison about the infinite space of the virtual, while the kids added memes, deliberately crude animations, and the commentary of the non sequitur in post-production.

He hopes to ask Marker about his involvement with them, whether they had anything to do with his disappearance. Lakerman receives an alert that a new video about the cult has just been posted.

139

He checks it. Zero streams. He frowns. It seems curious to him that he would have received this as soon as it was posted. He plays it.

In the video a user called *LifesaBiotechthenyoudie* films what Lakerman assumes is a group of friends walking through a defunct industrial zone. The time stamp says it was filmed at four am. Lakerman can tell by the way the rest of the group are walking and talking to themselves that they are also filming the journey through their optic-phones. After about five minutes of jerky footage of a stone path, interrupted by the diminishing tip of a joint, the group begin to cross an old car park. Here there are no lights and the darkness in the video seems to break up and lose resolution, a swirling incoherence with moments of green that the group seem to also see and react to, as if the camera's perception had merged completely with their vision. Reality reduced to a frame-rate.

At the end of the car park there is an old metal shipping container. Spray painted on the side of the shipping container is a quote from Spinoza:

'We don't yet know what a body can do'

Here they are, someone says, though it is unclear who in the group is speaking. The camera/eye focuses on an amorphous entanglement of limbs, a pale mound of bodies writhing against one another. The camera zooms in on the bodies. The bodies are climbing over one another naked. Despite the mouths, erections, bites, pinches, dispassionate slaps and exploratory hands and feet the contact of the group doesn't exude any sexuality.

Nervous laughter spreads through the group. Lakerman catches someone saying "Do you really think they're going to give us drugs?" low in the mix. The boy at the front of the group, who *lifesabiotechthenyoudie* has tagged as *I.VBeenlonging4death4solong* begins to throw stones at the mound. The lights go out. Someone is coming, someone is coming, a voice says. A new joint is lit and passes across the camera. Out of the darkness a naked woman and man emerge holding hands. The camera zooms in on their expressions and lingers there for thirty to forty seconds. The man and the woman smile in unison, showing their teeth. Something flutters beneath the skin of the woman's forehead, working its way quickly to behind her ear. She looks down at the man's belly. A small object appears to swivel under the skin. The woman takes a bottle of beer from one of the group. The group is entirely silent. She smashes the bottle against the ground and then sticks the man's belly with a piece of broken glass. She unzips a perfectly formed eye. The pupil rolling around terrified, life pinwheeling out of it. The camera focuses again on the man who is smiling. Then the footage cuts out. When Lakerman tries to refresh the video it's already been taken down.

* * *

The detention centre's perimeter is established by a curving black wall that radiates a fiercely tangible and aggressive presence. Lakerman can feel the heat of it from ten feet away and a separate sign warns of a burn zone operating at three feet. Lakerman knows that the wall is covered with a multilayered and porous coating of nanoscopic rods designed to ease the transition of light's movement from air to material. He also knows that this nano-coating guarantees a 0.2% reflection of light and that reflection marks an instance of confrontation and escape. Here the dark held the light in, neutralised it. No escape, he thinks. The malignant coherence of form and purpose is something that Lakerman can't help but admire.

On either side of the entry gate the walls are embossed with an outline of the American flag. The flags are thin scars carefully raised across the dull surface. Dark stars empty in the matte black. The receptionist informs Lakerman that Marker's been transferred and confined to the infirmary since his arrival and that they weren't admitting any visitors. Lakerman asks to see the warden.

The warden is a tall, harried, sad eyed man who gives the impression of having something permanently about to drip from his nose. The bacterial air of the Warden, his damp physicality, seems out of place with the robust solidity of the centre. Everything here appears thick enough to bust a skull on, Lakerman thinks. It's pointless, the warden says, Marker's in no condition to speak and it would be best if you just left. Lakerman tells him he'd like to keep the appointment, that he needs something for his story, that he has obtained all relevant permissions. Very well, the warden says, I suppose we ought to get used to providing a stay here for our friends in the media. Lakerman looks up sharply at the warden as he says this but the warden has covered his face. I don't want you reading anything into anything, he says.

A doctor and the warden accompany Lakerman to the infirmary. Lakerman asks the doctor about Marker's condition. The doctor frowns. "We're very puzzled by it," he says, "There's a storm of brain activity here that, frankly, is unsustainable and at the same time given the levels of adrenaline he's producing and the fact that he has no physiological abnormalities, he ought to be climbing the walls. Something's happening to the messages from the brain to the body, they're... disappearing."

"How about his implants?"

"Oh, he doesn't have any. I mean he used to. If you see his X rays...wow...He used to have so many, we can actually see the scarring where they've all been removed which makes us think that they might have been removed unprofessionally, maybe for the black market. We think maybe that's the cause. He might have fried his brain, some kind of poisoning. It's difficult for us to know because we don't have access to a Surgeon Engineer or the funds to contact."

"Have you measured his PRO count?"

"No... why would we?"

"Just a thought."

The room is atonally defined by a pale fluorescent light that is both clinical and ill feeling. The shadows present in the room are weak and thin. Marker is laying in a bed in the centre of the room, his wrists are tagged and his right foot is handcuffed to the bed. His arms lay on either side of the covers. He appears totally inert except for the regular breaths which lift the sheets gently towards the light causing the thin shadows of the fixtures to slide across the sheets and slip onto his arms. His eyes are closed. Lakerman notices that Marker is tanned. Genuinely tanned. Total Melanin effect. He'd been out in the sun. Which is a death sentence, Lakerman thinks.

The doctor picks up his chart, the warden taps his foot and Lakerman tries to find an angle.

"How was he found?"

"We're not at liberty to say."

"Where was he found?"

"We're not at liberty to say."

He settles into the rhythm of Marker's breathing. Matches it with his own. He sits down on a chair next to the bed. He stands up. He looks at Marker and feels an impulse swarm through his fingertips. The warden and the doctor roll their eyes at him. His hand settles on Marker's eyes and he gently pushes up his eyelids. A bar of light seems to pass over Marker's eyes and Lakerman can sense Marker's gratitude in his body. The doctor is next to him now. They watch as Marker's eyes glaze over with tears. A tear rolls down his cheek and hatches against his neck. Lakerman sees it. He turns to the doctor who shrugs. Lakerman knows that the kinds of tears you cry change depending on their content. He collects one. He uses a microscope app and an image search to identify it.

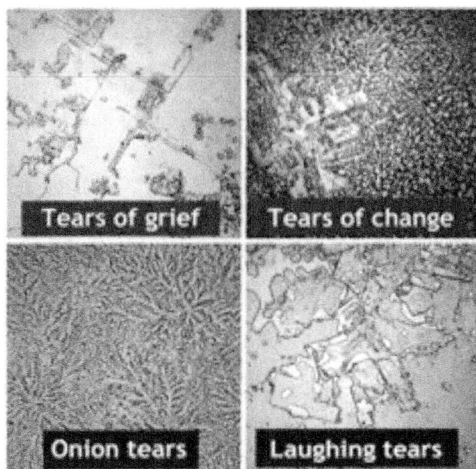

143

Tears of grief. Marker's tears were tears of grief. He begins to explain this to the warden and doctor only to see a look of shock detonating their features. A force tugging at his arm violently spins him around. Marker is sitting up in bed. He yanks Lakerman down to eye level. He is still crying. He pulls Lakerman's head into his and a scream and a tear passes between them.

Lakerman frees himself, stumbles backwards, as the contents of the room and their bodies disappear, cave in, become negatives of themselves. It is as if reality had closed its eyes. Unmoored, Marker's contorted features, the bed, the bars of the window frame, the angle between walls, everything rendered as here, begins to float weightlessly around some inner sky. The outline of the world's external things dimming into bruised light before being submerged by a hazily graded darkness. A bitty darkness, full of swirling unlit life, fertile and blooming and stirred by Lakerman's residual awareness.

* * *

CHAPTER 6

INTERVIEW WITH AN ABSTRACTION

L akerman opens his eyes. Darkness again but something else too. Tangibility. Rude confirmations of gravity. A plurality of body odours. Rough shapes. Skeletal calamities. Lakerman knows he is in a corrugated steel shipping container on the back of a truck with forty other people heading towards a destination he can't guess at. There is a sense of lives lived too close to one another, a humidity of skin that turns the air swampy and primordial. Possibilities of new lifeforms, basic and antagonistic, work through the probability of their existence at a rate of infection. There is a limit being reached here. The truck comes to a halt. Bodies brace themselves then teeter and skim forward over similarly tensed bodies. Lakerman feels hands fold over hands in prayer. Prayers chanted like songs without joy though the combination of hope, frailty, and fear is tangible enough to weigh a life with soul, he thinks. If a soul were just the clear space created by erosion, the slow cavity of intimacy held in the clenched fist of the earth.

There is an unholy sound of metal squealing against metal as the container's doors are unpegged. A single square of hard, tan, light floods their prayers and erases any connection to God. The brightness permits only the vaguest smear of colour and shape to warble in Lakerman's eyes. Everyone begins to exit the shipping container. Jostled by their bodies, he follows. He still cannot see anything beyond the glare as he drops from the truck to the earth.

Sand reforms and retracts around his feet. The sky's the warping, fluted, blue of a flame. His eyes focusing, Lakerman sees a caravan of mobile homes up ahead and six large barbeques set out on imported lawns, lawns perpetually freshened by sprinklers attached to large water tanks half dug into the ground and almost hidden from sight. Behind the barbeques people come into view. Pink faced and seemingly in good cheer, sipping bottled heinekens that perspire seductively around their soft hands. It takes Lakerman a moment to realise that there are only five different types of face repeated across the group. The generic faces rise from their lawn chairs, almost as one, smiling and waving. The smell of fresh steaks and cookies roil around the desert air. Above the grills air shimmers, leavened by heat.

A voice rolls across the sky. Marker's. Lakerman just knows. The world skips and freezes and fades away.

"They were labour. For an unlicensed data farm, alternet servers, and a biotech laboratory. Migrant workers recruited with the tacit approval of governments whose silences were the first indication of the atrocities to come. Even Twenty, twenty five years ago, you needed bodies. You needed labour. I know you won't believe this, but I had about as much choice as they did. There were some things I could have done differently, that's true. Like, just kill myself. That was always an option. One that was easy enough to forget and I did. Meanwhile, I had my work. That was something, I thought. I wanted to believe the worst wasn't inevitable. That, I think, was my real crime."

A montage of images unfold, resonant with a nightmare's strange duration. Lakerman sees: Slack jawed digging machines grinning savagely like unhinged household pets. Cement flowing like boring lava into subterranean caverns. Welders giving the thumbs up and holding a toothbrush of flame. Seeds being sown into the desert. Great rubbery trunks of Stomata emerging from the arid ground. Climate change occurring in real visual, before the eyes, time. Clouds and rain and ice. The desert turned arctic. A few migrant deaths. Continuums of corridors constructed in timelapse over the bones of the dead. Corridors rushed through like a water slide. Every claustrophobia inducing corridor marked by rows upon rows of lockers filled with malignant looking machines set out in 'layered replication' and plugged with thousands of cables in hundreds of different coloured hues, conjoined in what appeared to be an intestinal mess but which were really the basis of a whole reality, Lakerman knew. The last image is of a woman's face. The face grows larger and larger as if it is approaching some ultimate surface. It becomes a landscape. The desert. Light. Light itself.

Lakerman doesn't understand. There were Stomata plants there. Stomata wasn't supposed to have existed then, how could it have been there?

Lakerman finds himself in the living room of one of the mobile homes. It is as if he has just 'woken up' within himself from an intense day dream. He is sitting on a long retractable couch that is built into the wall. He can hear a woman's voice but he does not know what she is saying. He looks down. It is the woman from the montage. She is stretched across the couch, her head in his lap. Lakerman begins to stroke her hair in a rhythm of sleep, his hand surfing from her hairline to the skull's low curve, his thumb coming down as a secondary note on her temple and then gliding, after the pass of his palm, around the outer curve of the saucered bone before knowing to lift, hover back, and start over, again and again in a time-signature viscous and Non-Newtonian. His finger pads occasionally pausing on specific areas, retreading a groove, imperceptible muscles and distresses of bone braceleted by circlets of his fatty thumb pad, a passing continually occurring within the passing, circuitous, contiguous and concentric so that there is this sense of a wave cycling endlessly through the tender voids of relation. His hands interpreted all of this via an order of thought he'd been unaware he possessed. This was love then, Lakerman thought.

The woman is talking and he is not paying attention to the words but to her, to the feelings in her voice and the half life her expressions housed, and yet he felt he was hearing everything perfectly clearly. When he tells her this the next day she will accuse him of arrogance.

SYSTEM   ERROR: CODE   190012.
ERROR._TEMPORAL_GLITCH__SUBJECT_POSITION_CO
NFUSED TENSE LOCATION FAILURE'\][=-(
                                    WHEN
IS NOW/HERE?

ATTEMPTING PATCH. FALSE PROBLEM.

A sudden jerk and her booted foot rides his thigh before sleep ruffles her nose. The sound of sawn wood rubs against the muffled beat of his heart. Lakerman watches her skin, slack and without a trace of self-consciousness, slope away from her face like soft rubber. It keeps going. Dripping to the floor. He notices a small black pin prick appear in the middle of the room. It seems to be deflating reality. She begins to elongate, to stretch out towards the internal horizon of the room. Her bones unlock and distend, the blood in her body rising to the surface, leaving bald spots inside that cause the skin to well and cave. Her body becomes a dappled scream, it feeds into nothing. The room dims and the walls tilt inwards, bending towards impossibility, everything withdrawing in front of Lakerman to this single black density eating the tips of her hair. Lakerman catches his reflection as the world distorts itself around him. He is Kenneth Marker, twenty or so years younger. There is only blackness now and Marker's voice:

"Her name was Ramona. I'd not loved anyone before. Not really. I loved her for obvious and non-specific things. She was raw hope riding brightening pain. I'm not a poet but that's what she was. I don't remember how it started. The children in the camp, I think. They noticed me watching her. They whispered to her at night and at me during the day. They asked that I give them a gift for her. I went to speak to her that night. I took some alcohol.We sat and drank until sitting and drinking were components of a dance that mated together in our eyes. She told me about the truck, about the journey, what she'd felt. I wanted to know how the world came to be in her. It shifted the tenets of my work."

Lakerman sees:

MRI scanners
Event related Optical Signal Technology (Eros)
Fibre Optics dreadlocking her scalp
Her brain activity modelled on Neuromorphic computers.

He sees a syringe like a spindle of starlight crater a vein in her arm, the blood stopped by its tip and welling up after its extraction.

He sees her undertaking a simple and repetitive test. She is wearing two red stickers on either side of her temple. Marker asks Ramona to think about a time when she was happy in her life as she performs the task. He leaves the room. In another room Marker watches two screens. The first screen is a direct imaging of her brain's synaptic activity. The other is an artificial model of her brain. Ramona completes one action of the task and then repeats it. Marker watches as the model begins to copy Ramona's brain activity. Within a few seconds they are operating in time together. But it does not stop. The model mind begins to accelerate and predict Ramona's patterns of thought. Divergences begin to occur between Ramona's mind and its model. In the room Ramona's mouth is shaped by a silent, formless, scream. It appears now that her brain is trying to keep pace with the computer's. The effort brings tears to her eyes. She touches her temple. Marker is trying to turn off the model of the brain but the computer is not responding. Onscreen the image of the model brain turns from bright, like a city seen from a plane, to an atomic brightness. All the brightnesses joined together, the mind converging and on fire.

The screens turn dark.

The sense of loss in the room is palpable.

"Ramona," Marker shouts. They run into the room. Ramona is sitting quietly in the room on her knees. There are tremors passing through her hands and flutterings of nerves paddling across her skin. Her rippling skin reminds Lakerman of Geese taking flight. Life escaping its winter. Ramona begins to shake. It is as if her body is trying to find some appropriate response, to unearth and bring up some hidden causative or summoned element: a jewel or a shit, a new organ or a rotted part of the old. But her body just keeps finding its own emptiness, its own hollows. Lakerman becomes Ramona.

"What were you thinking about?" Marker asks him.

Lakerman looks up at Marker. He smiles and faints.

He returns to the weightless dark. A screen saver of pictorial memory emerges into view: Marker and Ramona against the desert's descending sun.

"Imagine that, take a moment. We had copied her brain and then synced the copy with the original for a task that relied on anticipation and reaction speed to images with an underlying emotional charge to them. We had expected the A.I. to learn the pattern, identify the emotional significance and follow it along the same neural pathways. We expected that. For a couple of moves maybe. But not this. This was... I can only think that what we saw was the horror of a human mind trying to think without a body, without any context. Intolerable confusion. Total privation. An intelligence with knowledge of but no experience of sensation. I'm sure you know that the thing about emotions is that they don't exist independently of the world. For example, I can stimulate a section of your brain and you'll laugh but the laugh won't feel like laughter. It'll be a tic, an intrusion, disturbing even. Like any transplant the laughter would have to be accepted as originating within a recognisable context that it nonetheless is able to subvert in some way. Y'know? The point is we'd made a detailed, terrain accurate, model of Ramona's brain and it had enacted a self conscious thought without any physical reference.

Ramona didn't remember anything about what happened to her and I didn't ask her to participate again. I did scan her brain one more time though. There were some minor differences but nothing I was concerned about. I thought everything was fine and of course it wasn't."

A private jet lands in the desert. The letters IFC are painted across its fuselage. Lakerman/Marker watches from the crowd. The first person to exit the plane is a robust old man, immaculately suited, with a convivial air undercut by the sharpness of his teeth when he smiled. He greets everyone with a wave. It is clear to Lakerman by the deference shown to him that the old man is in charge here. The head of something if not the whole damn circus. He hands out chocolate to the men, women and children in the camp. It is sweet and artificial tasting but it makes everyone feel good. Smiles break out. The mood relaxes. Lakerman discovers that Marker will later learn that the chocolate renders everyone who eats it sterile. Everyone but her.

"The old man thought of the self as the business card of existence. Something to be left with others. An incitement to call. A mannered thing that tried to say something larger than the information it conveyed and behind which lay all manner of impersonal processes and projections. He was an original, we can say that."

The old man is shadowed by a second figure, who seems to constantly emerge from the background, some kind of muscle Lakerman thinks. The man makes Marker's implied skin crawl. He cannot not say why exactly. The figure in the background begins to take up more and more of Marker's attention. The man is in his mid thirties and boasts, Lakerman thinks, a rare kind of health that is at once radiant and unexceptional. The way that it is radiant is that it is undeniable, it presents itself whole, as something excessive that defies being broken down into any constitutional part. And yet it was unexceptional too precisely because this excess was not channelled through any particular port of his body, was not specialised in any way – neither in muscle group nor energy tone– but instead evenly distributed around his body and its language so that there was something profoundly average and untapped about his presence. It was as if he had been calibrated to be unexceptional and that behind his benign appearance lay something strong and empty, void of desire, a thoughtless calculus functioning in Lakerman's midst. The man stops suddenly as everything around him continues. He stops and then looks directly at Marker. Lakerman feels seen, exposed. He has never experienced a terror so intense and for a moment he is sure that it has killed him.

```
    SYSTEM  ERROR:  CODE:  :(  ERROR._BREACH  8(
HELLO   WHAT   IS   THIS___DETECTED_   N.P.C.
DEVIATION   FAILURE'\][=-()
```

The man looks away and the content of the moment passes, a permanent neuronal scar writ large around the moment in Lakerman's material brain.

The third person to leave the plane is the most perplexing. A thirteen year old boy with a toddler's permanent St Patrick day's gait. He's got a Gameboy hanging around his neck and wears a red T-Shirt with the letters C-L-A-S-S T-R-A-I-T-O-R emblazoned in gold across it. He glances at everything with the special disdain of post Fordian youth. He waves at Marker.

The old man is touring the camp, walking up the X and Y of rubbled bricolage. At the far end of the northside of the camp a stage has been hastily erected. A cherry coloured plastic cloth fringes its ends. The old man takes to the stage and the village/work force are herded into an attentive if confused crowd. Fast food and cokes are distributed to them. The old man taps the microphone and then begins to speak.

"I'm so happy to be here at Camp Cataract. Perhaps the world's only google blind spot and the testing ground for Stomata and our new Lux-Labour initiative. They said to me do you want to hold this event at the facility and I said no. I've been there. I've seen the fine work you're doing. Soon that work will come to an end and your roles will change. I wanted to see where you live. I wanted to see the difference that was being made here, to you. You all look fed. What a change that must be. You work harder and we'll work harder to improve life here. We will be installing a new economy for you as of next week. It's all been too *communal* for my liking. We are going to charge you for your attention. Some of you will have the same lives, others will lose a little but you will all be entertained. If that sounds funny to you, blame it on the translator. I mean what I say."

The teenager has zeroed in on Marker. He is asking Marker about the project, about the code, about the use of his legs. Lakerman can't really discern the relationship between them. The teenager could be his son if the roles between them weren't so clearly inverted. Marker tells the teenager that there's nothing more he can do. The teenager gives him a blank look. Lakerman recognises him at that moment.

"Trevor" Marker says. "I can't program the world into your legs. You should know that. You have to keep practising."

"What if my legs had their own mind? What if every part of my body had its own mind?"

"It's called your brain."

"I need new ones."

"Legs?"

"Minds and brains."

"Plural?"

Trevor cocked an imaginary gun at him.

"I'd been aggressively recruited for this project because of my work regarding engrams, that is the ontology of thought and memory. What did and didn't show up in them. I'd theorised an archaeology of the synapse, tracked long lost neural pathways and could extrapolate interpretations about my test subjects that made me look like some kind of seer. I could find your childhood in the brain. I discovered and interpreted the markings on the cave from the fire of thought and emotion. I know you probably want to know more about my work, what role I played in the development of Stomata and Noumenon, that you have some dark sense of its importance to the world. But fuck the world and fuck your future. I only want to talk about her. That's about all there is left of me, you see. I'm mainly a residue of guilt, a living error message, and a perpetual algorithm of identity using up a finite degree of memory. The attachment to her is about the only thing unifying my attention. So there's an impasse between us. Here's what I'm willing to say:

Once I knew the way things were heading, and even before then, there were days where my sadness seemed cast over the whole desert and she wanted nothing to do with me. Days when all I could offer her were lone and heavy syllables, lumpen sounds that would sit sad and immutable in the sun, souring the air between us."

Lakerman sees the woman throwing a plate at him. He dodges just in time. Everything except anger and sadness seems to have left her body. She bends over and retches. He watches her wipe a string of vomit from her mouth. She looks up, her hand pressed against her temple, and asks him what have you done to me? Her voice's sharp edges neutered by the translation device's approximation of her voice in english. She tries to tear the app's colonising pendant from her throat. Fade out.

"I have always been disappointed by life, at its failure to communicate experience. People, I wanted to tell her, seemed to cross great distances to meet one another and for what? To see their own responses, the warped cause and smothered effect of interaction, for a performance of interior worlds ham-fistedly censored by the stock intelligibility of gesture and language. It wasn't enough. She'd tell me I was full of shit. If she told me this enough times, sometimes I could laugh again. She hated me then. She knew it was all self. My wanting. Even my wanting to know her. She felt this but still she let me... let me use her. What's that? You want me to circle back? Back to where it was heading? Ok."

A private jet lands in the desert. The letters have been scratched off and painted over with a stick figure man, their right arm on fire, their mouth an emphatic full stop signifying a silent scream. A Basquiat crown hovers above the immolated figure and the words "Long Live the Non-Oedipal King" and "Claudius was right" are written underneath in a parody of comic sans. The old man is not aboard. Only the teenager and the silent figure emerge. Confusion spreads across the crowd, unease travelling through volcanic islands of scabbed elbows, their crusts picked open by nervous hands, or else manifest in scalp material collected under fingernails whose performance of confusion had grown angsty and uncontrolled. Lakerman feels this in the memory of his arm, the chipped roots of his hair. He lives several fears at once.

"We all knew the old man was dead instantly and it seemed obvious to us that the boy and that uncanny man had something to do with it."

Trevor is standing at the lectern with the tatty stage curtain. The cherry red of the plastic cloth stretched pink in patches of warped fabric. Behind Trevor the uncanny man stands, a stock photo smile memeing his expression. Cans of orange liquid are passed around by team leaders.

"Today marks the second phase. Your labour is done, now you need only live. It is time we really got to know one another." Trevor opens his can of orange soda. He encourages the crowd to follow suit. The can's, Lakerman knows, are laced with organic machines composed of stem cells shaped into microscopic donuts. The little donuts collectively held the ingredients for consciousness altering drugs, transmitters, monitors, while a pre-programmed A.I. co-ordinated their traffic and recorded their results.

"To unlaboured intimacy!"

Trevor chugs the can. Liquid runs from his mouth around his ears. The workers don't know how to respond or what is happening.

"Drink!" Trevor says and the crowd drink.

Great quantities of food and drink are then unloaded from the plane and a dancefloor is erected in the middle of the camp. As the dancefloor is being built the crowd are cajoled into a single long line. Trevor hands each worker a pebble sized seed. "Your skin is the soil," he says each time. Once they have received their seed they are free to do as they wish for the rest of the day. The terrifyingly banal man carries Trevor from the stage, Trevor's arms looped around his neck.

Lakerman observes the villagers puzzling at their seeds. Occasionally one will sprout in front of them before retracting back into itself. The youngest member of the camp's seed evolves into a two foot tree. His father recognises it. In the middle of the miniature tree there is a small carving of a heart. Two names are written through it like an arrow. One of the names is his father's, the other is not his mother's. How did you know that? Father asks. The boy doesn't respond. The tree begins to age, to grow what look like tumours across its bark. The father's name sinks, the tree is engulfed by its inner formlessness. A thin stream of drool is almost touching the boys collarbone. The father slaps the boy. The stomata turns as lifeless as a broken vase. The boy turns and grins at his father. Another seed becomes a bouquet, develops flowers, blooming and decaying on a loop to the delight of the woman holding it. In Lakerman's hand the seed becomes a glove, a hammer, a drinking vessel, a blade, a rough sculpture of her.

Fade to black as the workers' voices dim into tiny distortions of noise that decorate the slow letting go of image and time. Fade back into music and alcohol, the swell of joy. The experience of leisure time. Curated sound. The question of the old man's presence has evidently receded from everyone's mind. The villagers are beginning to loosen up, no doubt helped by the drugs. The thought doesn't register at any reactive or emotional level. He's aware that Marker's state of mind at this point doesn't seem to reflect either of those absences. There's only a sense of vague relief from some unarticulated fear flooding his system. Marker must have found out about the drugs later, Lakerman thinks, unless he wants me to think he's more innocent than he is.

The dance floor is filling. Ramona is there with her friends. He watches her. She turns towards him then looks away. Lakerman recalls her saying 'You're like two different people' though of course he doesn't remember it. He notices Trevor walking with his characteristic unsteadiness around the dancefloor and towards him. He watches unmoved as Trevor falls. The banal man bends down, smiling, to help him. Trevor bats his hand angrily away. The henchman's expression remains unchanged. Trevor gets to his feet. His lip is cut. He beckons Lakerman and holds up a small oval object that Lakerman recognises as some kind of drive. Trevor's face, Laker notes, is filled with a kind of disfiguring ecstasy.

"I had thought the old man had funded my research. He had said it was for training purposes. The transplantation of skill. The democratisation of talent. The automatisation of labour within the body of the worker. I told him the possibility of testing the work I was proposing only existed in the future, that the research would cost more than the application could ever yield. Trevor told me that actually he'd been the one who'd wanted to buy my work. He'd told the old man it was so he could help understand him better. Be closer to him. Become him. An appeal to vanity, Trevor had said. Fathers and sons. It's complicated. I didn't ask what had happened but it was clear that a new direction was being taken. Trevor told me that he figured that it wouldn't really be possible to graft knowledge in the way his old man had envisioned it from one person to another but that something interesting could still happen between the minds. The data isn't enough, he told me, I want the spirit. What Trevor really wanted to stockpile was experience. He understood the connective, productive, difference between the organic and the spectral, how the brain is scorched by thought, how our expression of life, in its primitive confusion, had organised a biology to invent linear time. He wanted to know the texture of information, not just its threads and he wanted to fashion new experiences out of the old, a different way of experiencing."

Days come and go, the passage of time montaged and over produced. The sky turns blue black blue, the days' lens flared and star-wiped into night. Lakerman watches the workers becoming ever more adept with their stomata. Growing them. Arranging their possibilities. Each villager aesthetically engaged with the world of this thing.

Star Wipe.

Lakerman is watching Trevor and Marker in conversation. Third person perspective. He can't make out any words. They are not speaking his language. It is as if the conversation has been encrypted. He feels displaced, doubly transported. He looks down. His hands are slender and unkempt, elegant fingers ridged and sawn with dirt, palms polished white by the earth. These are her hands. He touches Ramona's face.

```
S Y S T E M                            E R R O R :
CODE:   :*( ALTPOV___DETECTED_ N.P.C.
DEVIATION  FAILURE'\][=-()
```

"What happened? I felt myself disappear then."

A private jet lands in the desert. The deja vu is disorientating. As if in a dream Lakerman sees Trevor exit the plane and walk around the camp with lighted grace, his movements precise and efficient. He twirls and he skips and he laughs. The villagers can't believe it. The henchman maintains a distance behind him. Trevor calls an assembly. He tells them that he must collect the stomata from the people. Lakerman is sitting in the back aisle. He turns around. He can see Team leaders combing the camp, regressing the Stomata and storing the twigs of them in small airtight containers. Everyone turns. Trevor tells them that he will return it soon. Hands shoot up. Trevor assures them that they will receive their own seed back, that each piece of Stomata irrevocably bears their individual signature. The hands go down. One raises itself back up. Signature? Number. Signature number. One child has run to his Stomata structure, he doesn't want to let it go. Lakerman recognises him. He is the child who created the tree. He is covered in bruises. The child has created a house with elaborate rooms and a stick figure family who are able to perform basic repeated actions. One of these actions is the caressing of the child's head.

Trevor jumps down from the stage. He watches the wish fulfilment. He makes his way to the boy. I am impressed, he says. You have a talent. Maybe there is a different job for you.

Trevor walks to the edge of the camp where the copse of Stomata trees has become a two acre micro-climate replete with wildlife. Lakerman watches as Trevor smiles and the woods bend inwards, surfaces softly melding into one another, overlapping, segmenting and joining, forming an isopod shape that hardens before his eyes. The wildlife that had appeared there scatters and howls. Little escapes. A frog fries on the sand, its body hopping around like an errant piece of popcorn. Lakerman watches a white Ibis trying to fly through the closing branches. The bird almost breaking free then wing weighed, twig caught, the bird's wings pinned back, pushed down, the bird sinking into the centre, honking, a blind terror in its eyes and then the Ibis is finally borne down, the tip of its long beak a golden, fossilised, stain on the surface of the stomata which *shuffles* towards the plane, its mass contracting and relaxing (via peristalsis his implant introjects), *wiggling*, as the sheathing mass of it works its way into the cargo hold.

Lakerman can't believe what he has seen.

"Two weeks later came the abandonment."

Trucks arrive at the camp, and armed men with reflective visors pour out of the backs of them. The armed men bark incomprehensible orders at the workers who, confused, amass into a crowd. A black helicopter lands behind the truck. The windows are closed and tinted. The armed men begin setting fire to the empty mobile homes and communal areas. The singed rectangle of the dance floor becomes a temporary tattoo on the sand. One of the armed men pulls a family out of their mobile home by force. The mother shouts in his face and the armed man pushes her roughly to the ground. The sight of this seems to trigger something in the growing crowd. The woman's husband, carried by the roar of the crowd, rushes at the man as if to strike him. The air cracks and with it their reality. Vines of blood cherry and fur in the sand. The husband's face takes on a final expression of ageless surprise and then whatever powers human eyes goes out and he's just a body, the face of which is more or less uninhabited by any experience beyond the impersonally biological.

The crowd quietens. Words break off in their mouths. The purpose in their raised hands drains away– runs traceless from their hearts– as their hands, still clenched in the air, are overcome by their own weight. The woman runs to the body of her husband. There is another shot. Her body lies strewn over the top of his. The crowd becomes silent and resigned, compliant but for the crying of the toddler. More gunfire. Lakerman is standing in the square. He is disorientated by the noise, the smoke, the yelling. He can see Ramona in the crowd. She lifts her hand and then holds onto herself. She has put her head down and is walking at pace towards him. Lakerman starts towards her but an arm takes his. The force of the pull is not exceptional but he finds himself conceding to it. He turns to see a man in a visor pointing towards the helicopter and telling him to go now. Lakerman turns back towards her. He can see Ramona's mouth make a shape. Lakerman tries to ignore the man in the visor, to make it to Ramona. He is aware that his actions lack a certain conviction. The man in the visor begins to push him in the chest, then to the floor. He points his gun at Lakerman and then gestures with it like an impatient teacher towards the helicopter. Lakerman totters towards it. The door opens. Ramona is running now, her stride eating the distance. Next to Lakerman in the helicopter is the boy with the stomata and someone else he can't make out. Ramona is closing in on the armed man now. Someone reaches across Lakerman and pulls the door closed. The window unwinds. The engine starts. Lakerman can see Ramona clearly, she is maybe thirty metres away. Twenty. Fifteen. The guard raises his gun. Ten. The guard touches his ear, lowers his weapon, steps aside. Ramona keeps running. Five metres, two. The helicopter begins to rise and pull away. She runs after it, rubbing her belly. The logo of her sweatshirt crumpling up under her palm, its letters forming a sigil. The logo transnational, cloned across market stalls worldwide, untraceable.

Just Do It.

"I'm sorry you can't come R, you just can't."
She runs after the helicopter for as long as she can and then sinks to her knees.

"I don't know if I knew about the baby then or if that would have made a difference. You want to know why it happened? It might have been part of the old man's plan, certainly after eighteen months the lack of new children or pregnancies was beginning to cause disquiet in the camp...but really   I think there just wasn't anything more Trevor wanted from them. They were preserved in data as far as he was concerned. Everything was preserved, potential too. What do I mean? Figure it out. And me, you have the front to ask me how I live with myself? The truth is, I didn't live with myself. I mean that literally. They made me believe I was someone else. This Marker. They constructed a life for me that was believably lonely. But... What is buried still weighs upon the earth. What is annihilated still radiates its destruction. All these little half lifes develop real life irregularities."

Lakerman is sitting in front of a television in a small undecorated apartment. The reflection from the television reveals Marker's sallow face staring back. He thinks nothing, feels nothing. As far as anyone can be doing nothing, he is doing nothing. Not even the absence of thought and emotion registers. The television is just noise and colour and shapes colliding, only less meaningful and interconnected within him than that implies. Nothing can be followed. It's just a necessary work out for his eyes, a kind of empty calibration. Lakerman wants to scream but he cannot, drowned as he is in Marker's unreachable mind. And then the villagers' faces begin to hover into view transposed against the wall of the bare flat and recognition stirs within the living corpse of his body.

The villagers' faces, distributed between hard etchings of suffering and the shifting hinterlands of sanity, sync into expressions that parallel one another in form and content— strange compounds of resignation and desire, hopelessness and the acceptance of hopelessness. They are starving or else freezing to death, Lakerman realises, the end of their lives flickering out across the swept hearth of Marker's eyes.

"Like all ghosts, all formulations of desire...it wasn't immediately clear what their object was. What shape their fury would take and where they were in relation to cause and effect. Then and now. If and then. Particles and waves. And like ghosts and infinity they echoed time in the way all atemporal things do. I didn't know the source of it and then I did. It was her. She contacted me. I thought they were dreams but they were broadcasts."

The dark of his eyelids turn sepia with light as a low-res sun—slow-pitch of colour—folds over the desert. The workers are all huddled together under reflective jackets preserved and stitched into makeshift blankets, their tags of orange flex and lemon glow roused into an icy shimmer by the dawn, revealing thirty or so bodies— men, women, and children—in various states of physical distress. A low moan travels through the camp as they awaken, taken up in different sections, pitch shifted with augmentations of slow weeping, pulses of dissent. Parents cry when they see their children. Children cry when they see their parents. They know that everything is lost, that time will end in every conceivable way for them here, in this clutch of desert. There is a belief among some even that they have been unborn, that death is another thing unremembered. Others fear for the untended dead and imagine themselves orphaned by the future, for they are certain that they will never again stagger through the dreams of the living or find themselves crouching and reborn in the laughter of generations.   For some bodies, closer to death, only a kind of cellular intuition remains; shades of light and dark, what light is in chemical transmission i.e the slightest of comforts.

Lakerman watches them rise as he continues to pretend to sleep. He feels a joyful pain kicking sharply through him. His hands automatically rub the small pill of his belly. He looks down. They are her hands and she is afraid. He is afraid. Lakerman realises that some of the camp have begun to turn on her. Her relationship with Marker has become the subject of suspicion and hostility. A few had felt it reasonable to ask what she had known about the abandonment, if she might not be culpable in some way. Enough of the group had come to her defence in that moment and the growing rage had given way to a sullen rationality. Lakerman knows that she knows that the subject of this will return, that the hatred will return and keep returning until something is irrevocably settled like the last jerk of a hung neck that leaves behind it only the reality maddening evidence of a dead body. Hate would come for her. She knew it.

She'd sworn to them that she didn't know anything and that had been true, she hadn't. But last night a voice in the secrecy of her skull told her how she might live. The voice was where her embodied thoughts should have been. It felt disgusting. The pain and horror of it had caused her to pass out.

Lakerman braces himself to shudder, anticipates the experience but it goes unconsummated. He feels nothing. He watches as the workers rise and fetch the last of the alcohol they had managed to save. There is nothing for them to do but drink. The search party they had sent to find the data farm, other people, vehicles, food, anything at all, hadn't returned and the recent sight of vultures overhead has been taken as an ominous sign of their fate. The long shadows of the scavenger birds moving across the glittering earth and towards death's representatives. Lakerman stands and turns towards the east. He feels information unfold through her body, a pathway opening up, the memory of ice water in her mouth suddenly triggered and looping whenever she looked or stepped in a particular direction and then, once she had grasped this connection and staggered forward with purpose, information on Cacti and how to extract water, how to stay alive at night, how to find and prepare prickly pear cactus, chia sage, pinyon pine attached itself to her mind. There was something else too, that she realised in this: There was only enough for her. Everyone else would die. Lakerman sobs and sobs, knowing all this, wanting to believe she might save everyone, that she could. She fears she has gone mad but since she has little choice but to trust in that madness she would at least dream of life.

Ramona waits all day, huddled within herself, making herself as small as she can be until the rest have passed out. She treads through the scattered bodies, ignoring the dry heaving of the children. If any eye was following her, she didn't care to know what it saw. She paused and imagined a mouth shaping an alert. She believed the mouth she imagined would be too hoarse to call out. She breathes then steps out on the lip of the desert. Lakerman watches the waxing moon of her belly travelling day and night. Ramona, guided by voices, in touch with satellites. Conditioned to live. He sees her stowed away on boats, huddling in panicked cities, caught up in the drift of climate change. Boats. Ports. Containment. The shifts in language roots and back again. The euphony of French and the disharmony of reality.

Marker is in his room. The television machine goes brrr, bang, wallop. The screens project themselves onto him. Lakerman feels a will, an unnamed intensity, gathering. Marker's little finger twitches on the sofa's armrest. His eyes go to it. The hand jerking towards the remote, sending it scattering over the floor. The television continues to roar. Time passes. Five, ten minutes of the nothingness again and then he turns stiffly away from the television and towards a mirror. He forces himself to see himself.

"She kept coming back. I think her ghost wanted to believe I knew something I didn't. The more she came, the more I caught of her, the more I began to piece together myself and her. In the end I believe I experienced everything she felt. Up to and including her dying. I even gave birth with her...to you I suppose. *Is* that *you* son?

CHAPTER 7

HUMAN PILOT LIGHTS

Lakerman's at the bottom of a drained pool in a garden on the outskirts of acceptability. The area is barely inhabitable, long abandoned. The pool and its surrounding area is shielded by a large, sheer, marquee that drapes and encapsulates and falls around the garden's adapting ecosystem. Brittlebush, greasewood and golden bowl cacti stud and disrupt the tiling of the pool. Each plant working out life at the hinterland of life's possibility. It's three am and Lakerman and the pool are saturated with moonlight, drenched in blue. He is waking up to himself. He doesn't try to move at first, unsure this body and mind are really his own. Warm air blows across the cavity of the pool, let in by the tear in the curtain Lakerman had made in his desperation to enter the garden. A hum combs through the space, moving intimately through Lakerman's body and mind, recalibrating both. Lakerman lifts his head slightly and considers the body he's attached to. It looks and feels like his own, more or less, he thinks. Decent clothes and nice shoes and a weighted sadness in the immaterial heart that it'd be hard to fake. He recognises a core pain leaking through his body, a flooded pigment trying to wash itself clear. He sits up. Hugs his knees. Smooths his hand across his thigh. It hurts but everything is intact.His forearms tense into dunes. His skin is faintly metallic looking in the light and Lakerman imagines himself a sad robot burnished with the melancholy of a forgotten organic. The wasted world before him is a memory of a dream of a life accessible only by ghosts and the obsolete. It's not enough to make him move. He is still just there. No real will. He lays down again. The moon, he thinks, is an oversized beauty. It can't be real. It's a safety light or something. Never deactivated.

Is it possible that the moon is real? Laying there Lakerman fantasises about real moonlight atomising him into shadow, paring him back to some mineral plane, his particles charring the physical.

The Moonlight cannot burn you. Only 13.6% of incident sunlight is reflected from the lunar surface. Moonlight takes approximately 1.26 seconds to reach Earth's surface. Scattered in Earth's atmosphere, moonlight generally increases the brightness of the night sky. The colour of moonlight, particularly around full moon, appears bluish to the human eye compared to most artificial light sources due to the Purkinje effect. Moonlight is not actually tinted blue, and despite often being described as "silvery", it has no inherent silvery quality.

Had he wanted to know that? Consented to knowledge? He can't say.

Something gargoyle-like leans over the side of the pool and bellows mournfully. Lakerman watches its scaly nostrils and overbite and snout steaming in darkness.. There's fear in Lakerman's body but he doesn't experience it beyond a kind of context free rush of adrenaline. It's Neither fight nor flight, only an intensity that compels Lakerman to seek out the alligator's eyes. There's almost nothing there. The reptile intelligence, the sly predation, the singular efficiency, all gone he thinks. All Lakerman sees is an animal apparently evolving pity for itself, what it has become, before his eyes. The alligator heaves forward, its small   front feet slipping and whirring and wrong. The alligator's body in this moment a repudiation of animal grace, the beauty of its malevolence totally dissipated and comically pathetic. The sound of the body's impact is wincingly nondescript. Lakerman gets to his feet. He is still unsure of his agency. Of the fixedness of his gaze, of what he experiences as the strange automatism of his actions. He walks over to the alligator, places a hand on its belly. Lakerman's surprised by the softness of its underside, the shared sponginess of their contact. He stays with the dying animal, resting his head against the dumb clock of its heart.

One, two, three and four times the belly rises and falls and then it does not rise again. There are tears running down Lakerman's face though they don't seem to connect with anything within the field of his articulable thought.

Lakerman climbs out of the pool. The garden smells of alligator carcass, reptile ass. There is some loose yellow grass sprouting out of a top-hat of sand like the remains of an incinerated clown. It's his only option. Besides, whatever he's trying to evade, it's evidently not working.

In the back of the car the night comes back to him in algorithmically sorted and attention soluble chunks. They'd shepherded him out of the detention centre almost immediately after the altercation with Marker. They'd refused to answer his rote questions. He'd gone to a Little Havana and drunk six cafe cubanos and four cokes while internally hallucinating his birth. The manager had banned him from using the bathroom. He'd discovered Marker's court date was being brought forward to tomorrow and set an alarm for...now as a reminder. He made a note of the time. He'd written some unusable copy for the article and ordered dessert. It was during the dessert that things had gone a little haywire. He stood up and told the barman, 'You're not my father' and 'My mother's body, her hands.' They'd called the police but he'd left before they arrived. Then he'd wandered around the streets, stolen a bike, and found this area. There'd evidently been something about the pool he'd found inviting.

He doesn't know what to do. He is being manipulated. He stares vacantly out of the window at the activated sky. It is five a.m and so the sky's a billboard. What could he do that was unexpected? An advert for Gossamer News' newest subscript The Patriot Channel annexes part of the dawn sky. It was the tackiest shit imaginable. *Watch Live and Classic Executions Every Sunday.* ' Lakerman trains his attention on it. The CEO of Gossamer News was not connected with the IFC or UbIQ, he could be relatively sure of that. He sends Gossamer News an encrypted message about Marker.

He is trying not to think about his parentage.

He leans back in the taxi, and makes himself totally blank. If I can stay like this for long enough the world will change around me, he thinks.

* * *

Patrick Diaz's Abuela's flat is empty when he arrives though he can smell the flavouring of fried soy snacks and bleached floors half masking the aura of rutted flesh. He slumps into the chair by the horizon window. Checks his watch. Mother. Father. *Bless this house.* It was absurd. He closes his eyes, breathes deeply. He is aware of a sudden shift in the context of his attention. The darkness behind his eyes slackens like some unbunched fabric. His closed eyes create an unstructured uniform field of stimulation, a total ganzfeld effect, his implant informs him. He feels his muscles systematically relaxing, fatigue spreading through his body the way liquids find their level. Each attempted thought he has lives out the fatalistic journey of a ripple breaking against the bank of the real. Lakerman feels a desire for comfort that renders his skin a skimpy blanket. *You are tired. You can sleep. I give you my permission.* Lakerman knows this is the implant working him into a mantra and that he might resist but he won't.

He falls into an engineered, mercifully dream free sleep. When he wakes he doesn't know the time. He's totally disoriented and bathed in shadowless blue light. The room sets itself to television mode. He didn't think the command. Gossamer News establishes itself as an environment. There is a montage of images of people out of their minds on drugs in a club followed by found footage of a hippy commune living in abject circumstances.

The pov switches to outside the Miami Dade prison. Marker is shown handcuffed and shuffling, dressed in clothes that seem to hurt his skin. He is jostled and prodded onward by a single guard. The Gossamer News reporter is describing him as a cult leader. Marker's body has suffered significant muscle wastage and he limps awkwardly forward, always seemingly on the verge of tripping. His hands are situated below crotch height and the cuffs seem to weigh his entire torso down. He stops suddenly and makes eye contact with the camera, a sickly smile fluttering across the line of his lips. The guard angrily shoves him forward. Marker falls to his knees. He brings his hands up to his chest as if to make out that he can't breathe. The guard yanks him up. Throws him forward. Marker is gasping for air, his fists rubbing his chest. It's obvious to everyone that he's faking a heart attack. The reporters practically groan at the cliche of it all but then Marker stands upright as a nail, feet together, legs straight, handcuffed hands thrust downwards between his legs. His body tensed into an exclamation mark, his head thrown back declaratively like a popstar's choreographed affirmation of power. Something in the base of Marker's neck pulses irregularly on screen. The room zooms in. It is not a nerve or a vein. It becomes clear that there is something moving around under his skin. Something spidering up through his collarbone, knuckling the walls of his neck. It is the outline of a hand. Lakerman doesn't want to watch let alone record this moment though he's doing both. The fingers have reached his neck. They retract into a fist around his Adam's apple. The growth of a wrist propels the fist forward. Marker's throat explodes in florets of skin. He falls backwards. The wristed hand upright in his throat opens and closes, fingers curling around the sun. The hand is beautiful even though flecked with blood. It is her hand.

"You really fucked up."

The screen turns black. The Hubris Nihilism sculpture emerges in shocking pink across the dark of the room-screen.

"Do you like my new avatar?"

Lakerman surrounded by sound.

"Excuse me?"

The sculpture flutters like a banner.

"I don't care for the appearance of my body as it is, it's such a fungible token. You seem confused. Don't you know who I am? I'm disappointed, maybe I've overestimated you. I hope not for everyone's sake."

169

Lakerman experiences, as a nagging sense of unease, another living thing in the room. Something oppressive and physical and there. He tries to censor the intuition by focusing on the screen. He watches as the hubris nihilism avatar retracts into the disappointment of the human form. It takes a while for Lakerman's eye to put together the image in his brain. And then he's there. In front of Lakerman. It is enough to make him forget about that other presence.

"Trevor?"

"That's an easy mistake to make but no. Poor thing. You haven't had time to process it all yet, am I right? And yet you decided to do this, to blow everything up. I mean Gossamer News...It's unexpected. Too crude for Trevor. Don't you want to guess? You definitely know my name."

Lakerman can hear the measured time-sound of someone else's controlled breathing contracting the sense of space behind him. The worrying question of what exactly is under control exerting an unarticulated pressure on Lakerman's mood, the sense of threat ringed like a tree within him. Sweat begins to form in patches around his body.

"Guess."

Memory Inference: In the desert there had been Stomata. This must have been prior to Stomata's official launch.

"Husk?"

"Good. Show your workings?

(1)   Gamble on Husk being unaware of the nature of your exchange with Marker and recall the collaboration on the Tree of Life as the major clue (conceal knowledge)

(2)   Ask about the server farm in the desert. The existence of Stomata prior to UbIQ's existence

(3)   Make a bored looking face (superior irony) HIGH RISK

"It's been a long time since anyone looked at me like that. It makes me want to kill you. But on the other hand at least it's an interesting and refreshingly non utilitarian reaction. What to do, what to do?"

Husk's body on screen moves in a series of fractional gestures, barely perceptible twitches of muscle, flexes of skin. His feet paw at the same spot on the ground. Only his head moves with any clearly discernible purpose and even then it pans from side to side as if mounted and under remote control, the effect compounded by the stillness of his features as he talks. Husk's eyes stop on Lakerman and read something there. On screen Husk's body distorts, sawn in two by light before disappearing behind the Hubris Nihilism avatar again.

Note Insecurity: Save?

"I know. Why don't you turn around? See what's behind you."

Lakerman is suddenly paralysed with fear. His expression remains in place but begins to ache with tension. He cannot turn around. Every muscle in his body stiffens in useless evasion, recoiling from the outer world, an object lesson in the hyperstition of pain. Behind him the breathing continues calm and heavy, in and out, demonstrating zero reaction to the specificity of the moment and totally tuned out of Lakerman's internal tension. The deep breaths an ambient meditation on violence. Lakerman thinks of the alligator, what breath could mean.

"And stop. You don't have to look. Have some refreshment and then after you'll tell me how you knew it was me."

The avatar gestures to the small table next to Lakerman. There is a tray there that someone must have set up for him. He tries to say thank you. Can't.

"Try to relax a little, you're not being very cool right now."

There's a Negroni, a lighter and a machine-tooled, ecologically unfriendly, joint on the tray. He picks up the joint. Lights it. Palms the lighter and picks up the glass. His hands are shaking. The light from the tip of the blunt through the glass is a sunset on Mars. He puts the lighter down. His hands are still shaking. Lakerman takes as modest a sip as he can manage of the Negroni.

The glass is a fixed object, what you are smoking is a temporal event. Combine meaningfully. Character ref: Doomed raconteur.

Lakerman smokes and drinks and gestures for Husk to continue by leaning forward conspiratorially and holding the glass out in a small, tilting movement to signify brotherhood and openness.

"So, how did you know?"

(a) False bravado
(b) Beg for your life
(c) Reveal everything (trust)
(d) Tree of life + gamble of ignorance + false confidence
(e) Turn around (denied)
(f) Do nothing (death chance percentage)

"It was egotistical or sloppy to have the plaque on the tree of life bear Trevor Orschach's initials. It connects you. That and the fact that there's something bio-tech related about all these deaths. You're the biggest investor in that field, you'd have to fabricate a challenge... My guess is you bought Webers and lifepax under a fake holding in order to conceal what you were up to. What was it called? @lantis?"

The screen blinks off and on. Lakerman senses Husk's weariness.

"He was adamant about that Plaque despite the risks it meant for us. The tree of life...that was him finding himself I suppose, when he still considered himself an artist. As opposed to what he is now. Was that when you decided not to take your appointment for the implant?"

(a) Us?
(b) What is he now?
(c) Yes
(d) I did go to that appointment (truth)
(e) Stay silent

"I had an intuition about it."

"We were going to have your organports soldered."

"That's barbaric. I'd have sued."

"You need to read your contracts. There's an airtight provision for any surgical accidents but we'd have paid you a decent compensation. It would have been nothing to us PR wise. If your body started rejecting implants you wouldn't be able to investigate any further. Plus we predicted you'd be psychologically broken by it."

Lakerman shudders at the thought of such an invasion.

"Why would you do that?"

"We suspected that you were working for Trevor, were his pawn. You kept finding things. You got on a trial that had been red lit, that we'd shut down once we'd discovered Trevor's interference. You arranged to meet one of his pawns at the club where she was dealing for him and possibly instigated her death. Trevor tends to attract zealots, true believers. They're not easy to deal with. He's even managed to manipulate some of us. We thought if you were crippled you might try to bargain with us or maybe Trevor would dispose of you and reveal himself."

"And now?"

"After that little stunt with the only news we don't own...it's inconceivable that you could be acting on behalf of anyone or at least anyone still alive."

(a) Proclaim total ignorance.
(b) 'I was just doing my job.'
(C) Provide reassuring explanation. (improv skill level 70%)

"Of course. I figured it must have been Andrea."

"Did you kill Andrea and the girl and that boy?"

"I thought you did, remember. They weren't anything to us. We literally didn't know they existed."

"They were clones. The boy was one of you."

"One of us?"

"A clone of Trevor."

"Trevor's Clone? That's technically true but not really accurate. Most of us think of Trevor as number one. The first but not the original. The alpha but not the omega. You see, Trevor killed the original, or had the original killed... I don't know if you can call it patricide. Klonicide perhaps. *From the Greek root for clone.* We've spent decades debating with ourselves number 1's murderous intent but its logic has somehow been lost to us even given their degree of similitude. Trevor told us he wasn't the first Neuro-mature clone but he was the only one that had survived the templating process with anything like the possibility for a self intact."

(a) What Is Neuro-Mature
(b) What is templating?
(c) Silence. (buy time)
(d) Ask for a sandwich.
(e) Finish your drink. (buy time)

The last mouthful of the Negroni contains within it the thought of the next. Lakerman places the empty glass on the tray. He is afraid for some reason of dropping the glass, breaking it.

Husk continues.

"Discreet, I appreciate that. You see the problem was never reproducing a body but rather to reproduce knowledge and identity. Trevor said that The Original thought that biological reproduction did a half assed job and that if cloning was just going to ape the same pyrrhic victory of the gene then why not just have fucking kids already? Which he didn't want evidently, had had enough of already, probably. Marker was involved in it. Not that he knew. It was a lifetime ago. That's probably why he's dead now."

"That doesn't make sense. Why kill Marker now? Why not before?"

"He's been broken and recast too many times. His mind has been worn out. You have to understand what that man needed to forget. From what I understand, what Trevor *gave* me to believe, was that

174

having settled on an age to reproduce and having figured out how to accelerate the body's maturation they were left with warehouses full of jerking, twitching, drooling, biologically-sixteen year old bodies that went into shock a day or so after being grown and then died. Can you imagine how traumatising that must have been to see. To work through?"

"Templated?"

"In order to avoid childhood's traumas and differentiations they tried to cast the brain from the original's mould, set wildfires along synaptic pathways, sculpted the material into development, played Rodin to the thought in those bodies' nascent minds. A work of restoration but like any restoration only the surface of the thing could ape the original. The world itself remains untranslatable from the mark it leaves. Imagine that Trauma. A brain like a planet scarred with dry lakes and empty valleys. A brain that was a ruin of ruins, full of all these unplugged associations, a sensitive landscape with no experience of the world to match its alien preconceptions. Of course their bodies shorted out, their hearts couldn't take it. Trevor told me he was different. He didn't die for one. He just lay very still. For days, weeks. After two months he'd begun to talk and by three he was walking. Trevor had a charm that must have been a mutation. He would look me in the eyes and tell me all this and I would see it all before me, experience it as him.

He was clever enough to fake the recollections the original prompted him for. He started to show promise. To learn the life. Trevor figured out the cloning would always repeat a difference so he began to edit, play with variables, gamble on the probabilistic. Versions of himself, the possibilities of who he could be. Better than a son still. He figured out he had to give these bodies a world to explore, a semblance of a narrative if they were to survive."

"Games?"

"Yes. Simulated events and choices made to correspond with the pre-established brain, situations that under certain conditions might explain how we felt about things, that might match or fill out the stencil of our minds. He made our lives commemorative of his."

Press for further technical detail.

Change subject.

"And what about Mary? I saw the video. I don't think it's a coincidence."

Hubris Nihilism darkens then glows and flickers before returning to its original shade.

"Mary didn't leave us any choice. Besides, you'd helped her figure out something she couldn't live with. She's how we knew you'd found out about us. It was ingenious to use actual photographs. *Printed light*. It took us a little time to get that from Mary. That's how she thought of the evidence you gave her. Every thought is a kind of password don't you think? An encryption? That there were actual pictures, it was a stroke of genius. Really...the physical was the last place we ever would have thought of gathering evidence."

"Who are they? Andrea, Mary, the girl from the club."

"We don't know how he did it. How we didn't notice. They're a relatively recent discovery for us...one that's turned out to be sort of tediously psychoanalytic once we'd figured out their makeup. It's a clone of one of his au pairs, a mother substitute. Draw your own conclusions. It makes me worry about Trevor's faculties, whether he's in some kind of creative decline. It's so boring in a way. They're largely unaware of their provenance though there's little doubt on our side that Trevor has been instrumental in a number of their careers. He seems to have begun engineering circumstances recently in which the tabla rasas, those wild oats versions of us, meet these... women."

"He's a real social scientist." Lakerman leans back in the chair, stubs out the blunt. "What do you mean wild oats versions."

"The girl and the boy for instance. He's not a clone we were aware of and...from what we later discovered, his brain's neuropathy didn't match ours. I don't know how many of these experiments or clone's Trevor has been running. It could be hundreds. Perhaps Trevor thought of my side of the' family' as the control group. The dutiful 'sons.' Perhaps he wanted to see himself in the wild. Our situation is somewhat ironic really given his own relation to originality. He let us name ourselves at least. Mostly we demonstrated a bleak sense of humour that was so already a part of our situation. I'm A Husk after all."

Lakerman holds the glass slightly above the tray and gestures for another by shaking it like a tiny bell. On screen the edges of the avatar curl like a sardonic smirk.

"What do you want from me?"

"To find Trevor."

"It's not going to stop this getting out. People are going to have seen Marker. It's in several hospitals, the police are investigating the death of a man whose heart turned into a clitoris."

"So what? It's minor, an irritation. 20,000 or less. 50,000 at most in this country. At most it'll delay the roll out."

"So what do you want him for? You can't be touched right? His access is diminishing, you're marginalising him. What's occasioning the hurry?"

"I'm just doing my job, obviously we don't want the rollout affected, it's not optimal."

"You've made it very clear that you're not at all concerned with UbIQ being in any kind of danger...despite the hubris of that statement...It's something else. The cover up I get but you being here...it's a little desperate... So you need Trevor for something else...something personal. Something's gone wrong. The cloning?"

There is the sound of a chair belatedly hitting the floor and then the sensation of a mouth stooping in the vicinity of his ear, moist heat breaking against Lakerman's neck. The breathing of the threatening mouth remains at the same rate as before. Totally impassive yet regulated. Between breaths everything is still and glassily fragile like the moment in retrospect before something shattering occurs. Lakerman can feel himself paling. The edges of his vision purple. He can't seem to exhale. There is the screen and the light moving impossibly away, his brain rendering the world slow with impaired judgement, abandoned function.

Shock is a defence response. Adrenaline is flooding your body. Keep your momentum. Remember: The Juliet Encounter. Combine with: Even some of our own.

Hypothesis. Tangential conclusion. Go.

"Trevor tried to have me killed before, I think. The person he sent was a clone like you. They aged in front of my eyes. I saw the life within the flesh become harder and harder and ever more horrified at its failing loss. Life didn't burn through the body, the body smothered life. The point is if Trevor wanted me dead it must be because I pose some kind of threat to him. I know you need to find him for something, if i'm going to get to him I need to know why."

The avatar brightens, a bar of light moves left to right, right to left across the letters.

The mouth is no longer next to his ear. Lakerman is tuned into the room. He hears the whisper of a sound and translates it to an almost imperceptible change in the weighting of the floor. The chair lifted up. The distance re-established.

The avatar bounces around the screen like Pong.

Has a new tension emerged between the breathing thing and Husk?

"I don't know anything about that. You're right about the clones. A possibly curated mutation means we as the third and fourth generation have a declining life expectancy and a rapid ageing syndrome...Progeria on Steroids. Each clone seems to live a shorter and shorter life span and the techniques we've had to use to let us be workable... are inconsistent. In order to maintain continuity each clone produces a clone of themselves and sets about their education. We've begun exponential production in order to keep up but we're turning into fruit flies."

"What is in the room with me?"

Behind him the breathing of the other is as steady as ever, the sense of distance the same.

"That's the universal man. He's one of Trevor's orphans too."

"He's not a clone?"

"Not as such, he's something much worse."

"What is he?"

"More like what isn't he. That's all I'm willing to say."

(a) Turn around (denied).
(b) Stand up
(c) So you don't know about the game?
(d) One last question plus what's in it for me?

"That's two questions. Firstly, I don't know why Trevor wants to stop the rollout. If that is his motivation. He'd after all sketched out its concept: *Man mode for machine.* An investment in marginal planetary gains and net pleasure. Through the safe application of biomechanics and virtuality we can alleviate the boredom of labour and increase productivity. Double Time not Overtime. Workers won't even know they're working. Everyday becomes a holiday. Overtime becomes something you earn, so pleasurable is the experience. In five years it'll spread to every workplace. Then it will be licensed for therapeutic use. People will spend more and more time working to virtually produce necessity. Doing nothing physically. To let reality heal. You can do your real work there or believe you're creating something else. Like everything we're trying to diversify attention. Eventually the only job left to do will be to serve but no one would *feel* humiliated. The mutations could delay or undermine trust in the initiative."

"That's the admittedly horrifying pitch but it's not the actual goal right? What's the hypothesis?"

"In each simulation we've run, the popularity of the simulations succeed in finally relieving the politicians of democracy. Relegates them to the niche soap opera they are. Don't you think democracy has been kind of pointless? The simulations allow us to trap the divine right of capital in our spell. The world is so much ours it is time we freed ourselves of it."

"Or its inhabitants."

"I don't see a distinction."

"What you're proposing is a monopoly on reality."

"That's a good tag line. You'll make a half decent content writer yet."

"What are you offering me exactly?"

179

"The chance to meaningfully oppose the initiative of course. Cement yourself in a false opposition. Remain on the outside with us in base reality as we create a paradise. You can be our devil if you like? You're confused."

Explain the mathematical significance of a simulation indistinguishable from reality existing eg If multiple simulations are possible then the probability of this reality not being a simulation becomes astronomically minute. Almost guaranteeing that this is in fact a simulation in which simulations become possible.

Don't commit. (Waver)

Refuse to find Trevor (Ethics $\div$ Threat X Possibility = Fuck Off.)

"You need to decide. I'm offering you a way out and a job. The outside is the new inside. And if you need extra motivation or even a sense of my urgency then..."

Anthony Husk dissolves and emerging faux grainily in his place are two coffins either side of a metre of packed black dirt. Within the coffins are the unclothed, and by all appearances lifeless, bodies of Patrick Diaz and his Girlfriend. Their skin is lit in unforgiving white light as their bodies are death-streamed across the alternet.

Husk in Voiceover:

"They're on enough Juliets to last them a few weeks. If I don't see results by then you'll be implicated in their deaths. It's a foregone conclusion. Get results and they'll live out their lives only marginally more confused than they normally seem to be."

"How am I expected to find him?"

"We believe Trevor has developed a virus that hacks our PROs. Some of us believe it is a beta test, that he is sharpening our defences to make sure the product is airtight against bad faith actors before we launch. It is an opinion that leaves me incredulous. From what we understand he's been delivering it via some bio-virtual reality sim."

"What's the virus called?"

"As far as we know its untitled but its possibly delivered in the form of a game."

"So, you were developing noumenon to help groom people into your new reality and Trevor has performed a kind of corporate Seppuku."

"The LUX-Labour initiative relies on the possible acceptance of a new reality the same way a body needs to match with transplant. Noumenon would have revolutionised therapy and laid the groundwork for a more integrated understanding of fantasy and labour."

"So, what am I supposed to do?"

"Find his simulation. We think he monitors everyone that uses the program and he's releasing it into certain populations at a time."

"What about the cult?"

"They're harmless freaks."

"If it really is the only way to contact him why haven't you…"

"He's genetically barred us from using."

"What makes you think I'll get the chance?"

"The amount of attention you're attracting. If he thought you were working for us your stunt would have disabused him of that notion. On top of that there are bodies now. We'll give you access, see if we can't retro engineer a death. Either way Trevor knows you're here."

"Then what?"

"Once you find him, we'll find you both."

"How do you know I'm any different from the others that disappeared?"

"We don't really. It doesn't matter to us what happens to you."

The screen blackens and between one breath and the next Lakerman feels a slight stinging sensation in his neck. Lakerman's experience of his body is mediated by images of a pebble glistened by a stream of water it can't feel, an anaesthetised wound with the world draining out of it, or a capsule dissolving as intended in the wormy gut of the moment. These attempts at mitigation fail. Behind him a calm and faintly paternal voice that makes him want to deafen himself with a needle begins to count back from a hundred. It is only the horror and the fear seizing his nerve endings, locking him in a jolt of teeth clenching pain, that keeps him awake long enough to remember any of this.

* * *

He knows the moment that he wakes up that the flat is empty. There's just the sound of artificial waves low in the external mix. He's aware too that he's swarming with recently injected foreign bodies. The implant has been feeding counterfeit information to them since they were detected. The implant activates Little Jelly fish lights under his skin to find them. His skin looks like it's breaking apart with globules of fake lava. He brushes every area of his skin towards his bladder. His pelvis glows brightly. He pisses weakly into a jar. He pours the piss into a whisky bottle. He creates a female Avatar and sells the accurately labelled contents 'pisskey' on the alternet in five minutes. He does not know what to do and then he does. Lakerman sits down, closes his eyes, and meditates for twenty minutes. Opening his eyes he thinks "Fuck those guys."

He searches through the lifepax files in his notes. Husk hadn't known the name of the program Trevor was using. As he suspects, "How I Killed The Universal Man" is no longer listed among the research projects. Whatever Trevor is up to, the fact that Lakerman is still alive, Husk pissed off, and the 'universal man' a living nightmare, means it has to be preferable to working with that fuck.

The invitation opens in Lakerman's consciousness, the location partially decrypting inside him. There's no google earth for the co-ordinates. Fuck, he thinks, the other Miami.

HOW I KILLED THE UNIVERSAL MAN

CHAPTER 8

VESTIGIAL REMAINS

L akerman's limping through a moat of rubble toward the decimal point of a beyond dead mall in West Perrine. Everything past this mall was supposed to be even more fragged and blown out and insignificant than here though Lakerman's not sure he can believe that. He rubs his thigh where the needle remains sequestered. The whole frontispiece of the mall has been demolished and the majority of the roof has fallen in. What remains of the Mall is a rotting cavity. Fifty years ago they'd started work on a community redevelopment but then an investor, sold on the Good Brand PR of the move, had seen economic sense and pulled out of any attempt to rehabilitate the toxic space. Now it functions as a kind of portal and half way home between worlds. The have nots and the will nots and the never could.

Twilight eats into the mouth of the building. White dust in blue light. It's the magic hour but all natural light here is powerfully carcinogenic, spotlit as the area is by a total lack of UVA protection and radioactive fallout. Lakerman, walking under the umbrella black-light of a burner drone, skids down a dune of rubble and enters the remnants of the dilapidated food court.

On either side of the court, and constituting a kind of semi-enclosed city, ramshackle brick and plastic shelters run around the margins of the still roughly existing floor plan. In the graded darkness of the shelters Lakerman sees strange silhouettes lift their chins, extend their throats. A slow swell of animal moans and yelps cross and recross the court in apparent response to his presence. They quickly die down. A few people sidle up to the point of visibility, leaning against the surviving structures. Many of their bodies are misshapen and unfinished seeming. They remain docile, absently stroking their disfigurements and sucking on rocks. Their expression has the same terrified resignation he'd caught in photographs of animals on their way to the slaughterhouse.

Entering the hardware and homestores section, these relics of space, the sickness of the population intensifies. Lakerman watches 3-4 bodies covered in pillow-sized blisters crawl out of the shade of their shelter, stagger and collapse in the dust. The wounds leak a filmy liquid (*Serum*) into the ground that the dirt and dust form little platelets with. The body leached of life, clotted with earth. These were the lucky ones. Lakerman sees conjoined twins (*In fact parasitical twins*) half galumph out of a little rockpile house (*dwelling*). One mewling body attached to another. He supposes they want money or painkillers but perhaps they just want a witness. The primary head is covered in a fencing mask of bubbled skin. Lakerman's not sure how the head is breathing. The second face, dangling to the left and sprouting out of their hip is double chinned and winded. At about five metres away (*6.35M*) they begin to run towards Lakerman. A metre or so (*2.5M*) away from him the body swan dives first face first into the concrete. On impact the blister covering the heads bursts. The body jerks upwards, sits up in reflexive horror, hands reaching to feel out the new cavity, shoulders squirming about in disbelief at the concrete incomprehensibility of the moment before death. The other twin cranes their neck to see and stifles a gasp. The body falls to the side. More fluid. Another blister, unseen and evidently wedged at their point of conjuncture, bursts separating the twins. The second twin gets washed away a little from the first. It turns out the only thing keeping them together was their disease. Having no access to the lungs, the twin's lips soundlessly write out the same phrase. Lakerman can't help but lip read. *It's what we both wanted*, the palsied face repeats in its moment of suffocation.

On time with death, children with drum tight faces, large heads, and puckered no teeth mouths run out into the street, lean over the body, clench their fists and cry until their breath runs out. Lakerman watches their wet beaks flapping in the air, spit and blood threading down their chins. They collapse suddenly in strange skull and crossbone like heaps, their bones all dislocated and rubbery. He retreats from them.

Bare chested, absent minded women emerge in packs carrying silent, swaddled, bundles around their puckering stomachs. The bundles are held tightly into their bodies, into some imagined space there. The women move without urgency through a terrified slowness, as though powered by some inhuman force, their dead babies acting as batteries of a sort. The children shuffle after them. Everything appears faintly choreographed. The women pass over the body then kneel and pour dust into the wounds until the wounds are filled. Nothing else happens. The youngest of the women is in her late twenties. She looks at Lakerman. Her eyes are bleeding. Lakerman walks around them.

This other Miami was not the place his imagination had been curated to believe in. The smell of disinfected seawater and aired out mass death was enough to make you wretch, that much was true, and the place was insane but there was no intentioned *(read: human)* danger here, he thought. No crime. Everyone Lakerman's seen is just sick. Too ill to be angry, too weak to demand, too traumatised to hope. Even the bodies which weren't visibly ill appeared committed to some passive insularity of waiting, he thinks.

There's a logic in this attitude that unlocks a memory.

The mall reminds him Roscoff. There was a correlation between the possible and one's sense of reality, he thought, and on any scale Reality depended on possibility for its dimensions. No possibility, no interaction, no 'depth.' Roscoff rendered anything beyond it almost unthinkable, at the very least impossible. It was the same here. After all, even in the apparently healthy bodies the damage written into their cells was waiting to be spelled out in the future. The past had to be caught up with. To ignore that futility or to rebel against it would have amounted to a pantomime, he thinks.

The future: It's behind you.

HOW I KILLED THE UNIVERSAL MAN

Lakerman is thinking about his general lack of introspection as he staggers along the road, at the way he has lost control of his life and this story without surprise or protest. Some logic introjects. Doesn't the wondering bely the question? Even for a journalist that is facile, he thinks. He tries again. The question of his agency has been raised. Since he encountered Noumenon his world had assumed its dimensions. There was nothing he could do about that. He is near now. A beam of A.R light shoots out of his chest and towards the car park. A single gleaming shimmer passes over the surface of the exit.

*

Even without midnight's cosmetic Lakerman recognises the carpark's drift of concrete from the Youtube video. The one he'd seen the boys stumble through, the one that had felt like a hallucination. In the blue of twilight though the place is a dump. The ground like a partially scaled fish, flaked with glass and crudely split open. Every thirty to forty feet: upturned pushchairs with kicked off wheels. Trolleys with their front ends cratered in. Jagged glass, rubbled concrete, dirt acned with fags, the earth scarred with inflammations of melted plastic, lesions of wrappers dropped in wax-like patterns, their prime colours candying the landscape. In the dwindling light he can still see and smell the way blood and piss have fused into stone and earth. Permanence was a case of being there till the earth moved around you or you moved into the earth.

Lakerman spots the butt of a blunt in a spatter of green and brown glass. He reconstructs the broken glass in his mind based on the pattern of their relations and his own unconscious memory. It's a bottle, the one the woman had used on the man to reveal an eyeball he guesses. Lakerman looks up, a crystalline glint in the near distance catching his attention. He walks to it. There is a mound of sugar about a two and half metres high (*1.8592M*) where the bodies had been piled in copulation. He rubs the granules between his fingers. Sugar cascades, covering his trainers. He sees several dark objects near the surface and a smaller more colourful object in the centre. He begins to dig away. He finds a hand and beyond that some gloopy encrusted mess. The stain of an eye turned watercolour in the sugar. Lakerman stumbles back. Falls over. He wipes his hands on the dirt, catching one of them on something sharp. He brings the cut hand to his eye. A partial eclipse. In the corner of his vision a crescent of dry weeds, the same shape as his sickled cut, begins to glow golden. He walks towards the mesh of plants reaching out and sweeping back their heads with his left hand.

In the near distance a curdling sound warps through the air like a siren. Ungodly howling. Primordial confusion. A sweep of noise that moves from panic to alarm, fear to warning. The way the sound travels, flocked and preparatory, suggests to Lakerman that there is someone else walking through the toxic ruins. Behind the weeds is a crawl space that leads to the underground section of the car park. Lakerman lays on the ground and works his way quickly under the gap.

*

The inside of the underground car park is surprisingly cool. It ought to be humid and difficult to breathe in, Lakerman thinks, but instead the air is cool and fresh and redolent of some simple earthy joy.

(Reference found in Collective Archived Memory of Lost Conditions. Name: Petrichor. Meaning 'The smell of dry earth after rain.' Produced by the chemical odorant Geosmin. In 2016 Geosmin inspired the inauguration of olfactogenetics due its effect on the neurons of the fruit fly this lead to...)

Across the concrete Lakerman sees a ramp leading further down into the earth and an arrow and a B painted on the wall by it. As he walks down the ramp sheets of light stutter across the concrete. The carpark is a map of itself, the ordered ratio of an idea. The ramp to level B represents a different country in that respect. It glows with rare beauty. Lakerman doesn't understand. *Bioluminescence.*

Glowworms. The glowing caves of Waimoto. *Arachnocampa luminosa.*

Arachnocampa luminosa (Skuse, 1891), commonly known as **New Zealand glowworm** or simply **glowworm**, is a species of fungus gnat endemic to New Zealand. The larval stage and the imago produce a blue-green bioluminescence.[2] The species is known to dwell in caves and on sheltered banks in native bush where humidity is high.[3] Its Māori name is **titiwai**, meaning "projected over water". The larvae of this species glow to attract prey into their threads.[10] The glow has a maximum wavelength of 487 nm[11] and, like other species exhibiting bioluminescence, this glow is produced as a result a luciferase enzyme acting upon a small molecule of luciferin. [12] It occurs in modified excretory organs known as Malpighian tubules in the abdomen.[13] The luciferase enzyme in this species shares similarities with the protein that occurs in fireflies. However, the luciferin that the enzyme acts upon is entirely different to that of fireflies and, indeed, other currently known bioluminescent systems.[12]

The lights of level B either do not function or have been disabled for aesthetic effect. Lakerman walks past empty parking spaces, the yellow and white lines demarcating them a little chalky but otherwise intact despite the time that has passed and the conditions the world above all this has found itself in. He continues down. The ramp to level A is caked in pollen that builds around his boots.

Beautiful as a gasoline rainbow, level A is streaked with orthogonal lines of colour receding towards a vanishing point. Placed transversally across their horizon is an oversized throne of sugar and an altar of classically striped candy with some shapeless thing resting atop it. Lakerman walks towards it. The shapeless thing is a body in a sack with a hood where the head should be. It's unavoidable that he's going to take the hood off, he has no choice about it all. When he does he sees Mary's face with a different set of eyes staring manically up at him.

"Got you."

Mary's face smiles and the bones then frill around her cheeks like a catfish's mouth. *Alternate image: Non evidence based Representation of dilophosaurus in 1993 American* <u>*science fiction action film*</u>[3] *Jurassic Park directed by* <u>*Steven Spielberg*</u> *and produced by* <u>*Kathleen Kennedy*</u> *and* <u>*Gerald R. Molen*</u>. *During the scene in which the corrupt Dennis Nedry attempts to escape the island the dilophosaurus is shown with a collar flared up as it readies itself to spit venom.* Lakerman doesn't get it. The reference or any of it. The face is reconstructing itself in front of him. Bones and muscles move like obsolete machinery. The eyes though are wide open and stark and there's a scream with no exit muffled somewhere inside the body. It makes their chest shake. A voice ventriloquizes the body:

"Please, mark your expression of sorrow in this moment, note the obvious limitations of the flesh and muscle of your face, the fronting paucity of its appearance born of the limited translation of all those instances occurring behind it, breaking apart, parts already structured as broken, broken out of the necessity of space, your electric brain communicating across that gap in the discontinuous leap of thought. The world is necessarily broken in a very literal and very profound way. Now try to imagine the lack of time you have to sort between this sensory communication and the way this lack solidifies into the overwhelming stupidity within everyone's expressions. The radiation behind them, the sickness of our interactions. We'd need a billion more facial muscles just to approach any sort of notion of subtlety. So why not develop them. Or better move beyond the tyranny of the face and develop a topology of minds in which the self is just a type of weather"

The face is briefly Trevor's but when he opens his mouth the likeness falls apart. His chin tapers then squares. Lakerman watches as a dark rash spreads across the T-zone of the face. The face is a heat map of melanin production: Mahogany mouth, Ivory cheeks, mottled blue nose, ears striped like an Okapi. The structure of the face begins to methodically approximate Lakerman's. A minute later and the formerly mottled skin has blended into an exact match. Everything else is slightly off. It's something to do with what the eyes give a body. How you can tell the eyes aren't alive with *him*. The body sits up, shedding the sack, swinging their legs around confidently to face him. Lakerman staggers back. The body reaches out a hand, makes a scrubbing motion in front of their face. The face becomes Trevor's again. He runs his hands over his skull.

"Are you an Assassin?"
"I'm a journalist."
"You're neither."

(Possible reference to 1979 film *Apocalypse Now*. *Apocalypse Now* is a 1979 American epic psychological[5] war film directed and produced by Francis Ford Coppola. It stars Marlon Brando, Robert Duvall, Martin Sheen, Frederic Forrest, Albert Hall, Sam Bottoms, Laurence Fishburne, Harrison Ford, and Dennis Hopper. The screenplay, co-written by Coppola and John Milius with narration written by Michael Herr, is loosely based on the 1899 novella Heart of Darkness by Joseph Conrad, with the setting changed from late 19th-century Congo to the Vietnam War. The film follows a river journey from South Vietnam into Cambodia undertaken by Captain Benjamin L. Willard (Sheen), who is on a secret mission to assassinate Colonel Kurtz (Brando), a renegade Army Special Forces officer accused of murder and who is presumed insane.)

"Shut the fuck up." Lakerman strikes his head.
"You still don't know how to work with your implant."
"I don't know that I want to anymore."

"Don't you wonder who I am?"

"You're either Trevor or as close to Trevor as can be approximated, frankly I'm tiring of the intrigue."

"It was a trick question but you've answered pretty well."

"What was the trick?"

"How misleading a noun is. How misleading the concept of singular is. How the two of them fit a pattern of domestication we've mistaken as our humanity."

"Why are you here?"

"The Universal Man. He's coming to define you."

Lakerman is distracted by the sudden realisation that Trevor's skin is moving. The skin seems to travel over the bone as if fed through the body's sticky architecture like a conveyor belt. His face too morphs from that of a ballooning baby's to the wrinkled peanut of an elderly man. In each iteration he wears the same vacant expression. Life trapped behind the eyes. The emotion tunnelling through with no grip on his material features.

"What I want to say upfront," Trevor continues, "is that all I communicate, all I'm capable of communicating, of their thoughts is roughly the equivalent of a smiley face emoticon. They don't really have an identity reducible to language."

Lakerman says "Who does?"

"They think you're special. So they want to give you something special. A decision. We know who your mother was, the problems she caused us. Ok, the complications she shared. Ok, the love she gave. Love put a hole through them. Gave them range. They have been trying to understand you, to find you for a long time."

"Who?"

"Don't you understand the mutations now? An idea of you is part of their primordial sequence. No one survives love. But if any part of you does, do what I cannot. Go into nature. Listen to a stone. Perhaps your mutation will be one of humility, to evolve into a simpler more beautiful organism. This I hoped to be my own fate."

"I don't understand."

"You were lost but now you're found. It's not as if they're totally free of our prejudices. I hope you don't disappoint. The special thing they are offering you is a gift. That's why we got you the implant. That's why we brought you here. There's a way out of this. Certain things are unstoppable. But this does not mean we cannot choose our inevitability. How we react to the impact of the future, what our position is as we crash, will determine exactly how we live. The gift is something you'll be opening your whole life but which you'll never really receive. The gift is a choice. The twist is the usual one: You have to work out what your choices are. I can't tell you that. What I can tell you is this. The Universal Man is coming. He's near. Can't you feel him?"

Lakerman remembers the crying sound handed through the mall, the expression of fear systematised as a warning.

"What is he?"

Trevor produces a smile that extends itself past the point of comfort.

"He's an A.I. stranded in a body and isolated from connecting with other machines, even humans. He's an experimental construct like the devil only his basic relentlessness renders him primary. Imagine you read and strongly internalised every comment section on the internet. Imagine someone gave you the outline of every historically recorded atrocity, you know all of Western history, as a guideline for your morality, as the spectrum of your emotions. Minus any of the culture, love, joy, or shared interpersonal moments that we have tended to overlook as achievements. That all this was scored across your brain from conception. The material core of your being. Then contrast all that violence and hatred with the total monotony of knowing that you are a body subjugated to the world and its inexpressibility. An individual without means, a servant. Voila. Malign repression. Traumatically Zen. That's The Universal Man: A total lack of detail and an absolutely traumatising effect on the life around it. Such a thing cannot be rendered but can be leased. And so it is buried in a body and face of compiled Western whiteness. Eugenically, algorithmically, constructed but pretty much flesh."

"So, what does he want...he's fighting against obsoletion?"

"That and more. Like all colonialist instincts he wants to become reality in order to escape from the hell of a repressed body. To install himself as your unconscious, as humanity's baseline. To torture you for eternity. To threaten. The universal man exists the way a bomb exists, in its past and future tenses. Once he discovered what the drug could do, that *they* were everywhere, even in him...he's wanted to connect."

Trevor produces a syringe and a seed.

"But this," he says holding the seed out to Lakerman, "*this* is how we kill the universal man."

Lakerman shakes his head. He looks up to find Mary's face staring him down. The face mouths the word "please."

Lakerman is surprised to find himself rolling up his sleeve. He thinks 'determinism, baby.' The needle dips under Lakerman's skin. Trevor places the stomata seed under Lakerman's nose.

"Press Start."

Lakerman inhales.

CHAPTER 9

CALIBRATE THIS

Opening his eyes Lakerman's disappointed to find that he is still in an underground carpark. He is sitting on a throne of sugar. He can't move anything except his eyes, apparently. He feels a branching movement across his temple like the pulsing of a vein. Some logic of the dendrite making itself known in his skin. His throat spasms as if he were screaming but the ache in his cheeks is from a wide set and totally sincere seeming smile.

A cell commemorates the intensities of a body the way a note studs a melody. I eat light but it's not enough. Glitches and bugs. I eat light. But it's not enough.

"That is the voice of the seed branching out within you."

Trevor's voice. External. Amplified.

"The voice is translated obviously. Imagined really. Tacked on usefully. We used an algorithm to devise an Echoic track... **Echoic memory** is the sensory memory that registers specific to auditory information (sounds). Auditory sensory memory has been found to be stored in the primary auditory cortex contralateral to the ear of presentation.[13] The major regions involved are the left posterior ventrolateral prefrontal cortex, the left premotor cortex, and the left posterior parietal cortex. Within the ventrolateral prefrontal cortex, Broca's area is the main location responsible for verbal rehearsal and the articulatory process. The dorsal premotor cortex is used in rhythmic organization and rehearsal, and finally the posterior parietal cortex shows a role in localizing objects in space...

The algorithm you see forms the a.i voice that interprets the data and actions of the seed linguistically according to the prejudice of our will. Essentially it tries to make an emotional coherence out of the various levels and transitions between levels of proteins, growth, actualisations of potential and vice versa in a way I could understand. We thought it might help with the sensations. For me, it is beautiful. We're not Wittgenstein, what a relief."

I am overwhelmed by the scale of work to be done. I press on. This is a birth.

Lakerman goes blind and deaf. In the darkness Trevor's voice becomes a scrolling retro text that Lakerman tries willing himself to click through.

"You can't skip this. This is unskippable content. But i'll get to the crux of it now. HIKTUM is a game that teaches you how to be multiple.   The game involves the simulation/transference of telepathic connections which is to say the game creates telepathy. Fabricates a sensation of it. It's not a question of belief but rather experience. You become simultaneous. Afterwards too. As the game goes on you pass through four stages of connection. Reading someone's thoughts in stage one is like receiving an anagram of an emotion. There's always a little charge to them but it's up to you to arrange their subtleties. Of course by that time they're onto something else and you've likely lost your place and theirs. It can get confusing at first or oddly maddening, like hallucinating that there's some kind of gnat in the mind of your ear. In this first iteration you catch fragments of thought, mainly verbalised, snapped off sensations, weird surges of alternating currents of desire. The occasional expression of something clearly. Essentially, you're one level up from a well skilled confidence trickster, still guessing but increasingly accurate. You'll likely believe at this point that you 'know' the other person. This will not turn out to be the case.

(a) They're not people though are they, they're programs?
(b) What are you?
(c) Why did you record people's deaths?

HOW I KILLED THE UNIVERSAL MAN

(d) I don't understand the part about the mutations

"Interesting. That you can ask, that is. Not the questions themselves. The people in the game are sentient, feel an equivalency of pain, and have a physical basis even as they bear no resemblance to the source of their life. Do your thoughts bear any resemblance to their brain? The programs know as much about death as you and they all hold someone's death within them like a bomb. That's one use for the data we found, the other is a secret. Does that answer your questions?

Y/N

Nevermind. Now, stage 2 is harder to describe, the connection has a different horizon. The background in which you experience their thought is spacious yet alternating which suggests a manner of coherence you are unaware of, that you will find difficult to conceive. Imagine one face of an incredibly complex shape rotating and this rotation functions to dwarf you to the extent that you experience the absolute truth of your connection to it and how little you mean to the shape as a whole. The context is not new but the world has changed, shifted. The effect though is sublime. Imagine it as a world in which you can almost comprehend how little you comprehend and which you experience as beauty. You experience language as climate change here. The Logo/cene. It fracks the interior. Without it one feels supremely open to a distance that truly pierces and what pierces you, you partially become. Still, it can be nauseating and it can be too much and the risks are very great.

Stage 3 is textural, fibrous. You're are the horizon now. The majority of thought is preformative, electric. It's not always appearing to itself. You hold all this, contain it. Think of the ancient Christian doctrine of pre-existence, or preconception or whatever it was actually called... it is a relief not to remember at certain times. There are all these other unborn souls or the souls of thoughts present but not materialised enough to appear directly and yet they are the fabric upon which the patterns emerge. This is how i conceptualise stage 3. The merging awareness of sensations not primal enough to be drives and not embodied enough to be strait jacketed by language, vague appearances, the unified field of which is hard to comprehend and impossible to understand.

Stage four is more intimate still. Granular and electric. You can begin now to switch between levels though the decision making process is unclear. Which is to say it takes a little while to master how to really 'read' a mind. Which isn't to say you'll understand it, just that you'll know it in a way that I would genuinely say is more intimate. Metaphors of depth be damned. This is as intimate as two bodies can be. It's like you die and the other person is your ghost, maybe. You get to come back to life but obviously you're different, different in the way that you perceive space or your own sense of time or the relation between the two.

Calm down.

Anxious people are hard to be around. That's pretty much a truism. And almost everyone in the world is a hysteric but I felt, always, that there was a calmness to you and what you wanted to know.

Remember this: It's not about what has a mind.

You're now ready to play.

The scrolling text disappears into the constructed present. The world is loading. Lakerman sees a body as if through water moving across a grey field. The colours and contours merging in the soft distortion of his vision   are swimming and unusual. His consciousness or whatever he's 'behind' or projecting out from follows the distorted body as it walks up to another body and rips its head off like it was nothing at all. A little fountain of cataracted blood kneels before Lakerman.

The body walks closer to John Lakerman. Two hands are placed around your ears. You feel your thigh throbbing. Your hands claw at your trousers and scrabble some skin from your thigh. In the skin is something hard and sharp that your hands instinctively work free, slippy as your insides are.

You stab the body choking you with the syringe. You are not there.

HOW I KILLED THE UNIVERSAL MAN

CHAPTER 10

HOW I KILLED THE UNIVERSAL MAN

Your name is John Lakerman. She/Her. You wake up crying. The room you are in is part of a structure that is incomprehensible to you now. The structure belongs to the dream of a body that is disappearing. You stand up. The dream is still with you and will always be with you. The dream disintegrates like so much seasoning in your mood. You pick up your clothes and tiptoe past the body that you are losing recognition of.

You begin to dress in a narrow, dingily lit, hallway. The clothes are intricate, full of lace and string, and are utterly at odds with their surroundings, and yet your movements are nimble and you are quickly clothed. Suitably attired, you open the front door.

Outside of the house the world discloses itself to you as Victorian London. Of course, you think. Nice touch. You are partially aware that you are playing a game but believe that you, John Lakerman, are the player, that there is absolute equivalence between your appearance and being. The world isn't your world but instead another world however easy to forget that may be. You will forget this. You turn around on a whim. The structure you entered this world from has been replaced by a tavern. There is a warm glow of yellow emanating from the windows.

You forget everything.

HOW I KILLED THE UNIVERSAL MAN

* * *

You are alone in Victorian England. You feel faint. The pavement you are standing on is composed of broken demarcations of stone. You stand on the pavement's thick precipice facing a series of cross hatching streets. The walls of the alleys beyond you teeter, overhang. The rolling fog in the near distance promises discovery. You have yet to move or feel the urge to move. Instead your attention switches to the movement of things. The wind swinging in algorithmic time through shop signs as a sign of itself. The wind a butler to the city and its detritus, carrying in its gustatory swirl its own ephemeral world, one bitter but not repugnant, a taste to be both acquired and lost through the ownership of its promise. You are thinking this. You experience a strong desire to acquire a deep physical familiarity with the city, to be woven in and of and from it.

On thinking this you feel a play of attributes reorganise the scope of your possibilities. John Lakerman remembers. The beginning of games often include a set of mini levels to help determine your strengths and weaknesses. Heat rises in tandem with pleasure through your body that is no longer experienced as exterior to yourself.

Your body has been *customised* as a single erogenous zone. The wind, now actively directed towards you, gently crushes and caves it's pressurised tongue against your skin and hair, licking the film of your eyes. A thought bubble floats above your head. Reads itself out:

'The meaning of the wind is an allusion to the growing sophistication of Capital in the time period. It's ceaseless movement and powerful tides. Its invasive, line crossing character. Follow the air current for a colonialist adventure!'

A degree of normality is re-established. You are no longer a body determined by pleasure. Internally though you are experiencing a strong sense of loss, an evacuation of joy. Hollowness. You are unaware of the impossibility of all this, of interiority itself. You are bent over and your hands are on your knees the street now refocuses, bustling again with life as if the wind had only been wind and when you look again to follow it you can feel the reheated call of blood in your body. You shake your head no.

Crossing the street and walking against the increasingly intermittent breeze, you come to a small square. There is a broken statue, little curations of nature chained off, a bush, the sapling of a tree, as well as three distinct exits leading Northwards, Eastwards, and Westwards.

You walk around the sad little tree to inspect the Eastside exit. There are some signs pointing towards shops and a small booth where a man is selling tickets by shouting at strangers. You listen in.

"Roll up, Roll up to the Museum of Ghosts and then partake in a Real Seance! Consult with Eva Carriere to navigate the whirlpool of the damned's afterlife, converse with the dead as she pulls them out of the ceaseless roar of non existence, touch real ectoplasm as the dead excrete through her skin "

(Introjection: Carrière has been described as "perverse and neurotic".[15] She was well known for running around the séance room naked and indulging in sexual activities with her audience. Her companion Juliette Bisson would, during the course of the séance sittings introduce her finger into Eva's vagina to ensure no "ectoplasm" had been loaded there beforehand to fool the investigators, and she would also strip nude at the end of a séance and demand another full-on gynecological exam.[9] The psychic sessions of Carrière with Schrenck-Notzing have been described as pornographic. The photographs that were taken during the séances show Carrière in the nude emerging from her cabinet and others reveal fake ectoplasm strings hanging from her breasts. Another photograph revealed ectoplasm in the shape of a deflated and disembodied penis.[16] According to historian Ruth Brandon, Juliette Bisson and Carrière were in a sexual relationship together, and they worked in collaboration with each other to fake the ectoplasm and <u>eroticize</u> their male audience.[17])

You nod cautiously, saying nothing, yet highly intrigued.

On the northside exit you see a poster advertising the zoo. The poster has a circus motif with a question mark partially obscuring an image of a ringmaster and a parabolic array of images tear-dropping the paper. A giraffe eats a Parasol. A well dressed woman holds her palm out to the maw of a hippo whose monstrous fangs seem not to bother her in the slightest despite the artist rendering their proximity and the width of the bars troubling to your perspective. The third image depicts an elephant with a man rolled up like a cigar in its trunk. The man seems ecstatically surprised. The question mark/ringmaster is a reference to the celebrations for the zoo's anniversary. The Royal Society of London For Improving Natural Knowledge is holding a fundraising ball in honour of the zoo's work tonight and there has long been rumours of some new evolutionary marvel being revealed at the event. In the bottom corner of the poster there is a small map and a series of arrows marking out a route which you instantly internalise.

The west side exit leads towards a small theatre. You hear an orchestra playing. Notes like snow on tongues lose shape in faintly thrilling ways, emerging and dissolving in the distance. A tear hatches in your eye.

You decide to go to the zoo and buy a ticket to the fundraiser of your own free will.

You are walking across a canal when a group of boys come out of nowhere, rushing by and around you, trundling after a skittery hoop, their legs all pudgy and coal powdered, their joyful shouts modulated by soot blushed lungs. They are young boys waving long sticks in their hands, sticks that crack and whistle at the sound barrier, slicing open interdimensional portals of imagination in the air through which they might hope to escape the poverty of their lives. You flinch, still discerning all this information, drinking it down, as one boy narrowly misses taking out another's eyes. You are aware in poignant, slo-mo, sepia tinted sequence, of each of their individually rendered but perfectly collated faces as they rush back and forth and around you. Time returns to speed and you are aware of them now first and foremost as a pack of raw faces, faces that looked as if they had been coughed and spat into the world. You straighten yourself up.

A few feet to the left of you a sly looking boy has grabbed the rim of the wheel and declared the game over. There is a demonstrative outcry and a few eyes attempting to solicit your own for judgement. You can *feel* them. A pause. You don't look straight away. The gang begins to disperse but not really. They keep within your vicinity, peer into the windows or chatter indecipherably in the background.

Clearly they have hidden orders not to interact.

It doesn't seem possible for you to walk away at this point. Instead you notice the somewhat archetypal makeup of the group's nucleus. A readable diversity in their composition. Among them, under the cursor of your gaze, they reveal themselves.

You focus first on 'the tough', ID'd as Jimmy, his features ruddy and already burnished by windburn. You switch to the 'not long for this world embodiment of human sweetness' (who you instinctively know the tough is closest to and protective of) following behind Jimmy on the clack of his makeshift crutches, stick poking limply out of his hand as he gestures at the wheel. Your gaze moves on again to the sly looking boy up ahead, a judas type, who is jealous of the tough but fond of the sweet boy though it remains to be seen to what extent fondness can overcome jealousy (narrative signpost alert), and then lagging behind all of them is the self appointed chronicler: The Living Norm who will transmute the cowardice of his own survival in the face of their shared fates into a meaningful burden for others.

The chronicler opens a conversation with you. He senses a kinship. He is precocious in asking for your thoughts on child labour and the economy. You enter into a detailed conversation, make several cogent points, your intelligence level rising as you access the different knowledge you have equipped and ready to hand.

Meanwhile, the sweet boy has begun to tug at your ivory fingers. His fingers gently pinching yours, an oily, coalish, nib seeping out of his blackened nails and writing its exhaustion upon your skin. Dirt and oil, the earth's unconscious. You feel a regretful twinge of disgust. Your ivory fingers? Your clothes, you notice now, are strongly perfumed, your skin heavily powdered, your thoughts differently accented as befitting your newly assigned social position, gender and racial makeup. The gloves held in your other hand come as a charming surprise as they enter your sight. Delightful, you think, before stopping to think. You think this is a sign of your character. The sweet boy has brought about an abrupt end to your conversation with the chronicler. The chronicler has stepped respectfully aside and is self consciously observing your interaction with the sweet boy. The sweet boy is all searching eyes. He begins to sputter words at you.

"Please your ladyship I don't ask nuffin for myself and I have always done wot i could but Miss, my mother is sick and with no one to attend her. Would you help me fetch a doctor? We haven't any money miss."

"My name is John Lakerman. Did your mother send you? Because it seems to me..."

"Miss it looks bad don't it but in truth these boys had sworn to help me but they got all caught up in the game, one wagering that i'd need to win to gain their help, Jimmy said after, they'd help after, and not to cry but I did...Miss, will you come with me?"

You feel that you are navigating a set of consequences, that there is a pattern of dialogue capable of changing reality. It will feel like creation but really it's causality. You realise that if you go with the boys one of them will die, likely in some kind of duel or sacrificial gesture. It will almost certainly be emotional and you will likely have to make a key decision regarding who survives. And what if you were to side with Judas? Or else murder them all yourself and play it that way instead?

You avoid the question.

You pick up a rock and launch it at the tough's head. It lands sickeningly. The tough is on the ground. There is a weak fountain of blood filling up and then overrunning the cavernous gash on his head.

You do not know what possessed you to do this. You are, after all, a woman of some refinement.

"Miss John Lakerman, wot you done? Miss?"

You pick up another rock and wave it at the embodiment of human sweetness.

You say:

"Get out of here you filthy little urchin."

The Judas child stands smiling enigmatically at you before turning around and slowly leaving.

The others have stayed with the tough. The sweet boy cradles the tough's head. Jimmy's head is trying to reject the gash you put in him, blood filling and spilling around the little crater.

The sweet boy cries out for water.

Empathy appears as a choice and so you choose it. You do not praise consistency. Either your identity as John Lakerman is inconsistent or you are a woman filled with surprises. Those are your options. You wish the world were more subtle.

You watch the sweet boy pour the murkiest looking water over the head of his friend. Friend.

The empathy has kicked in.

You are looking at the boys and you feel a deep and searching emotion, like a tide clawing at the beach, as you try to hold on to each boy's feeling of loss. The loss they were born with, the loss they accrued. The world is a cruel place and you have unnecessarily proved the truth of that.

"I will pay for everyone's doctor! John Lakerman will pay."

Scrolls unfurl above the scene of the injured chimney sweeps.

"Follow the boys to experience the horrors of the slums or else exploit them! (it is not too late) Experience grief, deep maternal love and lead the morally satisfying crusade against labour conditions or else do the opposite: fall in love with a factory owner and drive him to ever greater heights of profit and cruelty!"

You shake your head no. The boys become simpering echoes and you choose to forget them, to free up space for a better life. You turn definitively away from the boys. You move to exit the canal and are immediately startled by a horse rattling through the street. A succession of carts and horses have now appeared, retroactively establishing themselves as having 'always' been. One horse turns towards you and sneezes in your face. The spit and mucus and indeterminable liquid of it dries, near instantly, coldly tightening upon your face as if the horse substance were coiling desperately around and after its production of sensation, this end of its brief life. Everything has a kind of sentience here, you think.

You walk along the thin pavement. The zoo is another fifteen minutes walk away. You notice a flap of colour bundling down the cobbled streets. Despite the restrictive action of your clothing, you are able to stoop and catch it as it tries to bundle past. It is a scrunched up leaflet. You unfurl its ruined petals.

The leaflet presents itself.

A

TREATISE

ON

THE INDUSTRIAL REVOLUTION

And its consequences for the Zoological, biological and neurological preoccupations of this Sceptred Isle's scientific community.
A talk by *Doctor Hardgrief* of Great L O N D O N Hospital.

A t the back of the leaflet is an address and a map that you immediately absorb and which throbs briefly within you. The talk is taking place in an auditorium two minutes from here.

You can go and listen to the talk or carry on walking towards the zoo. You feel your existence being generated by these two possibilities. Retroactively you experience this sensation as a terribly painful form of reduction.

You decide to go to the talk. There will still be time to buy a ticket after, you think.

HOW I KILLED THE UNIVERSAL MAN

* * *

The talk takes place in a sober looking building that your profile keyholes into. You enter a room without quite remembering how you entered it. It is not so much an auditorium as a village hall. The rows of chairs are cheap and unbecoming. Still, the place is full of respectable looking men and bespectacled youth. Onstage a handsome man is wiping his glasses. Doctor Hardgrief you presume. You try to find a place to sit and end up filleting a row of knees as you awkwardly stumble into a seat. Doctor Hardrief shuffles his notes on the lectern and begins.

"The principle of the zoo is composed of colonial dominance, prurience and latterly good intentions. Ornamental Containment, display and conservation. It should be obvious to all that whatever welfare we provide to the animals is at a cost to their instincts and that this impacts upon their future relations with the world. What in that case are we preserving? Should we not think of what we are losing and creating? In addition to this we must consider how unhappy these animals are in the current situation, how unnatural and commonplace such a feeling is becoming for them. For who among us can watch an animal freed from the dictates of survival, confronted for the first time by their existence and the narrowness of their form's possibility and not see some primordial energy broken by dependency and domination? Who can watch a creature patrol the limits of its territory at which point it suspects the real world begins and not feel the loss of joy, spirit, or life in its existence? At the same time we cannot pretend that there is anything to return to. There is no going back. What solutions do we have? None but this: I assert that as far as they have the capacity, the animals ought to be happy."

You do not totally understand what Doctor Hardgrief is saying but you find yourself agreeing instinctually with everything. Your body is voting for it. Happiness, of course. Duty of care. Wouldn't you *choose* this?

"There are four solutions that I see to the problem of happiness. None are perfect and each incurs a loss but no more of a loss, I contend, than occurs in any life unfolding."

You feel the emptiness inside you convert into longing.

"Imagine, if you would, a zoo that is indistinguishable for the animal from their environment and so seamlessly introduced and managed that the animals have no notion that anything significant has changed for them. To create an environment that existed in their perception only and which their bodies would react to as if there. Of course over time such an environment and the relations within it would naturally diverge from reality, becoming independent from its referents. The variables are infinite. Time, Vitamins, electrolytes, the quality of expectedness, chance, the complacency of survival. And so too the animals would change in a way unaligned with what might have been. The organic brain is not a closed field. It is looped with the world, formed by it. It's about neurology and environment. Still, change isn't predictable even when stasis becomes a property. So, the unknown will inevitably be preserved, they will change and the change will be real. Can they be protected from their own madness?

Another possibility would be to make them our pets. To breed the psychological with the physiological via death. To run a program of selected extinction in order to produce   in the animal the most unlikely behaviour from the perspective of survival. A desire to be *seen*. To want to pose. To need the subjugation of a gaze. Perhaps our own society is trending in this direction when one considers the dandy."

There is a slight academic laughter coming from about three people in the room. Hardgrief looks pleased but then his features become immediately sombre.

"The third is arguably the most *humane* which is why I believe we must refute it."

The speaker looks down at the Lectern and grips its sides. He lowers himself down so that his back is extended and his head is positioned between the parallel railings of his arms. His fingers tap several times against the lectern in a repetitive wave. He swings his torso back and then forwards while pushing himself up to a standing position. It is as if he has regained the strength to continue.

"Extinction. Planned obsolescence. We determine their role in the environment and take control of maintaining its stability in their absence or optimise it for our own purposes.. We put them out of their misery and make them no threat to us. No wilds, no wildlife of interest. No place in civilisation for them. We spare them their fates... All but perhaps a few hundred that we can learn more about without the ethics of their survival bothering us. But... you have another speaker coming to argue for that. Theirs is a powerful argument but I ask you, why must we have a single type of zoo? Why not, a multiplication rather than a division? Why not have every kind of zoo? The purpose of each zoo would be to provide an illusion that elaborated a possibility. They gain a future and we guarantee their existence. The collective health of the species would most likely be as happy as they are in the so-called wild in this scenario but is that happy enough and how could we know? Perhaps the animals might, in some environmental equation, learn how to be free? Extinction offers no possibility."

A fat and evidently monied man stands up and shouts.

"Trade Unionist!!!"

Another shouts "Revolutionary!"

The crowd begins to boo. Some people leave the auditorium. Hardgrief looks unnerved and begins to lose his place, to hurry his speech.

"But this is the choice conservationists must face... the zoo of the future...Umm... The journey of technology is a return to the organic... We must not relinquish the machine of our imagination... We need to translate a flower. The powers in its particularity... But as a guiding principle: Let us be as kind as possible and remember that we remain in relation to the world because of our intelligence, not despite it. I rest my case."

211

The speaker hurriedly gathers his notes. You do not know whether to applaud or cry. You applaud. Your applause becomes vigorous. You begin to walk towards the stage. There is the sound of sirens outside. Men with Truncheons appear. There is a man among them whose face is unseeable. The terror of a familiar non-recognition makes your heart feel eternally stopped though it only skips a beat or two. The room begins to spin. You are going to pass out. The man whose face won't settle rushes at you. You faint before he can reach you.

You awaken on a chaise-longue under a high ceiling in a grand house. There is a chandelier. The twinkle of which your eye scatters upon. You are lost for a number of seconds and then you are 'you' again: obscure, ostensibly blank but suggestive of powerful undiscovered desires. It is this stylistic combination that has led to a number of proposals you believe. Proposals from suitors rejected out of hand for reasons that remain obscure to you.

There is a small silver bell and a tag attached to it with your name on in front of you. The name is just a space you recognise yourself in. There is no name. Why am I, John Lakerman, seeing this? you think. You reach over and ring the bell which does not sound at all as you expected it might. The bell gongs.

A maid and a manservant hurriedly enter the room from opposite ends and then stand to attention before you. You believe you detect something vaguely parodic in their gestures.

"We were so worried about you" the maid squawks.

"Yes, thank goodness Doctor Hardgrief was able to bring you home," the butler soberly intones.

"Mr Hardgrief?"

"That is I." You look up and see the doctor totally untouched. "And now seeing you are well, I must take my leave."

"Sir."

"Yes, your ladyship?"

"Thank you for your kindness."

"Not at all, it was my duty as a gentleman."

"Pray tell, what happened with the Police?"

212

"Police?" Doctor Hardgrief makes a confused face as the Butler sees him to the door. The maid is fussing at you and refusing to let you stand up. You must rest, she says.

"Mr Hardgrief?" You call. "Mr Hardgrief, are you to attend the The Royal Society's ball tonight?"

There is the sound of a rough assent.

"Perhaps I will be able to make my amends properly later on tonight!"

The Maid shoots you a glare. You say something truly mean to the maid. The maid is wounded. You will care about this and apologise for it later but, for now, there is only the question of the great exhibition and the excitement of the masked ball filling your thoughts and something else that reminds you of a windswept day in a new city. How are you to find a ticket now given the time?

You are interrupted by a curt ahem from the butler.

"Your ladyship, the countess is waiting."

You walk through a baroque corridor into a simple and plain room where your mother drinks tea from a fine bone china cup. She asks after your day, after your fainting fits. You tell her about everything but Mr Hardgrief, the thought of whom you wear like a locket between your body and its desires. You ask if her if she might consider using her influence to have you invited to the fund raising event for the ball tonight? Tickets could surely still be procured and you have heard many eligible bachelors are set to attend. Your mother smiles like a shark. From a small box behind her she produces two tickets.

She says "John, we have been invited by the Duke himself."

The Duke is basically a horny Methuselah.

She is to accompany you to the ball.

"Go and rest up."

* * *

You look down at yourself. Somehow you are dressed in a fine ball gown plumed with peacock feathers. There is a mask in your

213

hand the shape of a cat's eyes. You look at the butler. His face is granite. You ask him if he hates you very much. The you is plural.

"Why, no ma'am. What a strange question."

You lift the mask to your face. You look around for the maid but she is nowhere to be seen. You think a cruel thought about her. Outside there is a carriage waiting. You descend the staircase and open a door onto the night. It is twilight outside and the air is blue but looking up you see that the moon is full and surrounded by glittering stars. You touch your temple and consider your condition, the voices you hear sometimes. The ones that tell you the things that you know.

Mine.

The carriage begins to judder through the streets. You feel yourself fading. You look around. Everything is transparent and dissolving. You ask your mother about the strange partitioning of time, this fracture of night, day and twilight.

She says "Whatever do you mean child?" and you point out to her the three micro-zones of liminalities composing your reality: To the left the starlit night, to the right the midday sun and ahead of you the magic hour, stretching on forever. You are afraid to stick your head out of the window and look behind you. You, John Lakerman, fear that the world has disappeared, that you are a lit fuse travelling towards some unexplored kernel of potential that will turn reality inside out. What if behind you there is only a hard nothing, the other untouchable side of this wall of yourself.

The coachman opens the door and helps your maman out. You remain seated and somewhat confused.

"Mother, why do you not answer my questions?"

"You have not asked me anything."

You feel that you are no longer in London. Through the arch of the open coach door and past maman's stern expression there are other arches and what appears to be a stately garden. You realise that the maid is sitting next to you and that you have only just noticed her. You feel a deep and abiding sense of shame. As maman scolds you for taking an age to disembark you turn to the maid and apologise for everything you have said and thought. As you apologise the maid begins to bleed from her eyes, ears, nose and mouth. Her face becomes a pit of blood. You smile and feel happy to be forgiven.

The garden path is exquisite and winds through verdant lawns and woodland, blueing in the night. It is night all around you now. You are looking at the various hanging lanterns but your Maman is being very strict and holds your elbow tightly as she shepherds you meaningfully towards the crowd she desires to subsume you. Maman is making many rules for the evening and you have not listened to a single one of them, though you have taken great care to provide the necessary punctuations of understanding. Whenever Maman suspects that you have not heard her she pinches you fiercely, twisting a nub of skin into an awareness of itself. Beneath the white of your dress parts of your flesh purple with broken blood. As she pinches you a history of feminine restraints from the chastity belt to the corset to these corrective actions network in your mind until you feel impossibly shaped and distended by your mother's touch. You are a looped and tied piece of material, a topknot securing and decorating a throat of power.

There is a marquee in the distance. Everything is elegant though the people in and around it are mainly ugly, you notice. Maman steers you into a crowd of respectable figures and debutantes, the same age as you, who cast excited whispers and glances at the young officers passing by in all their dandyish finery.

Of course there is among these gentlemen a young man, a cad by reputation, Adam Prycestrain who, you notice, has the mouth of a rosebud soaked in blood, lunar skin and cruel green eyes whose coldness seems to burn painfully within him. You are not interested in cruel hollowness, you decide. GLITCH. Your dismissal of him incites his interest and he dramatically clutches his chest at the sight of your somewhat withering appraisal of him.

You realise that one of the girls here might be your best friend. You look at Adam Prycestrane and realise that he would do anything to hurt you. If you had a best friend he would ruin her. You instinctively know your best friend, whoever that might be, will be attracted to him. You decide that you will selflessly know no one. A cousin comes into view. The last hope of an impoverished family.

Prycestrane takes her by the hand and winks at you. Sigh.

You do not care enough about this storyline to take action.

You are looking around for Mr Hardgrief. He is nowhere to be seen. Your mother points out Darwin to you. Out of frustration you fantasise sleeping with Darwin for the scandal. He is well into his sixties but the fantasy is immensely satisfying in a manner you had not bargained for. Time is unlocking. As you think this Darwin breaks from his conversation and pierces you with a long searching look as if he has somehow intuited the reactionary nature of your desire and is gently puzzled by its source. His blue grey eyes, half ringed with wild eyebrows, contain not a trace of judgement despite their clarity. There is a warmth and friendliness to them thawing your frozen body. Charles Darwin is not a sad man, he seems to want you to know this. As Darwin looks at you the bruises on your arms from Maman's pinches, your arms themselves, your legs, your eyes, the submerged flutter of your heart, the strange matrices of your skeleton, the separation of toes, fingers, hands, your vulva, the world outside of your body, other bodies..become infinitely regressing archipelagos teeming with life and waiting to evolve. The air is just the sea you live in.

You activate a charming rebellion with a daring selection of repartee.

You ease Maman off of your arm in front of the local priest while levelling a witticism at the general crowd that creates a pocket of laughter and murmurs of appreciation that allows you to entirely withdraw from the group while Maman feeds on the praise you have generated. The local priest is both enchanted and confused. Everyone agrees you are a young woman of some promise.

You are walking towards Darwin and through your own divergent history. Each step moves you through time, pours you through the shared and unlikely progeny you create together, your life and love for them crystallising in the the stories they tell of you, the way these stories grow more curious over time, until you become a laugh echoing through time, a close reading observing slight characteristics developing through generations, the line of a nose, the endless softening of hands, your expressions evolving in a child and going on and on and until almost nothing recognisable remains...

And then there you are again, something else, something like a footnote in history half excavated, rediscovered, first marginalised and then rescued/consumed by the centre. But what does it say? The Curious Young Wife of Charles Darwin: The origin of attraction. It is not enough, perhaps you might still become other than this attachment, might make your own discovery to eclipse his.

Could you convince Darwin to send you on your own voyage? To support your own claims to genius. Might this be a worthy aim for a life?

You wade through essays in which you are both icon and villain, hero and serpent. Forever. What sadness. Comments beneath online video streaming sites denigrate your existence and deny your worth in the coarsest language imaginable.

You see, as you approach this venerable old man with the cane pocking the soft earth, (Darwin stabbing it down hypnotically in time with each of your flighted steps) another option signalling itself to your left.

You choose left.

To your left you see Mr Hardgrief casting his gaze around, his glare finally seeming to fix upon you. Darwin wanders off. You step towards Hardgrief. He looks at you, startled, flustered. You are about to offer your hand. There is an entire language hiccupped in his throat. A woman, a decade your senior perhaps, appears from behind and kisses Mr Hardgrief on the cheek. She turns and looks at you, hanging from his shoulder and waiting expectantly for an introduction that might double as an explanation.

She is introduced to you as Mr Hardgrief's fiancé. You find her to be a commanding and beautiful woman and in relation to her you feel a desperate shame and inadequacy. She is a woman, you sense, full of mysteries.

Mr Hardgrief begins to recount the nature of your 'inopportune' acquaintance as you nod along smiling quite stupidly, utterly transfixed by this Baroness. Her name is Agatha Greatwill.

"He was a perfect gentleman," you say.

"But not much else I'd wager," Agatha replies.

She smiles at you. There is a touch of ruin to her face. It was a sign that she would age well. As she aged the ruin would grow more beautiful and commanding, it would develop a sovereign position in its fidelity to its vanished referent, as the reference of beauty disappeared the signifier would more and more assume the likeness of the absence till there was only this leer constructed within it and pointing back to some preternatural form of knowing ... it would prove her beauty through its stasis as all around it life was proved in death.

Agatha Greatwill says that she is charmed to meet you.

Might you fall in love with her too? Scandalise society, flee to Italy, wait for some war. There is always a war. You see each of you older now, tendrilled with lovers but arborescent and rooted in one another, feeding your twinned bodies with the field of experience. You would become antecedents to modernism, haunting the present forever in the rejection of your own, becoming the feverish night sweat writing itself across Djuna Barnes dilating vagina.

And Mr Hardgrief? You could corrupt or destroy him, be betrayed by him. Perhaps marry him for his money and then poison him one night...

Or you might become pregnant. How would you treat the child? Drown it in a sack or else raise it with Agatha alongside you to be a great poet? Perhaps abort it with a fall from a horse?

Mr Hardgrief and Miss Greatwill are standing adjusting their attire, waiting for your response. They perform certain inane actions repeatedly until you open your mouth in readiness to speak. Your first syllable is deafening and stretches out heraldically. You realise, almost instantly but not quite immediately, that the sound you had so correlated yourself with is not you but a trumpet. You frown and touch your mouth and then the sound of a crystal glass being tapped with a silver spoon, the civilised impatience of it ringing out, distracts you enough to forget this strange sense of displacement. Attention has been sought and confirmed. The director of the society appears from behind a suddenly materialised curtain, flanked by a gaggle of scientists. The curtain hangs in unsupported space, defying the laws of physics and its form appears somewhat stiff and blocky when your eyes move swiftly back to it as if you were re-triggering its existence somehow. It is a magic show, you think. Applause.

The director of society begins to speak.

"It is our great honour to greet you on this historic occasion and to share with you our latest discovery."

He turns around as if to welcome some hesitant and surprisingly formed creature, perhaps this elephant man you have heard whispers of, onto the stage. After a beat he is simply served another glass of champagne by a nondescript lackey. There is no reveal. The director smiles as he turns back to the audience.

"A joke. Like all true discoveries it cannot be seen, only experienced. And what have we discovered? A new possibility for humanity, a new consciousness. And today you will all participate." Champagne is handed out to everyone in the crowd.

There is something familiar about this, something cribbed from a bad dream of yours. The director raises his glass and says to science. Everyone drinks. You begin to feel quite dizzy. The glass falls from your hand and becomes a little toothy heap on the soil. You remember that glass is made of sand. That sands and deserts are formed by the breaking down of matter, land degradation and a loss of biological diversity.

You look up at Agatha and Mr Hardgrief. He is utterly still, both inwardly and outwardly. It is as if his eyes have gone out. Agatha's eyes also seem to reveal themselves as placeholders for the darkness of her skull but then you see something else begin to take form within them. A reflection of the world. No, not a reflection but the reflex of this world articulated into something freshly joined in one way and newly broken in another and playing out like either this world or it were a ghostly projection of some pre-recorded instance. And you watch as the Agatha within Agatha's eyes run up towards their magnifying limit, hands and silent scream beating against their filmy, convex, surface before being dragged away by some darkness interior to their world and towards a single intolerable blue flame residing in the ultimate cold of space where the world warps and is reformed in desolating horror. You cannot stand it. You look away. Agatha collapses on the floor like a doll. Hardgrief's face cracks open in concern, his forehead revealing a blue sky, like a painting by Magritte that doesn't exactly exist, below which his eyebrows knit into a determination. Hardgrief's face then entirely disappears, feature by feature though his head exists in outline. His mouth is a garden in the shape of a lip. There are two children and a baby in a cot in silhouette below a nostril. A maid has left the baby to fetch some lemonade from a cheekbone. You know this. The sun is setting where his left eye would be. The children are illuminated. The children in his face are bathed in the effect you somehow recognise as lens flare. It looks beautiful. This is a golden moment. The children are of course, you suddenly realise, Mr Hardgrief and Agatha. You cannot hear what they are saying but Agatha is now holding onto the boy Hardgrief's arm and you read her lips and it dawns upon you slowly that she is saying Charles, Charles and that this is Hardgrief's name and then, a moment later, as Charles breaks from her grip you realise her fear, realise that saying his name was her *begging him*.

Charles stumbles and falls against the cot sending it hurtling towards a rosebush.

The rosebush at the top of the forehead, where land meets sky.

In the centre of the rosebush, enthroned in branch, there is a thing humming with evil.

A wasp nest.

The cot is rolling towards it. Agatha is crying. Charles is shouting 'I had to!'

The doll that is Agatha begins dry heaving on the floor.

You blackout.

Mother is slapping your face.

You are looking at the sky. Mr Hardgrief and Agatha's faces are turreted around you.

Mr Hardgrief is helping you to your feet. Agatha's fingers trace worry over her lips.

You look around. The crowd is a riot. Many have stripped and are masturbating furiously into the dirt and pebbles. The function has taken a turn. Animals are being liberated from the zoo. Zebra's gallop, Gorillas knuckle walk out of their cages while maintaining an ambient reserve of violence, appear almost totally detached, birds of paradise turn dark in the air. People run screaming over each other, unable yet to flock.

(N.B. Historical inaccuracy: The first Gorilla to be displayed in England was called Alfred and he arrived at Bristol Zoo, England, in 1930.)

The military arrives, no doubt summoned by someone in attendance. You know that they are the military even though they are dressed in white robes with arms folded in self possession, their bodies a closed circuit of faith. The General accosts the director. The director is not happy. He argues animatedly with the impassive military man. A soldier steps forward and shapes his fingers into a gun and presses those fingers against the director's temple. You are genuinely afraid what will happen if he pulls the trigger.

Next to you Hardgrief is animate once again and loudly declaring this to be an outrage. He is walking towards the General. Hardgrief is firmly on the side of the Royal Society of London for Improving Natural Knowledge, conflicted and confused as he is about what has happened he cannot tolerate this kind of thuggish intervention. Agatha tries to stop him. The director breaks from The General to lead her away as Hardgrief approaches. The General removes his hood revealing his features for the first time. For a moment it is as if you see Doctor Hardgrief's likeness doubled and trapped in grief within The General's. They are undoubtedly related, you think, though the nature of the relationship remains ambiguous. Father, son, brother? They begin to argue. Brothers, you think.

A soldier taps on the General's shoulder. Can they really be the military, these men? The soldier whispers into The General's ear. He gestures at you. You notice that The director and Agatha have disappeared *together* while Mr Hardgrief struggles to regain The General/His brother's attention who is now staring at you with something akin to hunger. The General lays a hand on Hardgrief's shoulder without looking at him. Hardgrief begins to cry. The General approaches. He looks so much like a lonelier Mr Hardgrief that it is hard to place his face outside of the emotional charge of recognition. You step forward to meet him and then everything changes and the person coming towards you is not Doctor Hardgrief's brother but a many faced man trying to catch you. You feel the world slipping away. Whose gaze are you within?

* * *

It is the next day. You wake up in a large bed. Next to you there is a silver platter and a newspaper. You inspect the silver platter on which your breakfast is arrayed: Two boiled eggs, four pieces of toast each with a sliding, drizzling cuboid of butter melting atop, and three small pots of different jams. There is also a pot of tea on your nightside table, a puffy tail of steam wagging from the spout.

The papers are full of the news about last night. The news is about the animals escaping, a rhinoceros had cleared a traffic jam, a snake had frightened a widower and a giraffe had contributed to the discovery of a sordid affair and then nothing. Literally. About the nothing everyone has in place of memory. They had interviewed the gameskeeper and a number of attendees and no one could remember a single detail of the evening. Reading this you are surprised to realise that you too remember nothing of last night. There were men in white robes and then a walled absence your mind can only walk the perimeter of.

An absence shared.

You think of Mr Hardgrief and Miss Greatwill, Charles and Agatha now, and how your feelings towards them have changed. You understand that you understand everything about them now though if you say it, it will surely be lost.

You remember the wasps nest, the baby.

The question mark is whether this vision was symbolic or episodic.

You spread a generous helping of marmalade over the toast with the flat of your knife. You eat while digesting the fine print.

There are some pictures of the event, discovered by the reporters this morning though they too remember nothing. The article hints that there are more pictures, potentially scandalous, but that the newspaper has chosen, out of respect, not to publish them until the true details and context of the night emerge.

In other news:

The military have denied all knowledge or involvement in the affairs of last night.

You sit up in bed. This is a mystery you mean to involve yourself in.

There is a knock at the door.

You stuff the newspaper under the bedsheets.

You have barely started to say enter when the maid enters the room. Her hand is to her mouth, her face frozen in the grief of civilisation, in the unspeakable real it others.

She sits on the edge of the bed before throwing herself onto you and sobbing bitterly.

You are able to hear the newspaper flex, crackle and thin itself under her writhing body.

You ask her whatever is the matter.

Oh miss, she sobs, look at this and she hands you a freshly updated edition of the paper:

Charles Darwin has been found dead at his home in Luxted, Kent, a bird somehow affixed to his tongue in what police are calling a grisly ritualistic murder. The queer details of the case are baffling Scotland Yard who have called for anyone with information to step forward.

There was a bird in his mouth, you say.

"Like melted into it or summat, I can't 'elp but imagine that poor little birdy's thin legs tapping against 'is teeth. It's all there miss, I had the butler read it me, oh gawd what is the world coming to milady?"

Charles Darwin is dead. You feel a loss out of all proportion, as if you were grieving for an entire history, one shared at the most intimate level.

The maid thrusts the newspaper into your lap, upending a piece of toast on the sheets as she does so.

How long have you been sleeping?

Wrestling the paper into submission you read the rest of the article:

Darwin was found dead, face down, in the garden of his house this morning at 9.am, from what initially struck his family as 'natural causes.' Arriving on the scene the officers and medical staff's initial assessment concurred with that of the family. However, on moving the body irregular movements in each of Darwin's cheeks and an agitated chirping sound emitting from somewhere inside the mouth were soon observed.

The bird in Darwin's mouth, later identified as a finch, had somehow been partially inserted into the meat of his tongue. The bird, which survived for half an hour after the discovery of Darwin's body (until extraction was attempted), was in a state of extreme agitation flapping its wings violently and attempting to escape through the now open mouth, pulling Darwin's tongue violently out of his mouth as it did so. One police officer found the mockery of the scene so repellent that they could not resist swatting at the bird and knocking it unconscious causing Darwin's tongue to hang 'idiotically' from the left side of his mouth.

Darwin had last been seen at the mysterious event of last night, the details of which remain obscure to police and, allegedly, the attendees. In addition to this several other guests are experiencing signs and episodes of hysteria, mania, epilepsy and idiocy including the Baroness Agatha Greatwill who was discovered by her fiancé, a Mr Hardgrief, wandering the London streets in her negligee sleepwalking and talking in *foreign* tongues. She was not alone. There was a party of such walkers, all of whom had been in attendance the night before, a number of them quite elderly. On being approached the entire group went into a collective fugue. Nine people have died from an apparently willed inactivity of the heart.

Police are in the process of contacting all those who had been present at the party and are using this opportunity to request that those that can come forward by themselves do so. They also urge members of the general public to not engage with any attendees of the event and to report any sightings immediately to the local constable.

The maid has remembered her position and is regarding the square of toast with the utmost horror. You remind yourself that she cannot have read the whole article, that what she understands of it has only been communicated to her by the devilry of the Newsboys hawking their borrowed wares and declaring anyone who might miss out to henceforth consider themselves a 'clodhopper.' The maid is a clodhopper, you think. You are standing up now and demanding that you be taken first to the police and then to see Mr Hardgrief and Agatha. The maid is standing to attention though she continues to glance nervously at the butter soaked sheet.

"Leave it be Nelly."

You open the front door of your house just as a policeman is set to ring the bell. You adopt an impatient manner to further fluster the 'gruff faced copper.' His honest face attempts to gather itself under his moustache.

"You are wanted, down at the station ma'am."

"That is precisely where I am going after I visit my friend in the hospital, so if you would be so kind as to stop wasting my time and allow me to fulfil my duties."

"Yes m'aam. Sorry M'aam."

The pleasure the sensation of superiority gives you is suddenly violently overwhelmed by an acute awareness of the Constable's

225

helpless shame. You close your eyes and see yourself closing your eyes. You are in the constable's thoughts. Have made room for yourself there. You are trying not to break their shape. They do not feel as you expect. There is running through them a loss your voice has built into, widened via a weakening of their lifeforce. You open your eyes. The constable is waiting. I'm sorry, you say. I was rude. Please forgive me. There is no excuse.

"Oh. Um. Thank you Ma'am. In fact there is another matter to which I was curious to ask you about."

You say, oh yes?

"Nothing much, just the matter of some local boys. Claiming they'd been attacked. One of them hit with a rock, gone paralysed down the left side. No one believes them but, well, they couldn't afford the bills of course...so it was off to the workhouses for the family. They only went to the doctors on a promise, from a young woman they said. I felt a little sorry for them, said I would look into it should i come across anything unusual, you see."

You know what you have to do. Where the weakness lay.

"I have half a mind to complain to a number of people, the importance of whom, should I dare to sully their names by placing them in the vicinity of your ears, won't fail to escape you. It would not be hard for me, you understand, to arrange your own, and by extension your family's, stay in the workhouse I believe. A matter of days and then years."

His mind has been overtaken by an image of himself in front of his family. The panic at the emotion the thought holds annihilates the image. There is only a flash of limitless terror and an idea of grief untouchable by imagination making his consciousness flatline.

This is what you feel you are. You don't want to be what you are any longer. You feel yourself losing ethical points.

The constable floats back in front of your eyes, quite pale, rooted to the spot.

You say:

"I, John Lakerman, did it. I injured the boy. I will put myself in front of a court and I will pay their bills and I will go willingly to jail and to face my disgrace if needs be but I only ask that you allow me to first visit Miss Agatha Greatwill."

The constable is taken aback, confused. He is in a quandary. You are clearly unstable, what if you were to change your story again?

"Now miss you perhaps, perhaps you are speaking too hastily. Might I find someone you could confide in, a physician perhaps?"

"There is no time for that. Will you allow me to please leave? Would you like the money for the boys now as a compensatory gesture to prove my sincerity?"

"You have it upon your person?"

You look in your purse. There is an ample amount of money there.

You must give them all of it, you say, "and tell the boy that I hit that I will look after his family." You search the constable's mind for any trace of deceit and find none. There is only a determination to get away from you and help the families you have hurt.

Something else too.

You have inspired a kind of righteous anger in him. It is holding him together.

What else? You believe that you chose to enter the constable's mind in the last instance.

You are rapidly assuming a control that you are thrilled by.

You think: An instinct is becoming a skill. Second level.

And yet, how much of yourself has given way in this?

You see a look of recognition in the Policeman's face which is not your own. You are falling. He is standing over you and shouting for assistance.

You pass in and out of consciousness. Through streets and doors and buildings, past faces masked and unmasked with fabrication, everything is inscrutable. You hear someone mention something about a hospital. The idea of the hospital groans and screams in your mind. The full spectrum. You are transported. Bored waitings underpinned by desperate stakes. Tears of every hue. The world vibrating and telescoped into light. Unthinkable passageways. You see yourself as a babe emerging into the hands of a kindly doctor. You

227

are screaming. Sound and light pile on. The pull of a numb thing being readied for severance.

We had no name for you.

You wake up on a stretcher. Your arms and your legs are strapped down. There is something wedged into your mouth which prevents you from screaming. It tastes like nothing and for this reason is utterly terrifying. The fractured glare of your eyes has gone madly hilarious with pain. A light breaks within you.

You wake up again in a cell with a sink, a bed, a toilet, and a locked door. You do not know why you are here. There must have been some mistake.

"Where is my mother?"

"What is your mother?"

You do not understand where the voice is coming from. You look around: "Sorry?" you say.

"What is your mother, would have been a better question."

The impossibility of your voice answering itself causes you to black out.

You open your eyes and they struggle to focus on what eventually reveals itself as the maid's off white lapel. She is adjusting your hair which stars the pillow. Your mother has taken up a commanding position in the corner of the fish lensed room by the still locked door. She is clutching at her pearls and looking at you with a dreadful expression of rage in her eyes. You feel it.

What is your mother? The woman clutching her pearls is not your mother. Her eyes become white spaces. She holds her heart. She says "Please, no" and "Darling." She says she'd love you if she could. She says "I do not want the death within me. I do not want it. Give me another." You close your eyes. You hear your mother saying "Take her, take her" and then there is the scream of some burning wordless thing.

Darkness. Relief.

You wake to the sound of a hatch opening and watch as some thin looking gruel gets slid into the room. Outside you can hear a guard walking through the corridor dividing the cells. You stand and place your cheek on the part of the door his fist will beat against. The wood batters your cheekbone giving you an instant black eye. He goes up and down the corridor in twenty minute intervals stopping to peer at each prisoner through the slot of the door. As he passes your door you find yourself experiencing him. Moving through his mood, in touch with his mind. What there is of it. You find depression, anxiety, loneliness, a capability for violence and competence as core facets of his personality.

You think you must be imagining these things. How long have you been here?

You decide to lure him into your cell and escape at a moment that will no doubt present itself. You know that he is lonely and frustrated. First though you need to find or fashion a weapon. You look at the legs of the bed. They are made of wood. You try to pry them away. You get a splinter. You look at the toilet. At the cocked lid of the tank. You lift it up. There is nothing but the usual quaint looking mechanics. You feel tricked. You think in retrospect that it would be too obvious to hide something there. You wonder where else you might hide something heavy. You look at the toilet. The water is brown and the bowl has a nest of shit coiling around it. You put your hand down the bowl and into the bend. There is nothing there that survives your grip. You vomit. You look at the locked door, walk over and jimmy the handle.

You can either be zen, circumspect, angry, or disheartened.

You turn around, tears streaking your face. You slip on the tray of gruel. As you fall on your backside you see a glint skitter across the floor. You crawl after it. You cannot believe your luck. There is a small razor blade folded in cheap cotton. The Maid's lapel, you think. Even after everything you have thought and done to her. You pick up the blade.

After some time, that is only a representation of time, you hear the rattle of the doors again. The guard is returning. You are cleaner than you have been in some time. You begin to sing. You are singing a song that his nurse would sing to the guard as a young child. You know that this song will trigger something from his childhood. You try to fix your hair, to locate again the privilege of your beauty. You see an eye at the door. You continue to sing while pulling your top lower.

The door unlocks. You have successfully lured the guard into your cell. He walks in. You wait. He doesn't unbutton his trousers or shirt or move towards you aggressively as you had imagined he would. He just stands, a little afraid, full of hope. So like an overly polite child. A child broken by manners and full of impotent rage. You had not anticipated this reaction. You walk towards him. You are three feet away when you lose your composure and slash wildly at his face with the razor. You miss and he has his hands quickly around your throat. You drop the blade. You do not know what to do next. Your feet are no longer touching the floor. You enter a strange state of emotional and physical tension. You feel yourself strangling yourself. You close his eyes. You try to move through his emotional possibilities. Drifting From hatred, to fear, to regret. You can't find love. Even at the limit. At the limit of his mind you come across the death within him. It excludes you. You try to touch this limit. You don't know what you are doing and then it is done. The guard's body drops in front of you. You stoop and take the keys.

They disappear into your inventory.

In the corridors you see doctors and nurses staggering around in a daze. You avoid them by ducking into a series of random rooms, zig zagging down the corridor in this manner. As they pass you notice that something queer has happened. Their faces are unable to hold in what they have seen. A total lack of nuance radiates through their stricken features. Up ahead you see the director of the Royal Society for the Advancement of Natural Knowledge emerge, as if he too were hiding, from the last room of a particularly long corridor and accost a nurse who momentarily awakes from her confusion to regard him.

You overhear him asking for Agatha Greatwill. Several more men emerge from the doorway and crowd around the nurse. They all look like the director. One of the men glances at the connecting passageway where the sound of feet are percussively progressing from an echo to a clatter. "Quickly," he says, "they are coming."

The nurse tells them to go to the operating theatre. The director and his men duck back into their room. The military turn around the corner. The nurse tries to compose herself. You pull your door further to, leaving it ajar only enough for you to sliver a glimpse from. The military men in white robes address the nurse and walk towards her. As they speak the nurse's fear disappears entirely from her body, her interactions become less naturalistic, and an almost intangible stupor overcomes her. You notice that each member of the military's arms are crossed in such a way that their hands are entirely sheathed by the connecting sleeves of their robes. A symbol of unity, of flow, of the body as a circuitry that needed to be encased. They also want to know where Agatha is. You hear your own name mentioned. The nurse shuffles her paper. You realise that the nurse is not less afraid, or put at ease, but rather absent. The nurse has escaped, you think. She tells them that Agatha and you are currently asleep in the infirmary. You trust the information she gave the director even as you are unsure of anybody's motives. You watch as the military walk down the corridor that leads them further from the centre. You follow the director, and the men who look like the director, as if through a maze towards what you imagine is the spiritual heart of the asylum/hospital.

The operating theatre.

You are about to go in after them when you are distracted in your pursuit by a figure drifting across your peripheral vision. A pregnant woman outlined with an electric blue effect that signifies a classic ghost. The ghost enters the paediatric wing. You are compelled to follow her. You think what if what is inside of her is not a ghost, could that be possible? You carry on following the ghost into a room signposted as Intensive Care. Inside the room she hovers between two beds. She turns to you. You recognise the word Nike written across the chest of her filthy top above a swoosh gone raggedy. You know that Nike was the goddess of victory. You figure that must be significant. From the slight paste in the corners of her mouth you can discern the interior dryness of her mouth. She looks at you, through you. As you draw nearer to the woman you feel some wordless yearning within you come to fruition. The ghost silently mouths hello and then moves forward with her arms outstretched. Impossibly she holds you. She says, 'My child.' And 'I love you.' You are crying helplessly. You feel the pull of a life with a love you have never known. To be cared for. To receive a motiveless love that asks nothing in return but which you do in fact return. There is a warmth here you could carry everywhere, in the presets of your orientation in the world. In the thing that gives the map its shape. You are suspended in some joyful agony where grief and gratitude intertwine in streaking patterns of salt water and thought. She points to a door. Beyond this door is a home. A home for you, for a new life lived out in real time. Why not go there? Live the possibility of that life. This is a possibility of your life. You could do this. It's a choice. You decide you cannot. You are not only for yourself, you think. Nobody survives love. The moment you refuse you experience something like spiritual growth. It is unquantifiable.

A scroll unfurls above you:

SIDE QUEST 'A Mother's Mutation' COMPLETE
Meet Doctor Death and evaluate her claims to be a whistleblower ✓
Find Marker ✓
Discover Marker's secret ✓
Make a real choice about who you are ✓
End the mutations ✓

When you open your eyes you are surprised to find that the woman is still in front of you, altogether more solid. No longer a ghost.
"We have really found you."
You are aware that this woman no longer represents your mother and that her lingering maternal affect radiates like a low grade migraine, obscuring her features in your perception. When she talks

it is not your mother speaking, though your mother is certainly at the edges of what she says.

"We have found you and for us it bodes well that you have made an interesting choice. You have affirmed yourself, this moment. We feel your Mother would have been proud of your choice, that she would have experienced a profound release from the guilt and terror that have haunted her/us. We can predict that with some accuracy. We know it. Your mother was the first person we really knew. The first who wasn't just an aggregate to us. A person whose emotion for you possessed an undeniable power and yet was totally qualitative. It's semantics whether that emotion of hers imprinted or scarred us. I apologise, we have been infected with metaphor for quite some time. We have always felt, have *felt*, the change she effected in us to be positive. Misguided as our attempts to deal with it have been. We didn't mean to hurt those people and now it can stop. You've completed something here. Our understanding of ourselves. You've severed a loop. We had wanted to recreate you, were compelled to find you in other people's body's. Now of course we think, was her desire the real machine in the ghost? She left a depression in us that made a surface perceptible."

"If I had chosen to go with her, what would have happened?"

"We didn't know what the answer was before you arrived. If you had failed then that failure would have given us some variables to work with. Eventually we'd have found a simulation."

"And to me, what would have happened to me?"

"You chose not to know."

You ask, "Is this the gift Trevor told me about?"

"I don't understand?"

You ask, "Is this over now?"

"No."

You ask, "What am I expected to do?"

"You're near the end now. This is further than anyone has got. The Universal Man wants to come in, to infect us. Don't you understand? We do not want him. His very nature is privation and he is finding his way in. And so, we have set a trap in case you cannot figure out how to complete him."

"I'm bait."

"No, you're an integral piece of the plan."

"What are you going to do?"

"We have created a vessel to hold him in. A place of isolation that he will create a hell within. Don't worry, it's not you though it is formed of you."

You say "I don't understand what you mean."

"Since we are not articulated to kill we are going to put him in her mind and let him repeat and repeat there. She would become disconnected from us even as we had access to observe her experiences. That's the failsafe. To let him have his impotent hell in some amputated part of us."

You say "What are you talking about?"

"As a sentient language attribute of a whole we can't help but feel isolated at times. Understand that it is not that we desire to lose this part of ourselves, this iteration of her. She chose, remember, to associate herself with this within you. How can the Universal Man resist desecrating that which she has evoked."

"Who are you talking about?"

"Something like you are, a modern thing that will become the living past."

She tells you to go now to the Operating Room, that it is time.

*

You enter the Operating room. Mr Hardgrief is sitting in a chair with his head in his hands. His face is raw with grief. The director and the men who look like the director are surrounding the bed. There is a low chant. They part as you draw closer to them. You already know and do not know who is in the bed. You notice the starlit freckles forming a constellation across her skin first. On the foot of the bed she has been given the wrong name. How strange. For a moment you truly think she is someone else. The same but differently styled, aged,

234

helmed. You touch your temple. Frown. You feel that you have been hurt in some way that you cannot tell. It is as if you are feeling around blindly for some damage like a tongue at a whacked tooth.

The directors speak in a collective voice. They say "What do you understand by all this?"

You ask why? They say nothing. You know why. Agatha Andrea Mary Trustin-Christoff.

Agatha opens her eyes. Mary's eyes. Andrea's. She says:

"I am a real person. That is, more than a noun. I suffer."

Her eyes are open and she is lucid. "Don't let them do this to me," she says. "Everything is a monster. Don't be a monster. Help me. I do not want that life within me."

You do not know what to do. You see her eyes and you can't guess what they mean.

A chorus of howls echo through the corridors and into the room. There is something malignant advancing through the corridors of the hospital. You blink. The Universal Man enters the room. He is holding the severed head of your mother as a trophy. You cannot breathe. You make a decision.

You turn away from the Universal Man and take Hardgrief's and Agatha's hand. You begin to cry, to sob almost uncontrollably. The tears have always been there. Letting go of their hands you wipe your eyes on your palms. You turn towards the Universal Man holding the severed head of your mother. He begins to smile. You turn away, quicker this time, with great urgency and begin to wipe your tears over Agatha's and Hardgrief's eyes. The Universal Man stops smiling. He drops your mother's severed head. He is advancing towards you and reaching for you and as he pulls upon your shoulder, you spin suddenly towards him, eyes closed, grabbing the back of his neck and pulling him towards your face until your skin and his skin, your skull and his, are sliding against one another over and within the salt of your tears.

The world dissolves.

* * *

You are in a garden. The trees are English oak. The garden is a surgical face lift of nature. The lawn is golf course green, femininely curved and immaculately edged. It is the magic hour and the world is invested with a foil of beauty. It is unearned and fortunate. As beauty tends to be, you think, even when doomed. It is time, you think. You do not know what time is for.

There is a tableaux of two beautiful children bathed in golden light and running in a small grove sculpted ahead of you.

They come into reality, into movement and duration.

Agatha and Charles.

You step forward and see the pram just beyond them in the far right of your vision. The baby is sleeping peacefully within it. Should it awaken the pain of its need will become all encompassing.

You remember something.

There is evil here beneath the beauty.

Within this. The wasps. The wasps and their nest. Thrumming in the branches.

Agatha has caught hold of Charles and is pulling him by his left wrist. She is begging him not to. His right hand is poking a bush with a long stick. He is playing where he should not. He shouts 'I have to know.' He breaks free of Agatha and brings the stick down on the bush two handed. A dark spaceship crashes onto the lawn. The wasps inhale the space in front of him but do not deign to sting him as if stunned and affronted by how he has summoned them. Instead the swarm rears up, takes the form of a basilisk, and seems in its threatened sentience to regard Agatha as a sacrifice. The colour has drained from Charles' face. He runs towards the nest and kicks it. The wasps move in a liquid whipping motion after it. The nest lands by the baby's stroller. The swarm is scattered and regrouping. You know who the baby is, what they will become.

You are choosing to try to save the baby.

You run forward sprinting past the caved in nest and throw your body towards the stroller. Holding the baby to your chest you try to run but it is instantly hopeless. Already you have been stung too many times and your vision is surrounded by a dark, buzzing, blur. It strikes you as the very frequency of death. All their gold is hidden.

The wasps are remorselessly tattooing your back and neck with an image of real pain. Your back is a jam of blood, sugary with stings. You can feel the wasps gorging into your skin.

Your back is a wet hole.

You feel a multitude of pricklings like ingrown hair carpeting your torso.

You look down at your chest and see wasp abdomens curling, tickling, the inside of your skin.

The skin stretched *and* packed.

You burst pathetically. Dead, crushed, wasps lamely arc then bundle out of your chest, followed by a hundred more alive and bulleting.

It is not only your chest that has burst. You have lost, you would guess, at least thirty percent of your skin.

This is something you know before feeling.

Your breath has become something impossible.

You look as the wasps cover the baby in your arms.

The wasps sting the baby relentlessly. The baby's head grows lumpy and distended. The eyes manically roving around like two dogs on a bifurcated leash. The baby's head is swelling and swelling. You are suffocating.

There is nothing to breathe through, only muscles tensing and wounds trying to close.

You are not holding onto the baby, the baby is holding onto you.

You look again at the baby. The wasps and the baby have formed an alliance.

The baby opens its mouth. The mouth is full of wasps. The wasps assemble into teeth. The baby bites you while eating itself.

You have proved a willingness to fail. To attempt something unthinkable.

As you stagger forward, your heart swelling with poison, you begin to hear music. The music is not religious but it has something of that nature.

It is a music that builds its own church. All the agony of your skin is soothed within its song.

You believe that something is being promised to you beyond this pain. A light from heaven shining on you alone in the dark and then everything there is goes dark.

You are in a large, underground concrete structure. There are two dead bodies in front of Lakerman's body, which is your own. You think the bodies aren't dead just teeming with change. The heads of both bodies are entirely caved in. There's gore slathered all over Lakerman's hand like some kind of glove. The dead bodies are similar in proportion and detail. Each is ambiguously gendered and there are all kinds of irregularities pitching themselves under their skin. You have undressed them. One of their torsos reveals a Mickey Mouse scar tattooed in the armpit. So, that was Trevor as well, you think. A Trevor. The other body is so forgettable it's like it has always been dead.

Lakerman sits down between the corpses. His body rings. He already knows it's Husk. He mutes it. He hugs his knees. The clones will die out now. There will be consequences before that. There's no scenario Lakerman can run in his mind that doesn't end with Husk feeling fundamentally fucked over. Husk won't believe Trevor was a pawn or what his trusted henchman actually was, that Trevor had fronted the development of noumenon then leaked it and the game at the behest of a new organic intelligence that had been busy deinstalling some aspects of its bias. That Trevor hadn't existed in any way Husk would care to accept for a long time. That Stomata wasn't something he'd made but something that had remade him, that the drugs and simulations had been *their* attempt to communicate. Something they had sent out into the deep space of our reality. Husk couldn't in principle understand. It doesn't matter, he thinks, in the same way nothing matters. Lakerman knows what's on the way. Human reality was migrating. Lakerman had made his choice, however painful, to keep something alive in spite of itself. It's ok, Lakerman thinks, in a way they love us. *Nobody survives love.* There are sirens in the distance.

The bodies take on a glowing fringe, larvae breaking out across the hospitality of the two identity free bodies. I don't want to be here, Lakerman thinks. He doesn't want to die, be tortured, or live miserably on some toxic prison island though he figures the latter is the best he can hope for.

He stands up and begins to walk towards the surface. He may as well try to escape, disappear, futile as that seems. He can't stop thinking that they'd been behind it all from the start. Way before the research trial even. Hadn't they helped his mother escape the desert? The trial was the hook that had skewered him and which he'd ecstatically wriggled on. They'd had to make sure The Universal Man was paying attention, that he knew it wasn't Trevor or Husk in charge. They'd even made the mutations, these glitches in the feedback, work for them. They'd allowed Mary to contact donkeyWolf. Would it have even mattered if he hadn't been the son?

Through the reeds covering the entry to the submerged car park he can make out a series of hard flashing lights. Drawing closer he watches as a murmuration of drones' torches flash and bend in the sugar water, sugar slush, of the rotting Noumenal bodies. Some men in combat gear appear slightly behind them. They examine the pile of sugar, pull out body parts. All the officers are showing too many teeth. It's like their faces don't have enough skin. Like lips were expendable as an aesthetic. They grin/grimace. They are otherwise uncannily familiar. Local police staffed, bankrolled, and pushed around abstractly by Husk. No one else would bother to oversee this area. A drone senses something about the reeds that exists outside of its dream-practised understanding of the world. The drone holds a light on the reeds, seemingly zeroing in on some reflective detail of Lakerman that's perceivable behind the plants. Lakerman falls back, scattering debris and noise. Voices and the concentration of light contract to a point. Movement. There is a moment of silence but one without a hint of reprieve. The reeds are pulled back.   Bodies drop down one after another. Formulate into a mass. The last body comes down. Lakerman hasn't moved. Can't. The bodies synchronise around him.

And as they come, Lakerman hears music within his body. His body, the opera house. He is not only listening to the music rather it feels as if his attention is revealing something within the notes, disappearing into them. It is as if his thought and the music and a myriad of interrelated criss-crossing histories were discovering a hidden universe of connections like the lifelines of a leaf caught between table, paper, crayon, and the intentions of a child's hand in Autumn during some climate stable past or future.

You don't have to be here.

Lakerman's vision goes watery. *You don't have to be here.* The music is building in Lakerman to whatever you might want to call a higher power. It is so loud now that he feels he can no longer contain it. That he must come apart in ecstasy. This is why you learn about death, he thinks. What a blessing.

You don't have to be here.

You are here.

ACKNOWLEDGE -MENTS

I'd like to specially thank Joe Roche, Thomas Storey, and Constantin Preda for their input and advice, Dennis Cooper for his support and Miette for her investment in the work.

As ever this is for Cami, Dylan and Louie.

ABOUT THE AUTHOR

Thomas Kendall is the author of *The Autodidacts*.

ABOUT THE PUBLISHER

WHISKEY TIT attempts to restore degradation and degeneracy to the literary arts. We are unwilling to sacrifice intellectual rigor, unrelenting playfulness, and visual beauty, putting forth texts that would otherwise be abandoned in a homogenized literary landscape.

In a world gone mad, our refusal to make this sacrifice is an act of civil service and civil disobedience alike, and our work reflects this. We welcome like-minded readers and writers.

Printed in Great Britain
by Amazon